Seeing JESUS

A Novel

Jeffrey McClain Jones

Seeing JESUS

Copyright © 2013 by Jeffrey McClain Jones

All rights reserved. No part of this book may be reproduced in any form by any electronic or mechanical means including photocopying, recording, or information storage and retrieval without permission in writing from the author.

John 14:12 Publications

www.john1412.com

Cover by Gabriel Jones -- Photos from Getty Images, via Photos.com.

For Norm: An extraordinary regular guy, who knows how to see Jesus in the people around him.

Chapter One

Philly Thompson stared through the jagged foil mouth of the instant coffee jar. He could see his chipped and stained countertop through the clear plastic bottom. The morning had gotten off to a bad start. Philly swelled and released a sigh. He would have to break open the vault and pay five bucks for a cup of coffee on the way to work. His sigh turned into a low growl. "Five bucks for coffee! How did that happen?" Philly dropped the empty jar into the kitchen garbage can with a clunk and headed for his bedroom, stepping over his big gray cat, Irving, who was begging for attention. "Hey, I fed you. Now I gotta go."

Finding his black-and-tan rubber-soled shoes, he sat on the edge of the bed, his two hundred pounds inducing a quick squeak of springs. He puffed against the weight around his middle as he stuffed one foot and then the other into his shoes. Two sets of rabbit ears and double knots in place, he bounced up off the bed, determined to show his invisible audience that he still possessed youthful vitality despite his untamed waistline.

Irving stood at the bedroom door, apparently unimpressed. He bent his head to lick himself.

Philly stepped over the cat again and stopped at his coat closet to pull a tan squall jacket out of the musty assortment. He headed toward the kitchen, pulled on the jacket, scooped up his wallet, swept up his keys, and slipped his phone into his pants pocket in smooth, practiced order, only interrupting the usual choreography to lift the last corner of toast off the white Corelle plate on the kitchen table.

On the back porch, he locked the door, noticing his hair in

the reflection as he chewed his toast. As soon as he pocketed his keys and began creaking down the back stairway, he attempted to brush his hair from left to right with the fingers of both hands. Wobbling on the third stair above the second-floor landing, he forgot about his hair and snagged the railing in time to steady himself. He swore quietly. He should have just stayed in bed.

Walking down the uneven sidewalk between his building and the one next door, Philly followed the well-worn path away from his refuge. That refuge rested on the top floor of a three-story apartment building constructed a hundred years ago. The dark reddish brick and white window frames fit it into a spectrum of similar buildings lining the densely-parked residential street.

Philly arrived at his bus stop on Sheridan Road in time to buy a *Tribune* from the vending machine. A North Sider all his life, he thought of the *Trib* as his paper, though he only read it a couple times a week. He looked unconsciously at the front page, not yet ready to actually absorb any real information. He was still getting comfortable being out of his apartment, out in the cool, damp April air, exposed to the eyes of strangers—if they ever stopped thinking their own self-conscious thoughts long enough to notice this nearly-six-foot-tall single man with bushy eyebrows and uneven sideburns.

Someone had told him once that he looked like Oliver Platt, the actor, and Philly clung to this assessment, though the resemblance required seeing him from a certain oblique angle, and though he might have to admit that Oliver Platt wasn't one of the better looking actors. Still, looking like an actor, any actor, was better than just looking like himself, a white man on the North Side of Chicago who blended into the crowds, the streets, and the weather as if he wore urban camouflage.

The bus moaned to a stop, a hiss and squeak accompanying the opening door. Having sheltered his eyes by the blind perusal of his paper, Philly hadn't noticed the elderly Polish woman nor the young Hispanic couple standing with him at the bus stop.

Only when he had to shift into mass-transit protocol did he glance at his fellow travelers—all three regulars at that stop on a weekday morning. The old woman looked at him to confirm that he was waiting for her to climb the stairs first. As usual, Philly waited for her to follow the spry young couple, and he intentionally looked away so no one would think he was staring at the old woman's backside as she scaled the stairs. Philly thought a lot about how people viewed him when he was out in public. Of course, that often slowed his response when directly dealing with real people.

Sitting on the bus, Philly had just begun to read an article about the city budget when he felt his phone vibrate for an incoming text. He sucked in his belly and stretched his leg to make his phone accessible. After a bit of struggling, he birthed the phone and confirmed the expected sender—his oldest friend, Raymond Carver, whom he still privately called Ray-Ray. That was how Philly had known him since first grade. Likewise, Ray persisted in calling Philly by that nickname, which his father gave him before he took his first step. His coworkers, on the other hand, called him Phil or Phillip, with rare exceptions.

While Philly worked near downtown every day, Ray sold commercial plumbing hardware and only visited downtown when needed. A trip to a client today prompted his texted lunch proposal. Lunch with your oldest friend could possibly redeem a dreary day. But the prospect of lunch with Ray soured Philly's stomach. At this point, Philly was only beginning to admit to himself that he no longer even liked spending time with Ray. He texted back for Ray to meet him at a sandwich restaurant on North Wells Street, near Philly's office.

After his usual bus transfer, Philly arrived at his transit destination and walked the three blocks to the two-tone gray building, constructed in the 1950s. It housed the architectural firm for which he worked. He liked his commute because it stayed above ground and required very little of him. Philly knew nothing about architecture. He served as the network administrator for the firm, part of a computer support staff of six. He liked his job because he had both a boss and an assistant, which made him feel covered on two sides.

Not until he reached the front door of the building did he remember his missed coffee. His shoulders slumped, he looked around to see if anyone had noticed his hesitation, and he turned to walk to the fast food place nearest the office. No coffee connoisseur, he would take what he could get. Walking faster than usual, Philly nearly knocked down an old, weathered man shaking a Styrofoam cup with coins in it. Philly made a note to give the old man his change on the way out, more as an apology for the near crash than out of charity.

While he stood in line, Philly spotted Brenda, one of the secretaries who worked in his office. Brenda was his most recent girlfriend, but lately they had been "just friends." She had stopped accepting his invitations to dinner and movies and had dated some guy from her neighborhood for a while. That transitional relationship had passed, as far as Philly knew, but neither of them had attempted to change the status of their relationship since.

"Hey, Philly." Brenda was the single predictable exception at work who called him by his old nickname.

"Hi, Brenda." He stood up a bit straighter and sucked his stomach in a bit.

"Gettin' something to eat, or just coffee?" Brenda switched lines to stand with Philly.

Philly genuinely liked Brenda—when she was in a cheerful mood. In that condition, she could get him to do anything, to be anybody. But she had a pretty dark interior and sometimes showed it, even at work.

"Just coffee." Philly made eye contact, conscious not to look at the tight sweater Brenda wore under her unzipped rain jacket.

"Me too. Didn't have time to make some before I left home."

Brenda lived in Evanston and rode the train down from there. To Philly it made no sense to pay the higher rent in Evanston just to live in a neighborhood that looked just like his neighborhood in Chicago. But he never criticized anything Brenda did, for fear of triggering one of her grave and disgusted moods. Philly nodded and shuffled forward in the line as a grandmother collected her order for herself and two tiny children.

Brenda brushed a lock of her brown hair back, attempting to tuck it into the hair pulled tight in her ponytail. "You got big plans this weekend?"

From this question, Philly could tell that they were more than just friends again, and Brenda wanted him to ask her out. She knew what a leading question sounded like and never offered one unless she meant it.

"Not really. You?"

"Nope. Maybe we could do something."

That made Philly nervous. He knew what to do with Brenda's obvious leading questions. It was like a role in a play. Her line invited him to take the ironic initiative. The play was both comedy and tragedy. However, Brenda had slipped from *inviting* to taking the initiative herself. She hadn't done that since the peak of their romance, two years ago. How could she act as if none of the intervening two years had happened?

"Yeah." Philly tried to disguise his discomfort with her breach of protocol. "Dinner and a movie?" He pulled out the old standard in order to push over the hump of awkwardness.

"That would be nice. What's playing?"

"There's that new one with Julia Roberts." When Philly had seen the trailer, he had instantly thought of Brenda, a soulful Julia Roberts fan.

Brenda's voice bounced with enthusiasm. "Oh, yeah. I really wanna see that one. That would be great."

Philly addressed the cashier as they reached the front of the line. "Two coffees."

Brenda jumped in. "Make mine a vanilla latte."

Philly fished for his wallet in the wrong pants pocket, feeling a flash of panic, and then remembered that it was in his jacket.

"Oh, I'll get this." Brenda plunked her black leather purse on the counter.

"Nah. I know how badly they pay you, remember?" This had always been Philly's means of persuading her to concede his manly role as provider, in a way that avoided openly admitting the gender bias by making it into a question of economics.

Brenda rolled her eyes, probably less annoyed by this subtle bullying than she was thrilled to see Philly reverting to their old patterns, as if nothing had exploded and crumbled between them. They collected their coffee and walked together to work, where they would probably not see each other the rest of the day.

After saying goodbye to Brenda, Philly checked in the network room before riding the elevator up to his little office. A Tuesday, this workday faded into anonymity even as its hours passed through morning.

At lunch, Philly swung past Brenda's cubicle just to say hello, but he found that she was away. His appointment to meet Ray kept him moving, and the disappointment of not seeing Brenda evaporated quickly. His dread of seeing Ray sucked the sap out of smaller disappointments.

Philly walked the three blocks to lunch without a jacket for the first time that year. The evasive Chicago spring made a cameo appearance that day. Philly even noticed the buds opening on some of the trees along the street. When he looked through the glass door of the restaurant, he spotted Ray sitting at a table and eating already. His face was bowed over his sandwich, so Philly recognized him by his expensive haircut. Philly briefly considered turning around and just enjoying the marvelous weather. But loyalty had been riveted to Philly's soul at an early age, among loud family gatherings and always-attentive neighbors. He tugged opened the restaurant door and nodded to Ray on his way to the counter, where he ordered the tuna on toasted rye he had been craving for the past two hours. Though loyalty drove him, the sandwich was his reward.

Ray was taller and thinner than Philly, but he had lately developed a tummy that resembled a medicine ball implanted just above his low-slung belt. Ray was maintaining something of the baggy, saggy pants look of his youth, even as he dressed up for his position as sales rep.

When Philly finally reached the table, Ray put down his sandwich, scrunched a paper napkin briefly, and held out his hand. "Hey, Philly. Good to see you." He sounded like the salesman that he had always been. The persuasive intonation he certainly now used in his job had been the catalyst for dozens of regrettable schemes in Philly's childhood. Philly had hit Ray in the face more than once—in revenge for dragging him into trouble—but he had always fallen back in with his oldest friend before the bruises even healed.

Philly sat down after shaking hands, unwrapped his sandwich, and took a sip of his iced tea before saying anything. A boost to his blood sugar would help with tolerating Ray for a whole lunch. "You couldn't wait for me?"

"Hey, sorry. I gotta get out to the suburbs by one thirty." Ray wasn't sounding sorry. "So, how is the network treatin' you?"

Ray always asked some version of that question, as if he could only understand Philly's job in terms of his own. Ray's job revolved around his relationships with his customers. Philly's job revolved around his relationship with his computer network. Though the repetitive question annoyed Philly, he couldn't argue with the analogy. He did wonder, however, if Ray meant it in a belittling way, as if Philly were incapable of relating to people as well as electronics. Philly offered an acknowledging grunt in response to the question, anticipating the sandwich much more than the conversation.

As he sat looking past Ray, chewing contently, Philly's phone rang. The old bicycle horn ringtone warned him that it was his mother. In most circumstances, Philly would have let her go through to voice mail. He didn't always want to hear from his mother, expecting the call to involve either nagging or worrying, both of which he preferred to postpone. But Philly had been relying on his mother lately to keep him posted on his grandma's condition, and he suspected this call would bring him news of her health, which had been wavering since her stroke the week before. "Hello, Ma." He just finished swallowing, so his voice sounded strange.

"Are you okay, Philly?"

"Sure, Ma. Just eating lunch with Ray-Ray. How's Grandma?"

"Oh, Philly, it's not good. She's gone into a coma now and they don't know how long she'll be that way." His mother's voice swooned.

"Oh." Philly wasn't prepared for something as decisive as a coma. That sounded too ominous to handle at lunch with Ray.

"She's getting help breathing, but her heart is still good, they say." His mother pressed on despite impending tears in her voice. "And they say we can still visit her, 'cause it might help her to hear our voices, even if she can't say anything back." Philly's mother broke down crying, a quiet, sniffling kind of emotional leak.

Though this grandmother was his father's mother, Grandma had been kind and accepting toward Philly's mother from the start and had become a reliable companion to her in their later years. Beyond that, every small difficulty expanded into a grand crisis with Philly's ma. Years ago, Philly had figured out that his dad was so passive and mellow because his mother did all the worrying for both of them. As a result, Philly had learned to interpret the world in terms of the average between his mother's overreaction and his father's inattention. He wondered how his dad was taking the news about Grandma's coma—watching a baseball game, perhaps.

"Eileen's coming into town to see Grandma." His mother puffed, recovering from her mournful moment.

On a bad day, Philly's sister would bring double the nagging and double the worrying. On a good day, she was an ally against his mother's siege on his life.

"Does she need someone to pick her up at the airport?" Philly's loyalty spoke before any fear of Eileen could stop it.

"Oh, I don't know. I forgot to ask. Why don't I call her and get back to you on that?"

"No, Ma, I can call her myself, thanks." Philly was glad to keep his mother out of the middle of any of his relationships.

Philly and his mother said their goodbyes, and he pocketed his phone once again. The tuna sandwich had lost some of its appeal in the meantime. For a moment Philly focused on his annoying mother and the further annoyance of having to tell Ray what the call was about, until he thought of his grandma.

Grandma Thompson was the saint of the family. Literally. Not only did the woman pray constantly for all her children and grandchildren, she managed to alienate none of them by meddling or prying. She just prayed. And Philly had always loved to sit and talk with her, no matter the generational divide. He loved his grandma and respected her more than his own parents, if he had to measure such things.

Even Ray could sense Philly's mood change and knew enough to ask, "How is she?"

"Not good." Philly made a half-hearted attempt at enjoying the sandwich again.

"Hmm, she was always a good grandma." Ray was probably remembering how tolerant Grandma Thompson had been when the boys got caught throwing water balloons at innocent pedestrians in her neighborhood one time.

Philly nodded as he chewed. He kept a cover on his feelings, sure that there would be a gusher if he uncapped them. He said little for the rest of the lunch and listened politely to Ray's latest romantic conquests and work complaints—the usual.

When Philly finally finished his sandwich and iced tea, Ray followed him outside. They both paused to bask in the sun for a moment. Ray pulled sunglasses out of the breast pocket of his light gray suit. Glancing briefly at his friend in those shades, with that suit and a winter cruise tan, Philly thought Ray looked pretty good. It seemed to Philly, however, like a disguise to conceal the weasel inside that suit.

Philly looked away and then switched into polite mode. "Okay, Ray. Sorry I wasn't good for conversation today. My grandma, ya know."

"Don't sweat it, Philly. You know I like to talk anyway." Ray laughed. "You take care now and tell your grandma I said hi."

Philly nodded, trying not to roll his eyes at Ray's unintended irony. They turned and walked their separate ways, Ray to his new Camaro, parked up the block, and Philly back to work, where he would struggle to focus through his anxiety about his grandma.

Just before he left that evening, Brenda stopped by the network room where Philly was testing new equipment. He looked up and brightened for just a blink when he saw Brenda wandering into the maze of racks and cables, apparently dazed by the array of flickering LEDs of green, red, blue, and amber.

"Hey, I didn't see you all day." Brenda seemed to be complaining to the fates for arranging the universe against her.

Philly shrugged. "You were gone from your desk when I stopped by earlier."

Brenda looked impressed that he had tried to make contact. She had sent an email which he hadn't responded to, his attention buried in the setup instructions for a new firewall device.

"Oh, did you go out for lunch?"

"Yeah. I met Ray."

"When are you getting off?"

"Soon. I gotta go to the hospital and see my grandma." He suspected Brenda had something in mind for that evening. "She's in a coma now." He stepped right back into his anxiety as he said "coma."

"What?" Brenda squealed slightly. "Oh my God. When did this happen?"

"Last night, I guess. I talked to my ma today."

"Oh." Brenda's vacant stare probably signaled the end of her cruise toward whatever she had planned for them that night. There was no screech of brakes. Just a little bump. "Okay, I guess I'll see you tomorrow then." She stepped up to Philly and kissed him on the cheek, placing her hand on his shoulder as she did.

Philly smiled with half his mouth and raised an eyebrow. "Thanks. Maybe I'll call and tell you how she is after I visit." He sensed the need for some consolation.

"Oh, that would be nice." She tipped her head and returned his crooked grin. Then she gave a quick wave before picking her way out of the room. She nearly bumped into Philly's boss who had apparently arrived at the door during that little vignette.

An awkward little check-in with Dennis, his boss, ended Philly's workday. He didn't even stop for supper, feeling the pull to his grandma's side.

After getting the room number from the kindly attendant at the information desk, a gray-haired woman who could say numbers in a sympathetic cadence, he scuffed down the marble-tiled hall to the elevators and then through the faintly nauseating odors of the patient floor. He should have eaten first. A full stomach would have been less vulnerable to those smells.

Hesitating at his grandmother's room, suddenly wishing he had checked that his ma wouldn't be there, he gently pushed the dark wooden door with one hand and peeked through the slowly widening gap. He stopped for a second when he saw that someone was there but then lurched forward when he realized it was just a man visiting the woman sharing his grandma's room.

Except for the medical equipment and a sort of reading light above her roommate, Grandma's room was dark. Philly eased into the darkness like a swimmer determined to do his laps in Lake Michigan in late spring.

The monitors, equipment lights, and neighbor's nightlight sagged beneath the weight of the darkness. That belabored light made it hard for Philly to feel comfortable with the notion that the old woman in this bed was really his grandma. For a moment he thought of his mother telling him at a funeral that the body wasn't really Grandpa. Maybe a coma was a step in that same direction. He sat down in the chair on the window side of her bed, keeping his eyes on Grandma, not to miss some fleeting sign of life if he looked away.

On the other side of the gold-colored curtain, he could hear the middle-aged man talking with his wife in Spanish. Philly couldn't understand what they were saying and blocked them out.

Sitting there looking at the still form entangled in plastic tubes, he felt as if he should do something. Prayer came to mind, because that's what Grandma would do. She told her children and grandchildren of her prayers for them as often as she got a chance. Philly wondered if she told him she was praying so he could look out for the answers to her prayers. He had assumed, however, that he would have a hard time recognizing those answers. Philly decided to talk to her about this.

"Hi, Grandma. It's Philly." He paused over how silly that sounded. Of course she could recognize his voice, if she could hear him at all. He almost gave up on his plan at that point, but silence seemed more depressing than talking.

He continued in a low voice, hoping the man and his wife on the other side of the curtain couldn't hear what he was saying. "Grandma, I know you say that you always pray for me, and I sort of feel like I should be praying for *you* now. But you know I'm not too comfortable with that sorta thing. And I've always wondered how you can tell if something you prayed for ever worked out because you prayed. I don't think I ever asked you that before, but I often wondered about it. Then again, I'm not really sure exactly what sort of things you pray for me. Is it just that I'm safe? Or maybe for all the things I need to be provided?" Not one to monologue in any setting, Philly was rambling. But maybe this was good for Grandma. He continued. "If you can hear me, can you pray for me even now? Or is it just listening that you can do when you're in a coma? I guess you'll have to tell me when you wake up."

Sadness, like a wave of vertigo, rose up in Philly at the unspoken question—*What if she doesn't wake up?* He sat in silence for over a minute. The voice of the man through the curtain rose a bit as he seemed to be saying his parting words. Philly stopped listening to that detached voice and leaned forward, trying to keep his composure.

He found Grandma's hand under the blanket and held it gently, feeling the warmth of her life seep through that thin layer of cloth. "I know what I need you to pray for me now, Grandma. I need you to pray that I survive not having you with me, not having you to talk to, to listen to. That's what I need you to pray for me."

Philly sat silently again, listening to the faint breathing of the body in the bed, the only sign of life, and barely enough to assure him that he wasn't alone. He sat there for half an hour, until his mother arrived and he pretended to be on his way somewhere.

He never did eat supper that night, staring at the television for a couple hours and then going to bed early. He forgot about calling Brenda until too late. His head spiraled with inarticulate fears for his dearest relative, still wondering about Grandma's prayers.

Chapter Two

Philly's alarm clock rang at six thirty as usual. But he already lay awake, staring at the pastel patterns of light emerging on his ceiling as the sun levitated off Lake Michigan. He sat up and flipping the alarm off, ending the piercing alert from the little plastic guardian of his employment.

Irving stood at the foot of the bed examining Philly for signs of intent regarding the very important matter of canned cat food. Philly's eye contact with the cat started a prolonged session of mewing.

"Yeah, yeah, yeah. I got you covered, old boy."

Standing in the kitchen with bright light beaming from the basketball-sized white orb in the middle of the yellow-stained ceiling, Philly squinted and scratched. Irving wound in and out of his bare ankles. When he pulled a new can of cat food from the cupboard and set it on the counter, Philly noticed the empty coffee jar in the garbage can next to him. This time he considered brewing half a pot of coffee and even thought of carrying an extra cup with him for Brenda in case she ran out of time again. That would be nice of him.

Irving's mewing finally reached a crescendo. He followed his plate from its frustrating elevation past his nose to its usual spot on the green linoleum tile. The ringing clatter of the Corelle plate on the floor harmonized with the enthusiastic purring of the cat, as it did every morning. This service to the only other occupant of the apartment deposited a sense of purpose in Philly's heart, one that boosted him into his routine for venturing out into the world.

By the time he was showered and shaved, the coffee brewed,

his clothes on, and his hair mostly dried, Philly had once again witnessed the mysterious disappearance of nearly an hour. He wondered if some day he would find those escaped hours, perhaps lurking in a dark corner with several dozen delinquent socks.

This morning he grabbed two travel mugs for the coffee and added some vanilla-flavored creamer to each, knowing that was how Brenda would like hers. He had to sniff the creamer first, to make sure it was still fit for consumption.

Philly tightened the lid of Brenda's mug, his peace offering for not calling the night before, and took an awkward sip from the scarred black plastic lid of his own. He had to double back to grab his keys, checking for the third time that he had his phone. He planned to text Brenda about the coffee as soon as possible, though she might already be on the train by now. He slipped Brenda's firmly sealed mug into his jacket pocket, hoping to use his free arm to keep it from swinging wildly as he walked.

Walking and drinking proved challenging for Philly, the tan coffee filling the top of the travel mug nearly to the brim as he tipped it to drink and missed repeatedly. When he reached his bus stop, he sheltered his face in his phone and texted his offer of coffee to Brenda. She didn't answer before the bus arrived.

As usual, Philly boarded the bus last and found a seat on the right-hand side.

As soon as he settled himself, sucking the last bits of escaped coffee off the top of the travel mug, he noticed a man sitting in front of him on the bench facing the aisle. The Middle-Eastern-looking man, with long hair and a beard, wore a flowing white robe and sort of similar length blue coat. Philly tried to look at the stranger without being detected, thinking that he would usually have to go to Evanston or New Town to see a character like this. But the stranger startled Philly by turning toward him and speaking.

"Hello, Philly. It's good to see you this morning."

Seeing Jesus

Philly stared at him, now afforded a perfect view of the eccentric's face. The man appeared to be a bit over thirty years old, his dark eyes greeting Philly and the whole bus, it seemed. Such public friendliness from a stranger concerned Philly deeply, as it would most urban dwellers. But the most disturbing aspect of this meeting had just nestled into Philly's brain. The man had called him by name.

Philly spoke with the stilted rhythm of a man reading a cue card that someone else has handwritten. "Uh, how do you know me?"

The stranger smiled. "Oh, I know everybody. But I'm here like this to see you, just now."

Philly heard something dripping on the floor, and then he heard a kid say, "Hey Mister, you're spilling on the floor."

Philly jerked his cup upright, looking down at the little river of tan liquid on the dirty black floor. He glanced at the kid but said nothing, feeling that he had bigger problems to deal with. As he turned back to the stranger, he felt his phone vibrate in his pocket, presumably the answer from Brenda.

"That's Brenda," said the stranger. "She's very grateful for the coffee. That really *was* nice of you."

Philly stared at the smiling man, fumbled for his phone, tapped the message notification, and read the text.

Wow, thats really nicd of yu. Thx a bunch!!!

"T-H-X a bunch," said the stranger, who couldn't possibly see the phone display from where he sat.

"How do you know that? Who are you?" Philly spoke like he was in a late-night movie about a serial killer.

The bus stopped and a young woman who had been holding onto the handle on the back of Philly's seat stepped toward the door. She scowled hard at Philly, as if examining a crime scene that both concerned and repelled her. She looked away quickly when he returned her gaze.

"You might not want to respond to me out loud," the

stranger said confidentially. "No one else can see and hear me as you can."

Philly took a moment to comprehend what the stranger had said, and suddenly he understood the implications. He glanced around the bus and caught three or four people watching him suspiciously. Then he retreated, trying to find the moment his alarm clock woke him.

Surely he must be dreaming, so he wouldn't be able to find that waking moment. But he could. He remembered sitting up. He remembered the early light on the ceiling. And he remembered the belated alarm attempting to wake the already awake. But that must have been all part of the dream.

He smelled the coffee, looking down at his hand, which had collected a few drops of the leaking liquid. Philly couldn't remember smelling anything in a dream before.

"It's not a dream, Philly. I'm really here. But I'm only visible to you and to no one else." The stranger tilted his head sympathetically.

"Who ..." Philly started to speak aloud, but then stopped himself, casting his eyes about. Again, he found that haunted vigilance on the faces of his fellow passengers. For a second, he considered how to communicate without speaking.

"It's just like when you talk to yourself, when you play out those conversations in your head. Just do one side of that conversation and I'll do the other." The stranger was apparently reading his mind.

"*Okay*," Philly said inside his head. "*Who are you, and what are you doing to me?*" His inaudible voice elevated toward panic.

"I'm Jesus, and I'm here to keep you company."

"*You're Jesus?*" Philly still managed to keep the conversation internal, which was complicated by the fact that the stranger seemed to be answering with audible words.

"Yes. Your grandma prayed for me to keep you company and to talk with you."

Philly attempted to recall his exact words to his grandmother the night before. Would she do that? Could she do that? "*She prayed? When?*" Philly thought.

"Last night. She could hear you and was concerned about you. She knows she's not always going to be around for you, so she prayed for me to accompany you."

"*Accompany me to work?*"

"Yes, and to be with you *at* work and at home. Everywhere."

"*And no one else sees you?*" Philly glanced around again, more surreptitiously this time. He found his fellow passengers only watching him out of the corners of their eyes now.

"This is your stop." Jesus stood.

Philly scrambled to his feet, slipping slightly in the coffee spill. He looked down briefly but hustled toward the exit along with two regulars who got off at the same stop. Jesus followed him off the bus. The extra mug of coffee in Philly's jacket pocket banged against his hip like another delusion yanking at his attention. It pulled his jacket askew and added to his imbalanced feeling. Adjusting his jacket, remembering to hold his own coffee upright, and walking to his second bus as if chased by a stalker, Philly forced himself not to look left or right in case his impossible companion was still with him.

He tried to remember what he had said to Grandma and what his Jesus illusion had said to him. Instinctively, he turned to his right to check with Jesus about exactly what he had said. And there he was, striding along beside Philly, a smile on his face and his eyes taking in all the people around them.

Philly rode the LaSalle Street bus in silence, sorting out the disaster scene that his mind had become—bits of reality scattered about on the ground where they never should have been, shattered by a crushing earthquake or rushing tornado. He looked again at that stranger. That guy seemed to have no problems.

Jesus had taken a seat on the second bus just like the first. In that seat Philly couldn't help seeing him. Philly's heart rate accelerated. The guy was still there. What would happen at work? Was this Jesus? Really?

Philly didn't attend any sort of church, and his parents had avoided church for his entire life, having lapsed from the disparate faiths with which each grew up. Still, he couldn't conceive of simply telling his Jesus mirage to go away and leave him alone. That just didn't seem a good way to talk to someone who might actually be the Son of God, as far as Philly could tell.

Because his cramped mind led him wandering in circles like a man lost in the woods, the second bus ride passed quickly. This time he recognized his stop without help, sprouting some hope that escaping rapid transit would free him from his delusion, like escaping the crazy people he often saw on the bus.

Philly hit the pavement hard, as if forgetting to factor gravity into his planned escape. He felt a hand steady him before he stumbled, but he didn't dare look at whose hand that was. Instead, he strode toward his building with purpose, that purpose being to run away from this supposed Jesus. But, glancing over his right shoulder, he slowed down. There, walking step-for-step with him, was Jesus.

As he approached the front door of his office building, Philly could see Brenda waiting for him. "Oh, no," he said aloud. Then he turned to Jesus and thought, *"Please don't say anything around Brenda ... uh ... Sir."* Maybe the term he was searching for was "Lord." But he had little practice talking to God, or even an optical illusion of God's Son.

"She can't hear me. Only you can."

Philly broke free from the urge to clarify himself and get Jesus to not talk to *him* while Brenda was near, but he realized it was too late.

"Hello, Mr. Considerate." Brenda beamed an enticing smile—complete with fresh lipstick.

Philly fumbled for his pocket, found the second travel cup, and even found that his pocket was dry. Before he had started hallucinating that morning, his mind had been clear enough to use the most leak-proof mug for Brenda's coffee. Remembering that earlier moment of sanity prompted a brief nostalgia. He handed Brenda the cup.

"Thanks." Brenda examined Philly as if he had a Band-Aid across the bridge of his nose.

Brenda's mute inquiry reminded him of the suspicious looks from his fellow bus passengers, and he worried that he had said something to thin air without being aware of it.

"So, you gonna say hi or something?"

Philly nearly palmed himself in the forehead when he realized his oversight. But before he could say anything, his Jesus shadow stepped up right next to Brenda. The most distracting thing about that was the Savior's enraptured gaze, an odd contrast with Brenda's confused mask. This completely rattled Philly. Was his illusion making a move on his girlfriend? What *was* that look?

"Are you okay, Philly? You're acting really strange. You feeling sick?"

That was it. Philly had a way out. He could say he *was* sick and head for home, surrendering the field to the conquering armies of insanity and impossibility.

Jesus made a motion as if prompting Philly to answer Brenda.

Philly took the prompt. "Oh, hello. I'm sorry. My mind is somewhere else just now."

And here his delusion became even more complicated. Jesus raised his left hand as if to caress Brenda's face. But as his hand approached her cheek, it disappeared—as if the Christ were an amputee. Philly stared incredulously.

"What's wrong? What are you looking at?" Brenda's voice sharpened.

Philly covered his eyes with one hand and shook his head. "I'm sorry. I'm not myself this morning." He moaned.

27

"Oh, you poor dear. You saw your grandmother last night, didn't you? And you stayed there so late that you couldn't call me at a decent hour. So now you're all stressed and out of sorts." She hooked her free hand through his right arm and turned to walk him into work. "I'm so sorry."

Philly brightened slightly at this first bit of good luck. "Thanks." He accepted the role of the grieving grandson. Brenda's intuition, after all, wasn't too far from the truth.

Looking past Brenda, Philly saw his Jesus projection walking beside them. He made eye contact with Philly, and Philly nearly forgot to walk. Just in that moment, that brief expression on Jesus's face, Philly saw something like loving acceptance. It reminded him of his grandma. This was the second reason that Philly wouldn't think of just sending the apparition away.

When he sensed that Brenda had begun to drag him toward the door, he refocused on walking and maintaining a polite connection with her.

"Are you gonna be all right to work?" Brenda juggled her coffee to her left hand and pulled the door open.

Philly attempted to rally. "I'll be all right." Again, he thought about calling it quits for the day, to recover from his Jesus virus or whatever he was suffering.

Dennis Walsh, Philly's ghostly pale boss, caught sight of him in the lobby. This seemed to wipe out going home sick, maybe. Philly was, at least, relieved that he had broken physical contact with Brenda before Dennis saw him. And he reminded himself that no one could see Jesus but him. These qualifications in place, his slate was clean with Dennis. But with himself Philly was still inside out and upside down. In that state, he felt the pressure of his boss's disapproval of what he was *thinking*, even if Dennis couldn't read his mind.

Glancing at Jesus, Philly saw him cast a friendly eye in Dennis's direction, something Philly never thought to do. As a boss, Dennis kept his relationship with Philly strictly business and offered little room for friendship or charity. Jesus didn't work for Dennis. He seemed to feel no guilt or resentment toward him.

Brenda had increased the distance between herself and Philly when they saw Dennis. It seemed she truly didn't want to complicate Philly's work life. His personal life was, of course, a different matter. "Bye." Brenda gave Philly a wave with three fingers as they parted by the staircase.

"Bye," Philly said.

"Goodbye, beloved Brenda," Jesus said.

Philly scowled at his uninvited guest, now that Dennis had turned aside and could no longer see Philly's face.

Craig Washburn, on the other hand, intercepted that scowl. The twenty-eight-year-old African American worked for Philly as a network technician. He did lots of the redundant tasks that Philly didn't enjoy, making Philly's days more pleasant. "What's wrong, Phil?" Craig stepped into the traffic flow that would take them past the network room.

"Huh?" Philly hadn't noticed Craig next to the receptionist's desk. "Oh, not a great morning so far."

"Anything I can do to help?" Craig generally tight roped a line between sucking up and genuine helpfulness.

Philly could never see clearly on which side of that line his assistant tipped from one moment to the next. He just treated Craig at face value. "No, it's personal stuff. But thanks for asking." Philly changed the subject. "You got her computer switched over to the new patch panel?" He back nodded toward Donna at the reception desk.

"Yep, no problem. She's up and running."

"Good. Go ahead and start using that new firewall—I tested it last night. We can just switch over people who aren't in the office yet, up on the third floor."

"Cool, will do. I don't need to log in to it or anything, do I?"

Philly shook his head, distracted by the sight of Jesus in his workplace. The robe and sandals didn't fit in the business casual dress code, but it did look comfortable.

"Okay, see ya later." Craig kept walking toward the elevators when Philly detoured toward the bathroom.

"Yep." Philly spoke quickly over his shoulder. He wanted to wash his hands. The coffee he spilled had made his hand sticky.

While Craig had known not to follow Philly into the bathroom, Jesus apparently had no such boundaries. He leaned against the wall next to the paper towels and crossed his arms over his chest. That pose reminded Philly of high school and Ray following him into the bathroom between classes, or during some class they were skipping.

"You gonna follow me everywhere?" Philly's tone was just short of complaint.

"You can draw the lines wherever you want, Philly."

Somebody in one of the stalls flushed, and Philly rolled his eyes, realizing that he had asked his last question aloud. He sped up his handwashing, picked up his cup, and scuttled out of the bathroom before he could be identified by the other mortal occupant.

Jesus scuttled right along behind him.

As he walked toward the elevator, Philly decided he had better work on communicating with his hallucination without his voice. "*Are you just some kind of a mirage, or something?*"

"No, you're really seeing me. I know this is unusual, but Grandma and I have a very close relationship, and I respect her prayers." Jesus was still moving his mouth and seeming to use good old-fashioned sound. "You've been given a rare chance, Philly. Most people just have to assume that I'm really with them because they heard it in church. You get to see for yourself."

Put that way, this delusion seemed almost desirable. Philly got off the elevator and walked to his office. He unlocked the door with Jesus patiently waiting. He sloughed his jacket off absently and hung it on the hook behind his door, swung around his desk, clunked his cup on its surface, and dumped himself into his swivel chair. He tapped the space bar to wake up his computer.

Jesus took a seat across the desk in one of the aqua-blue woven cloth guest chairs.

Philly glanced at Jesus as he waited for his password to be recognized. He clicked on his email icon, again waiting, this time for the screen to update with his latest messages. He sat back and fixed on his visitor. He remembered not to speak aloud. *"Should I go home? I'm not sure I can work with you sitting there."*

"Why not?"

"Well, you're distracting."

"Okay, how about if I move over here?" Jesus got up and switched to the chair farther from Philly's field of view.

Philly shrugged. *"I guess that's better."*

He decided to work on purchasing half a dozen new computers—one of his favorite parts of the job. His boss took care of software licensing, as well as managing programmers and the help desk. That left Philly with the network hardware and software, and purchasing most of the desktop and laptop computers. Philly immersed himself in gigabytes and gigahertz, flat screens and purchase prices, aiming to buy the best computers he could fit into the budget he was handed. In this way, Philly started the strangest day of his working life. He was grateful that he had a consuming task to keep him from tangling with the meaning of seeing this apparition in his office. Jesus, sitting there watching him work, didn't bother him as much as the fact that no one *else* could see Jesus, impugning Philly's sanity.

At five o'clock, Brenda found Philly closing his office door and locking it. She had emailed him twice that day.

Of course, the fact that Philly didn't answer wasn't about Brenda, or even Philly's feelings about Brenda. For one moment, when he looked at the second email, Philly had longed for a relationship with Brenda—or someone—in which he could share exactly what was happening to him. The vision of such an honest and intimate relationship had blossomed and then withered, leaving only the specter of the God-man peacefully watching him check his email.

"Philly, didn't you get my emails?" Brenda's wounded accusation spilled all around her question.

Beginning to form his evasive defense, Philly sensed Jesus stepping up close to him, as if he were about to whisper in his ear. He couldn't stop himself from turning to check what his religious mirage was up to now. He made eye contact with Jesus, who seemed to project reassurance and peace.

On the impulsive strength of that gaze, Philly started to tell the truth. "I guess I wanted to be alone today. I had work to do that kept me in front of my computer. I didn't even go out for lunch, just ate peanuts and granola bars from my desk drawer."

His sincere response and melancholy demeanor must have melted Brenda's complaint, if not all her resentment. "Oh, I keep forgetting about your grandma. You poor dear." Again she hooked her arm through Philly's, as if to help him make it to the elevator.

And again, Philly fell into the role that Brenda created for him, thinking momentarily about whether he was being dishonest by not correcting her misconception. But he looked at Jesus again, and his apparent contentment with the resolution of Philly's situation reassured him that he had done nothing truly wrong. Perhaps he had fallen short of his own desire for that perfect intimacy that he had imagined earlier in the day. But was that a sin? If so, it was a different kind of sin than what he was used to regretting.

The day had turned cloudy and rainy while Philly worked in his windowless office. Instead of the rain, however, Philly focused on how to make a graceful break from Brenda. He needed to get alone with his Jesus stalker and figure out what was really happening to him.

"I'm worried about you being alone this evening." Brenda opened her umbrella.

Philly stood in the rain, his hair beginning to sag under the steady shower. He was struggling to decide whether to go see his grandma or just head for home.

Jesus responded to his thoughts. "Your grandma is fine. Your mother is with her now and will stay for a while. You need to get home and call your sister about picking her up at the airport."

His apparition seemed surprisingly well-informed. For Philly, taking advice from a specter seemed no less crazy than seeing and hearing Jesus with him all day. But he still wondered how to break from Brenda.

"Tell her about the call to your sister and that you need to get some rest tonight."

"Uh, thanks Brenda. But I need to talk to my sister tonight about arrangements for her to come into town. And then I gotta get some sleep." He zipped his jacket to the top and took a decisive step toward his bus stop.

Brenda's dejected face peered from under her pink, flowered umbrella as he threw her a resigned grin over his shoulder.

He began to jog up the block. Jesus jogged with him. That became somewhat annoying when Philly noticed that the long-haired carpenter showed no sign of getting winded or wet. Philly slowed to a fast walk, taking the rain as a small, deserved punishment for a life of disbelief.

Jesus skipped up the stairs into the bus ahead of Philly when they arrived two seconds before it left the bus stop.

Philly moved carefully, trying not to slip on the wet steps and aisle. The bus was crowded, and he and Jesus both had to stand, holding the overhead rail. Philly focused on Jesus for a moment as he watched his mirage looking around at all the other people. Something about the way he regarded them told Philly that Jesus knew each of them personally and had a compelling affection for all.

The survey of all who surrounded them ended at an African

American man in his late fifties, wearing a White Sox cap sideways, muttering through his ill-kept beard. He had been quiet when they entered the bus, but his attention now seemed to have fixed on Philly's hallucination. "Jesus, I see you. Jesus, don't mess with us. Jesus." He fired that name into the air almost like a cough, such that it clearly startled half of the passengers. "Oh, oooooo, oh, you're messin' with me, I know it, Jesus!" He shouted now.

The bus pulled to the next stop, and the disturbed Sox fan pushed toward the side door. As it swung open, he flailed both arms around his head, like he was shooing a swarm of bees. "I ain't lettin' you mess with us!" he screeched as he bailed onto the sidewalk. From there, he looked back repeatedly while running up the street. Unfortunately for him, the bus drove in the same direction. His panic kept him running for a whole block, as the Jesus-bearing bus seemed to be chasing him. Finally, he stopped running and let the bus drive past him, flailing at those invisible bees again.

Philly could just hear one last, "Jesus," barked into the rainy air as the bus swung back out into traffic and away.

Jesus looked at Philly, and Philly returned the gaze. Careful not to be associated with the escaped passenger, Philly remembered to communicate silently. *"What did you do to that guy?"*

"I didn't *do* anything. I'm just here, and I'm just me."

"I thought you said no one else could hear or see you."

Jesus nodded. "He didn't see or hear me. But the bees buzzing around in his head all recognized me."

"Oh." Philly let the whole incident sink in. That man's insanity—or demons, or whatever—recognized that Jesus was standing there next to Philly. Here was the first proof that this person with him was more than just a figment of his own fractured psyche. For the first time, Philly allowed himself to form the thought, *This could be real.*

Jesus, apparently reading his thoughts, smiled at Philly and nodded.

Chapter Three

Philly sorted through his mail as he walked up the stuffy stairwell toward his front door, stomping slowly on the light gray carpet stretched over the chocolate-brown wood. *The stairs will do you good*, he thought. This phrase often passed through his mind when he walked up the front stairs, though he couldn't remember when that had started and why.

"Yes, they will." Jesus followed close behind.

On the landing outside his apartment, Philly stopped and turned toward Jesus, who effortlessly scaled the last three stairs. Philly spoke aloud. "Are you like a ghost or something, so you can just do that so easy?"

Jesus smiled and shook his head once. "No, not a ghost, or even very much like a ghost. You see, the lightness of my step comes from being fully alive, not from the weightlessness of being dead."

Having never taken any kind of theology class, and barely passing a freshman philosophy course in college, Philly missed any deep nuances of that answer. But Jesus didn't seem discouraged by the blank stare he elicited as Philly stood holding his junk mail on the landing.

Philly broke from his paralysis and fished his keys from his jacket pocket, looking forward to getting into some dry clothes.

Jesus waited patiently, unperturbed by Philly's delay and totally dry despite the rain outside.

Finally, Philly slipped the correct key into the correct lock and cracked the front door open. Absentmindedly he left the door open for Jesus to enter, so Jesus closed it but didn't lock it. Walking toward his bedroom and tugging at his damp jacket, Philly wondered what that would have looked like to someone else. The door closing itself, perhaps?

Whatever the case, Philly was pleased to see his guest respecting his privacy and staying outside the bedroom while he changed clothes. The distraction of knowing that the supernatural visitor awaited him, however, repeatedly derailed Philly's attempts to change. He forgot what he was doing several times. Twice he started to leave the room less than fully dressed.

"Sorry. I kept getting distracted." Philly emerged from the bedroom.

"I know."

"You know? Oh, of course you know. I suppose you could see through the door." He dodged Irving, who stood staring at Jesus.

"I didn't need to see through the door to know everything you did in there. I've always seen everything you've ever done, without having to use my X-ray vision." Jesus's voice took a teasing tone.

Philly stopped in the kitchen door, trying to sort Jesus's response even as he puzzled over Irving's behavior. Obviously, the cat could see the otherwise-invisible man standing there. How was that? Philly clearly hadn't been adequately introduced to the rules of this experience.

Jesus grinned at Philly, who was staring at the cat, who was watching Jesus. Then Jesus said to the cat, "C'mere Irving." The usually suspicious cat took two steps and jumped up into Jesus's arms.

Philly reran the scenario in his head. "What if I filmed this with my camera? Would I get video of my cat floating in thin air?"

"I wouldn't let you do that." Jesus scratched Irving, who purred louder than Philly had ever heard in all their five years together.

Philly decided not to try that video experiment—at least not now. Instead, he switched to the comment about X-ray vision, or rather about Jesus always seeing everything. He cringed at several embarrassing things he had done in private in recent weeks.

He cleared his throat. "Uh, you said you've always been able to see everything I do, but you generally aren't watching, are you?"

Jesus let Irving down to the floor where the cat began purring in a tight circle around his ankles. "You need to understand that the way you're experiencing me right now is unusual." Jesus paced his words like a tolerant instructor. "You see me as if I were a regular human being in one place at one time. I do that for your benefit—a sort of optical illusion to make it easier for you to know that I'm right here with you. It's not possible for you to see me as I truly am, present everywhere in time and space. All that to say, I'm not limited to one pair of human eyes—or even a finite bank of security cameras—for watching over my loved ones."

The reference to security cameras connected with Philly immediately, since one of his responsibilities at work was archiving digital recordings from the seven security cameras around the office. He smiled at the notion that Jesus had a much larger set of security cameras. Then he bonked into the implication that Jesus had indeed seen him do all those very embarrassing things he was remembering, not to mention the ones he wasn't remembering. Repulsed by that idea, he veered toward the question of his own sanity.

"How can this be real?" He actually said this not as a question, but as a protest. He would at least try to fight the insanity.

"Why do you doubt that I'm really here with you?"

Philly stood with his eyes fixed on his delusion. But his mind was busy trying to find a fingerhold somewhere in all his catalog of life experiences that allowed for this thing to be happening. "People don't literally see you standing next to them. I've never heard of anybody that did, anyway." His belligerence faded. He couldn't maintain any kind of aggression for long.

"Have you ever had such a persistent delusion before?

Seeing Jesus

Besides the Cubs, I mean."

The Cubs? What did Jesus know about the Cubs? This very non-religious poke deflated Philly's rebellion. He released a short laugh at the indictment of his baseball loyalty.

"You think I can ignore all those frustrated prayers through all these years?" Jesus smiled. Then he turned more serious. "I see everything and everyone, Philly."

Again, this peaked Philly's guilt levels, like the totalitarian shadow of Big Brother, or the Matrix being plugged in all around him.

But he kept his eyes on Jesus. The look on that flawlessly loving face completely flipped being under surveillance to being watched over and cared for.

Wait, this man standing here in front of me is the one who's constantly watching me? This is the all-seeing God? He doesn't seem ticked off at me. He doesn't seem to hate me. HE is watching me?

Jesus just smiled in answer to the patter in Philly's head, his active eyes digging into Philly's soul.

Philly did something next that he hadn't done since high school. He began to sob like a child.

He clasped his face with both hands and simply erupted into tears. His breath lurched in cramping heaves, his sobs loud and unhinged. He wept a purging river of tears that drained all available liquids from his body until the tears smelled like ammonia, and his nose stung like when he tried jogging outside in the winter. After a minute, he was seated on the floor with Jesus holding his shoulders, another minute and he was on his face wetting the dusty wood, feeling Jesus's hands on his back. Those hands comforted him but didn't stop his tears. Instead, Jesus took part in them. Philly could hear weeping above him. He wasn't the only one sobbing in that apartment. And this broke his heart more.

Ten minutes of hard crying was exhausting. Being out of practice, Philly's ribs hurt, and his throat felt inflamed when he ran out of strength to continue. It took him another ten minutes to clean up his face and the floor, blowing his nose and drinking water. He gasped spasmodically to catch his breath and to calm himself.

During this whole breakdown and recovery, Jesus stayed close to Philly, seeming to know exactly how close he could stand, where he could place his hands to comfort and not interfere, and even exactly how loudly he could cry along with Philly so as not to be distracting.

As Philly began to recover his composure, he sat on his old couch, sunken into the soft cushions. His hair felt like it was twisted in eight directions. After the last sniffle, he mostly wanted to sleep. But Jesus, sitting at the other end of the couch, kept him focused enough to fight off the core weariness that weighed him down. Philly inventoried the possibility that this emotional breakdown might further prove that he was losing his mind. The need to call his sister about her trip to Chicago nagged at him, but he didn't want to call her in an unstable emotional condition.

"You should call her now," Jesus said. "She's not doing anything, and you could reach her right away. It'll be harder to get ahold of her tomorrow."

This self-assured advice from his hallucination fell into the nexus of curiosity and discovery twirling around Philly's head. He decided to test the information that this Jesus image was offering so confidently. Pulling out his cell phone, Philly unlocked it and found Eileen in his list of frequent contacts. Her number, with its suburban New York area code, displayed on the screen of his smartphone along with a picture of Eileen from the last time she came to visit, at Christmas.

Currently single and not seeing anyone, his sister would often be out at a bar or restaurant in the evening. Philly saw Jesus's account of her availability as a good test of his sanity. As usual, her voicemail kicked in after a few rings. Philly decided to wait and leave a message, giving Jesus a chance here in case she was simply indisposed for a moment. But, in the middle of Eileen's rote message about leaving a name and number, Philly heard a beep and a more spontaneous version of her voice.

"Philly?"

Philly glitched for a moment, looking to his right at Jesus watching him.

"Hello?" Eileen said.

"Oh, I really didn't think I'd catch you at home."

"Yeah, I'm surprised myself. Karen suddenly had something to do with her mother, and Rachel was kept late at work, so my plans for the night fell through."

"Oh." Philly wondered whether Jesus manipulated things in New York to make Eileen available for him to call.

"Have you seen Grandma?" Eileen seized the agenda, pushing into the gaps between Philly's responses.

"Not tonight. Ma's there. I saw her last night though."

"Well, how did she look?" From her voice, Philly guessed that Eileen had just lain down, either on her bed or her couch.

"Oh, I don't know. She was like asleep, you know, just still. I mean there wasn't much light, and she was in a coma. So I guess she looked the way you'd expect."

"I'm coming out Friday after work."

"O'Hare? What time does your flight get in?"

"Yeah, O'Hare. At 9:35 p.m." Her answer was accompanied by the sound of a sheet of paper slipping against another.

"I'll come get you."

"Good, so I won't have to blow a fortune on a cab."

Philly had a sporty two-door car that he kept in the fenced lot behind his apartment building. Given his public transit commute and the relative proximity of most shopping options, owning a car in the city was a marginal proposition. He strove to justify it with favors like picking up his sister at the airport. It also made a trip out to his parents' house in the suburbs less of an ordeal.

Jesus had a suggestion. "Ask her if there's anything new at her work."

Philly watched Jesus while mechanically parroting his question. "Anything new at work for you?" He tried to sound nonchalant.

"I'll say! How did you know?" Eileen cackled. "My boss got fired for falsifying his expense reports, and I got promoted to his job! Ha!" She inhaled sharply. "I wasn't gonna say anything—'cause of Grandma, ya' know."

Philly stared at Jesus, his eyebrows at maximum height.

Jesus smiled.

"Funny that you would ask me about that." Eileen sounded more introspective.

"Uh, yeah. Well, congratulations then. That's good news for you, right? A promotion and a raise?"

"Yes, they gave me a big raise too of course. But I don't think I've really let it soak in completely, with Grandma in the hospital."

"Mm-hmm. So, I'll see you Friday at O'Hare."

"Thanks, Philly. Thanks for calling and for picking me up at the airport."

Eileen might not have been as anxious to end the conversation, but Philly didn't know what to say, distracted by the psychic tricks Jesus had done. "Bye, Eileen."

"Bye, Philly."

He paused to set aside the questions he would *not* ask Jesus. Such as, *How did you do that*? He groped, instead, toward the meaning behind that little demonstration.

Jesus appeared to be waiting for him to say something.

"This is really happening, isn't it?"

"Yes, Philly. It is."

"Wow."

Jesus chuckled.

"Who can I tell?"

Jesus puckered thoughtfully. "You can tell anyone you want. But, of course, most people won't believe you at first."

"Is my mother still at the hospital?"

"She's just getting ready to leave."

Philly considered going to tell Grandma, the one person he *knew* would believe him. But that wouldn't be nearly as satisfying with Grandma in a coma. He decided to tell her the next time he visited her alone but chose to stay home. He needed to think more about what to do with his discovery that this Jesus was more than a delusional projection from his mind. His mind couldn't have supplied the sort of information he had been receiving from this walking-and-talking apparition.

"I wonder if I can tell Eileen," Philly said aloud.

Irving sat in the recliner across the living room, attentive to the conversation. Philly was staring at the cat when Jesus answered his question.

"What would you say to her?"

Philly considered for a second. "I could remind her about the question I asked her on the phone. I don't usually ask her about work. She just tells me when she has some story. I can tell her I asked because you told me to."

Jesus nodded.

"How will she react?" Philly wanted more than a nod.

"I can't tell you that. You're not responsible for the way people react, only for doing what you know to be right. Not to be rude about it, but it's not your business how she'll react. And I'll only tell you things that I think you need to know."

Philly nodded, glad to hear more of the rules to this game. "So, you'll tell me things if it'll help me out?"

"Yes." Jesus stood and walked across the room to scoop up Irving. The cat meowed when Jesus reached for him and began to purr when the Creator lifted him off the chair. "I'll also tell you things that will help *other* people."

Philly was intrigued by this possibility but couldn't imagine what it would entail. During the silence that followed he decided to call Brenda—after he ate some supper.

A half hour later, the remnants of his frozen dinner cleaned up, and feeling better physically, Philly sat in the recliner with his cell phone. Jesus sat on the couch across the room. Irving, who had been sleeping on the couch, woke up, stretched, and slowly stalked across two cushions and onto Jesus's lap.

Philly was considering telling Brenda about his visitor. He thought of her sympathetic eyes and hoped to find a niche in the conversation into which he could insert the leading edge of his most startling news. He tapped Brenda's picture in his contact list, a photo taken by him—using a previous phone—one sunny summer day at Navy Pier. He didn't follow that memory anywhere, however. He simply listened to the phone ring and waited for his opportunity to bring someone into his mind-rocking experience.

Brenda picked up. "Hello, you!" She sounded chipper, a promising sign for Philly.

Between chipper and sympathetic, he imagined that she wouldn't be able to reject his news outright. But a seeping fear made an appearance at the edge of his consciousness—fear that his story might conjure up the gloomy Brenda.

"Hi, Brenda. You busy?"

"No, just doing my toenails."

"Oh." That sounded sort of busy. But he could tell that she wanted to talk and expected she could do so with wet toenails.

"I'm glad you called me." Brenda usually didn't hesitate to coopt one of Philly's pauses. "So, how is your grandma?"

"I didn't go see her tonight. My ma was there, and I'd rather see Grandma by herself. I'd feel funny talking to her with Ma listening."

"You do talk to her, though? 'Cause I heard that someone in a coma doesn't really hear anything people say to them. But maybe that's wrong."

"I think she can hear."

"Yeah, who knows, anyway?" She spoke more carefully. "So, what kind of things do you say to her?"

Philly thought for a moment about how much to reveal to her. "Well, my grandma is the best listener, so I tend to tell her lots of stuff. Mostly, last night, I told her how much I missed her." He paused here and then took one more step. "And I asked her to pray for me, 'cause I know she's always praying for me."

"Hmm, who knows—maybe she can do that in a coma. I never did much praying myself."

"Me neither. It always seemed okay for Grandma, but I just didn't believe it made a difference." He stopped there, leaving that past-tense verb hanging. And then he chickened out, letting Brenda take the lead.

"Hmm. So, are you going to visit her every night? 'Cause I was hopin' we could go out this weekend, like you said."

"Oh, I won't see her every night. But I am picking up my sister on Friday, from the airport. You remember, Eileen?"

"Oh. Yeah, I remember her. She had that trendy haircut, all New York style."

"Mm-hmm. I don't know if she still looks like that. I think maybe she's more straight cut now. She has a better job." Three years previous, when Brenda met Eileen, his sister had just started in a pharmaceutical company as a researcher. Her recent promotion now put her two steps above that initial job.

"How long will she be here?"

"Just the weekend. Mostly to see Grandma and help keep Ma calm."

"Your ma's pretty upset, huh?"

"Yeah. Well, you know how she gets."

"Yeah."

Jesus sat watching Philly, no look of disapproval on his face, just watching. Philly tried to recover with Jesus and Brenda. "We could still go out Saturday night, if you're available."

"Really?" Brenda's voice squeaked. "You don't have to be with your sister?"

"No, not really. I don't plan on spending the whole weekend with her and my folks."

"Oh, okay. Dinner and a movie then?"

"Sure. Pick you up at six?"

"That would be great."

"Good. So, I'll see you at work tomorrow?"

"Of course."

"Okay. Well, good night."

"Good night, Philly. Thanks again for calling."

Philly looked at Jesus. "I could tell her Saturday night, right?"

Jesus nodded, setting Irving down on the cushion next to him. "Of course you can." He said that with no hint of irony or doubt in his voice, either of which would have been justified even if the Savior wasn't able to read his thoughts.

That night Philly had some difficulty falling asleep, having shut off a TV show that he normally watched and then going to bed early. A combination of remembering that he told Brenda he wanted to be home that night to get some extra rest and guilt over the content of the TV show prompted him to repent from his usual Wednesday night routine. He imagined that he could hear Jesus breathing where he sat in the dark corner of the bedroom. However, when he held his own breath and listened, he could perceive no other human sound. Just when he was contemplating asking Jesus to spend the night in the living room, he fell into a fitful sleep.

He seemed to dream all night about the people on the bus staring at him, sometimes people he knew, sometimes not. At other turns, crazy people shouted at him, driving him from the bus, chasing him down the street until he got lost in unfamiliar neighborhoods. He seemed to spend hours unable to find his way to work or back home.

Then Jesus entered his dreams. He ushered Philly out onto a familiar street where Philly realized he was only a few blocks from work. And Jesus showed him that no one was chasing him. There on the street, still in his dream, Philly fell into Jesus's arms and began to weep with happiness. At last he had someone to guide him, someone to protect him, someone to go with him and make sure that all his needs were met. After that he slept peacefully through the rest of the night.

Chapter Four

When he first woke up to the sound of his alarm, Philly didn't remember about Jesus being in the apartment. Flipping the alarm off, he rolled toward the side of the bed and sat up, his T-shirt twisted uncomfortably. He tried to tug it around straight but stopped when he heard movement behind him that didn't sound like Irving. Fortunately, his mind had booted up far enough to remember his visitor before he panicked. Philly did turn quickly to see Jesus sitting in the same chair where he had seen him before he went to sleep.

Jesus smiled. "I'm still here."

Philly rubbed his face with both hands and finished by running his fingers through his hair. He needed a haircut. Bouncing up off the bed, he waved a groggy good morning to Jesus and headed for the bathroom.

Irving followed, taking up his usual post outside the door where he recited his regular order for breakfast.

"Yes, cranky cat, I will feed you." Philly flushed the toilet.

After washing up, Philly opened the bathroom door and looked at Jesus. "Another day at work. I think I can handle you being there better today."

"I think you're right."

Philly managed to run through his morning routine, even brewing himself a cup of coffee, only to get a text from Brenda saying, **My turn to bring coffee**. He dumped hot coffee down the sink after debating with himself. He didn't need that much coffee.

On the way out the door, Jesus helped him remember his cell phone, which he had laid on the kitchen counter while contemplating what to do about the coffee.

"Thanks." Philly headed down the back stairs and toward the

bus.

"You're welcome. You better start practicing communicating with me without talking out loud."

"Oh, yeah." Philly said that aloud and then laughed at himself. *I'll get the hang of this.*

The April wind from the southwest undid all of Philly's coiffing, but he didn't mind. The temperature was over fifty already, and the wind was only moderately cool. In fact, Philly was in a good mood, coming to enjoy Jesus's company during the dull parts of his life—which included most parts of his life.

On the bus, Philly noticed a few of the people who had marked him for suspicious surveillance the day before. He determined to be as normal as possible this morning. Jesus sat next to him, facing forward. And for the first time Philly thought about the fact that he could feel Jesus's shoulder against his. For reasons he couldn't explain, this realization gave Philly chills to the point that he visibly shook for half a second. After he did that, however, he feared he might have alerted the freak detectors of his fellow passengers. He looked out the window and caught Jesus's reflection there. They exchanged small smiles.

At his transfer stop, a man with a raw, red face and bony hands shook a Styrofoam cup, soliciting donations with a weak, jangling rhythm. Philly, not generally a spontaneous donor in such situations, felt a surge of generosity. He found the change from the coffee he'd bought two days ago and dropped all of it into the beggar's cup. Philly didn't know the exact size of his donation, but he knew it was small—yet he privately congratulated himself for breaking out of his usual cocoon of protection from the world around him. As he turned away from the beggar, nodding to acknowledge the man's monotone thanks and "God bless you," Philly saw Jesus stop. Jesus stood next to the beggar, his garment brushing against the stained sleeve of the man with the cup.

Philly held up the line of folks boarding the LaSalle 156 bus as he stared at Jesus, who was looking sorrowfully into the beggar's glassy and bloodshot eyes. A short woman behind Philly cleared her throat meaningfully, breaking him out of his daze. He dutifully climbed onto the bus, fearing momentarily that Jesus wouldn't follow.

Before the bus pulled away from the curb, Jesus turned away from the beggar and stepped through the side of the bus and next to Philly, as if the world around him were a mere projection.

Seeing Jesus pass through the side of the bus startled Philly, but the bus rocking through a pothole probably disguised his spasm of surprise.

Jesus squeezed between passengers and took his place pressed up against Philly on the crowded bus.

Philly averted his gaze and then met Jesus's eyes over and over, unable to hold eye contact but reticent to look away. Only the general internal preoccupation of his fellow passengers would have prevented them from noticing Philly shifting his eyes back and forth nervously. Finally, Philly ventured to address Jesus with his thoughts. *"What were you doing back there with that beggar?"*

Jesus met Philly with his receptive eyes and peaceful smile. He spared Philly the strain of thinking in reply to someone speaking, by communicating mind-to-mind. "I was getting as close to him as you did and lingering there as long as you would let me."

"Why were you doing that?"

"I want to touch as many people as I can, in any way that I can."

"What do you mean?"

"You gave him money. In doing so, you acknowledged him as a fellow human being—someone who is connected to you in some way, someone who matters. You did more than make him a few cents richer. As you did that, you made way for me to briefly connect with that man, whose name is Ben, by the way."

Philly wasn't comprehending the significance of Jesus's

words, and he felt too constrained by the crowd around him to ask the questions to clear his tangled mind. He just said, "*I don't understand.*"

"You will. Just give it time."

Philly nodded slightly and then blinked self-consciously, hoping no one had noticed the nod.

Before the bus even stopped, Philly could see Brenda waiting for him, the breeze blowing a curl of her brown hair over one eye. She held a paper coffee cup in each hand.

Philly followed three other people exiting the bus and, just as the woman in front of him reached the top step, a young teenage boy pushed another boy into the woman.

The stern, thirty-something woman swore at the boy. "Jesus!"

When she said that, Philly looked over at Jesus, who was closely following him off the bus.

Jesus raised his eyebrows as if to say, "Is she talking to me?"

This little joke distracted Philly, who nearly stepped on the back of the disgruntled woman's shoes, having to dance delicately with his hands held chest high to avoid the collision. He caught a grim scowl from the woman as he regained his balance. Then he looked at Brenda, who was just fifteen feet away. He tipped his head to say, "Oops!" and then smiled.

Brenda mirrored his grin and shrugged slightly.

"Good morning, Philly. A close call there, huh?" She smiled as brightly as the sun, which dashed out from behind a white cloud.

Philly smiled in return, and they pivoted to walk toward work. He lost his focus for a moment when Jesus swept around to the other side of Brenda, as if the three of them were old friends, skipping off to work together.

Brenda tugged Philly back to her. "So, did you sleep well last night? Get the rest you needed?"

Philly wound up for a cogent response. "Oh, yeah. I did sleep pretty well, I think." He was uncertain what the right answer was until he remembered the anxious dreams. He chose not to amend his answer, however. "How about you?" He strove to pay attention to Brenda this time.

"I slept well, thank you." She answered with the whimsy of a girl skipping off to play.

"Hey, thanks for the coffee. You didn't have to do that." Philly raised the coffee shop cup. He really meant that he didn't want Brenda to buy him things. He knew she made less than half of what he did and that she wasn't particularly careful with her money. Restaurant coffee for two would add up to a problem if this pattern persisted.

"Oh, I know I should have brewed it myself. But I got a late start this morning and was afraid I'd miss the train. So I just bought some between here and the El station. I'll plan better next time."

Entering their office building, they reached the place where they would naturally part. All three of them hesitated. Jesus looked at both of them expectantly. Philly tried again to elevate his game. "I guess we better get to work. I hope you have a great day, Brenda."

"Oh, thanks. You too."

"I'll be thinking of you." He inserted this like someone who had forgotten his line until too late.

"Oh, wow. You too." Momentarily freezing in the middle of her turn toward the stairs, Brenda blinked her surprise.

That reaction, which Philly caught just before heading for the elevator, made him feel that he might have overreached. He glanced at Jesus, who seemed unconcerned. In fact, Jesus was looking at each of the people they passed with that intimate interest that Philly had noticed before, as if he expected each person to stop and greet him. He continued this on the elevator as well.

When they reached Philly's office door, and the hallway was

clear of traffic, Philly managed to ask a silent question. "*What are you thinking when you look at all the people you pass?*"

Jesus followed Philly into his office and dropped casually into the same chair he had occupied the first day. "I'm looking into their souls, connecting to what my Father is saying about them, or what he's trying to do with them. I'm essentially praying for them, as I always am for all people. You're seeing a very brief and local representation of my role as intercessor for humanity."

Philly swung into his swivel chair and tried to decipher what Jesus had said. Just then, Dennis poked his head in the door, which Philly had left halfway open so Jesus could follow him.

"What's wrong with your chair?"

Philly startled at the appearance of his boss and bungled his answer. "Wha ... my chair? I don't know. What's wrong with it?"

"I thought you were looking at your chair as if something was wrong with it."

Philly shook his head nervously, casting a quick glance at Jesus. He answered with a forced laugh. "Oh, I guess I was just staring into space. Nothing wrong with the chair."

Dennis still looked unsatisfied. "You know, your girlfriend told me yesterday about your grandmother. She was trying to find you by the network room. Feel free to take some time off, if you have to deal with ... things."

This uncharacteristic kindness caught Philly off guard. He very nearly teared up for a second, but quickly recovered. "Oh, okay. Thanks, Dennis. I really appreciate that. I may have to take you up on that, depending on how things go."

The boss, whose motivation for speaking to Philly was probably a desire to prevent any mistakes by a distracted network administrator, nodded. "All right. See you later." He retreated, closing the door.

Philly looked at Jesus again once the door was closed. He spoke aloud. "Was that a lie?"

Jesus looked back at him and nodded but said nothing.

Philly grimaced. "You know, I tell almost all my lies because I'm afraid of what people will think if I tell the truth."

Before Jesus could respond, someone knocked on the door. With the blinds closed on the long window next to the door, the visitor wouldn't know who Philly was talking to, so he picked up the phone. "Come in."

Philly held up one finger as Craig opened the door and waited. "Okay, that's fine. Thanks. Yeah, goodbye." Philly responded to the dial tone in his ear.

Making a mental note to only talk to Jesus silently while at work, Philly turned to Craig. "What's up?"

"Remember I wanted off tomorrow?"

"Sounds familiar." Philly had forgotten.

"Just wanted to make sure you knew."

"No problem. What are you working on now?"

"Antivirus software updates pushed out to all computers with nobody on them today, and then cleaning out the old boxes in the back of the network room."

"Sounds good. Make sure you come get me before throwing away any boxes—so we can make sure we're covered in case we need to return certain items."

"Okay, will do." Craig exited, closing the door behind him.

Philly sighed. He shook his head at Jesus, this time telepathing instead of speaking. *"That was kind of a lie too."*

Jesus nodded. "You're afraid."

Philly grimaced. Jesus had summarized far more than just two short conversations at work. Philly could list numerous fears that plagued him. Even then, he could only guess at the extent to which he lived by fear, so much of his life motivated by what others thought. Sensing the work-negating abyss that opened before him if he were to follow this introspection, Philly backed away. He sought refuge in his email and to-do list instead.

When he thought about it later that morning, Philly was amazed at how silent Jesus remained through most of the day.

He didn't preach or pry or interrupt Philly's work. Rather, he waited silently, patiently, always present, always ready, and never seeming perturbed. Jesus waited for Philly to initiate conversation most of the time, especially at work. *Perhaps he simply respects work and knows I wouldn't get anything done if we talked about the sort of things we should probably be talking about.*

Jesus looked at him and smiled playfully. "Did you forget that I can hear your thoughts?"

Philly had forgotten for that moment. "Yeah. I think it's time for lunch."

Jesus lifted his face a bit, as if he had an idea.

"What is it?"

"If you asked Brenda right now, she would go to lunch with you."

"Oh." Philly spoke aloud. Then he thought, *"I kinda want to, but kinda don't want to."* He twisted his mouth as he looked at Jesus.

"Yes, but fear is all that holds you back."

Philly considered his guest chair and the disruptive supernatural visitor sitting there and made an emotional lunge into danger. He reached for his phone and dialed Brenda's extension.

"Hello, Philly." The caller ID preempted some of the surprise.

"Hey, Brenda. What do you say I buy you lunch?"

"Wow, that would be great. When're you going?"

"Anytime you're ready."

"Okay, just give me a minute to save and close a few things. I'll meet you down at the front door."

After goodbyes, Philly hung up the phone and remembered something. He looked at Jesus, consciously limiting his communication to thought. *"When you first saw Brenda yesterday, you reached up for her face and your hand disappeared. What was that?"*

Jesus stood as Philly did. "Well, I wanted to caress her, to let her know how beautiful she is to me, and how much I love her. But I don't usually physically touch anyone. I rely on people to touch others for me."

For Philly, this was two cargo loads of information at once. Jesus was apparently passionately in love with Brenda, which made him want to touch her, as he wanted to touch other people. However, Jesus had to do that touching through human hands. Philly was well out of his depth. All he could do was respond to his own experience. *"But you touched me last night, when I, like, freaked out and cried."* He projected his thoughts as he stepped through his office door.

"I touched you because you wanted me to touch you. Though you didn't say anything, I knew you wanted comfort. Your heart had opened a deep well of pain so I could bring relief to that pain. Since you were conscious of my presence with you, you easily welcomed my participation in your emotional purging. You felt my touch as if it were a physical touch, just the same way that you've been given the gift of seeing and hearing me."

When they both got on the elevator, Philly tried not to look at Jesus while he answered. Walking and not staring at Jesus during this lesson took all the concentration Philly could muster. Absorbing the significance of what Jesus was saying overtaxed Philly's soul. He stopped by the front door and looked around the lobby, only half-aware of who he was looking for.

Brenda came down the stairs from her second-floor desk. Philly saw her face and remembered first how much he liked her face, its hint of girlish freckles, bright blue eyes, china doll lips that stretched easily into a thin smile, and her elvish chin. Then he remembered, of course, that he was having lunch with her. And he let go of what Jesus had been saying.

As they chatted, agreeing on where to eat, with Philly winning the battle over who was buying, he saw again that look on Jesus's face. This time Philly understood that the fraternal familiarity on Jesus's face came naturally. He enjoyed being with Brenda, as he enjoyed being with Philly. By now Philly was convinced that Jesus genuinely liked him and wasn't as angry as he had expected.

"You seem different these days." Brenda turned to address Philly full-faced. "Is it just your grandma? 'Cause I see something else going on with you."

Philly resisted the temptation to look past her to Jesus, knowing that Brenda had just flung open a door and shouted, "Please tell me the whole story." He didn't need to consult Jesus to know *his* reaction to that opening. He didn't want the extra pressure.

When they joined the line at the burrito bar, Philly made a deposit on full disclosure. "There *is* something going on."

"Good. Let's get our food, and you can tell me when we find a place to sit."

"Good." Philly felt considerably less invested in that word than Brenda had sounded. He did have the sense to order his meal in a bowl instead of the two-handed burrito, maintaining at least that level of commitment to actually talking. What exactly he would say remained the topic of an intense internal debate. When he sat down and Jesus sat in the chair to his right—which happened to be pulled out enough to not require a ghost mover—Philly finally looked at his constant companion for moral support.

Brenda slipped into a chair, arranged her bowl and cup, and opened the floor for Philly with clinical affect. "Go ahead and tell me what's on your mind these days."

In this relationship, an invitation for Philly to control the verbal agenda constituted an unfamiliar maneuver, like being required to write with his opposite hand. Adding that to eating, and to the controversial topic, Philly felt his shoulders tightening.

Jesus caught his attention and offered an optimistic smile.

"Well ..." Philly swallowed his first small bite of beans and sour cream. "... you know how religious my grandma is?" The question mark allowed him time for another, bigger bite.

"Mm-hmm." Brenda acknowledged this opening remark with her mouth full.

"Well, she always used to tell me that she prayed for me. Sometimes when she said it, it seemed pretty intense, you know?"

Brenda nodded, her eyebrows just beginning to edge toward each other.

Philly took another bite, corralling a fly-away shred of lettuce with his lips. Then he realized what an advantage the food offered. He had an excuse to stop and figure out what to say. He chewed thoughtfully, focusing primarily on his food.

Brenda chewed and waited, furrowing her thin eyebrows more intensely.

Feeling the pressure, Philly picked up the pace. "I knew she prayed all the time, though I never really put any thought into whether it did any good. But the other night when I visited her, I was feeling really desperate about her coma and all. And I didn't know what to say t' her." He foraged a mouth full of chicken but attempted to keep talking with his lips pursed. "So, I asked her to pray for me since she wasn't there to talk to me, 'cause I really missed her." Here Philly checked with Brenda but regretted it. Her tightening consternation slowed his resolve.

"Go ahead, Philly. I'm listening."

Jesus piped in. "She's not mad about what you're saying, Philly. She's just anxious to figure out what you're talking about."

The latter encouragement trumped Brenda's. Philly continued. "I really just asked her to pray because I missed her and was desperate. I didn't expect anything really to happen if she prayed." He paused. "But ... something did happen."

Brenda still scowled. "You told me on the phone that you asked your grandma to pray for you. Now you're saying that something happened that you think is 'cause she did pray?"

Philly nodded, glad to recognize his intended words in Brenda's reflection. He pressed on. "I've been having this ... sort of ... experience ... like sort of a spiritual thing, kind of, since the morning after I saw her."

"A spiritual thing?" Brenda sounded either incredulous or excited. Philly couldn't tell which.

"Well, I don't know what you'd call it." He huffed a short sigh.

Jesus offered some help. "You could call it a revelation."

Philly picked that up without turning toward the invisible man at the table. "I guess it's sort of a revelation, really."

"Really?" Brenda had stopped eating.

Philly, on the other hand, sought comfort in his burrito bowl. He chewed vigorously on a large mouthful, not wanting it to get cold before he could enjoy it. He continued talking while still chewing. "Since yesterday morning, I've been seeing Jesus with me all the time."

"Cheeses?" Brenda was studying something dangling from the corner of Philly's mouth. Maybe a shred of cheese.

To be fair, Brenda's parents had never been religious. And she had only gone to church for weddings and funerals, as far as Philly knew. She certainly knew much more about cheeses than she did about Jesus.

Philly swallowed.

Jesus was laughing.

"I said 'Jesus.'" Philly was trying to ignore Jesus being so irreverent.

Brenda took a bite of her lunch and began to chew purposefully. Obviously, she too could use her food as a delay tactic.

Philly's heart began to sled down a long slow slope toward his greatest fear—that he would never be understood, that he would always be alone in the world.

A memory hovered at the edge of Philly's consciousness, pushing him down that lonely slope. Philly had been a chess prodigy as a boy. His third-grade math teacher introduced him to the game, as the sponsor of the school chess club. Within weeks Philly was the top-rated player in the club, though he had only learned the game a few months before. Many disgruntled fifth graders stormed away from a match with the little third grader who said little before, during, or after dismantling them.

Philly could easily recall the time he came home to beg his ma and dad to take him to a youth chess tournament downtown. After his mother finally relented, making the drive down to Navy Pier, she stumbled through the registration and matriculation process. They nearly missed the first match, which would have ended the entire day for him. But, once he won the first match, Philly had only to follow the direction of the organizers to the next board that awaited his conquest. His mother huffed and puffed after him, dazed by the whole event so that even she was lost for words. When Philly won the tournament for his age group, collecting a trophy nearly as tall as him, he smiled for the first time that day. He had done it and done it on his own. Even his mother couldn't, and didn't try to, take any credit.

Not until he got home from that tournament did his ma catch her stride. "This is insane," she said to her husband. "Driving downtown, standing in lines, filling out forms, and then waiting around all day for him to finish. I'm not doing that again."

Philly tried to change her mind and even tried to move his laconic father. But his parents told him that it was enough for him to play at school. There they didn't have to be involved, and there they wouldn't have to explain how their son could be such a wizard at chess.

The defining moment came over dinner one night when Philly was ten years old. He tried to get them to sign a permission slip that would allow him to go to a tournament for local schools. At last they surrendered to his constant badgering and whining. But each of his parents said something in that conversation that impacted Philly's soul.

Ever looking to make a joke, his father had said, "You know, Philly, we might just have to admit that we found you in the ash can behind the house and didn't really bring you home from the hospital, if you keep this up." He punctuated his remark with a casual guffaw.

His mother nodded vigorously. "I know. I just can't understand all the sweat and tears over a board game. But then I never pretended to understand you, Philly, not even from the start."

With these statements, his parents sealed the feeling he had harbored all his conscious life—that his parents didn't understand him and neither did anyone else. In essence, he discovered at ten that he was truly alone in the world.

Now here he sat across from the woman whom he knew best in the world outside of his own family, and he fully expected to discover that she too couldn't understand him and would leave him alone with his delusions.

Brenda was investigating, rotating her eyes while keeping her head stationary. "Are you saying that you're seeing Jesus here right now?"

Philly looked at Jesus, who smiled and nodded. Philly looked back at Brenda. "Yes. He's right there."

Brenda glanced in the direction Philly was looking and then locked her eyes on him. "I don't know what to say about that."

Philly chewed another bite and raised his eyebrows. "I know. It's the strangest thing I've ever heard of. And it's happening to me." A rare squeak slipped his voice out of gear.

He could see Brenda weighing the spooky and disturbing implications, her eyes rolling back and forth, trying not to look at the empty chair.

"I could prove it to you."

Brenda gawked as if more frightened by this offer than by Philly's unsubstantiated claim. "How would you do that?" She had set her plastic fork down now.

"He could tell me something about you that I don't know."

Philly kept his eyes on Jesus during this part, monitoring whether he had overstepped his bounds.

"Like what?"

Philly cocked his mouth sideways in question, turning the onus over to his divine partner.

Jesus turned his compassionate eyes on Brenda. "Like that you had a doll when you were six years old that you named Nancy, and the neighbor boy threw her into a yard with a big mean dog, and the dog chewed her up."

Philly repeated this narrative and watched Brenda's face.

She sat up unnaturally straight, then she shivered. "Oh my."

Philly was pretty sure that she meant, "Oh my God," but had edited, considering present company.

When tears began to well up in her eyes, Philly began to doubt the value of his little demonstration. He consulted Jesus.

"She can handle it. It's just a bit of a shock at first. Mostly she's stunned at revisiting that memory."

Philly nodded.

Brenda was tracking Philly's movements, seeing his attention to that empty chair.

"Philly. How is this possible?"

Philly shrugged. "Grandma prayed."

Chapter Five

Back at work that afternoon, Philly tussled with distraction, searching for certainty where little seemed available. Lunch with Brenda had ended in a muddle of uneaten food and stunned brooding. Philly's only assurance had come from Jesus's face. He clearly had anticipated Brenda's response and showed no fear of the long-term impact. Throughout the neglected afternoon, Philly looked up from his work to find Jesus's comforting smile. He liked having a serene supporter, ready and waiting with an encouraging smile throughout the day.

As comforting as Jesus's smile was, and as reinforcing as the conversation on the commute home, Philly still longed to share his wonder with another mortal. Brenda hadn't responded to a gently probing email late in the day, and Philly felt more alone in his Jesus experience than he had before telling her. Therefore, right in the middle of his bus transfer, Philly changed direction. He headed up to the train station at Belmont where he could catch the line that would get him within half a mile of the hospital. That this would leave him with a longer walk didn't blunt his urgency to see Grandma.

His impulsive redirection didn't include a consultation with Jesus. Philly just assumed that Jesus would continue to follow him, and, of course, he was right. Jesus spent a good deal of the train ride reaching toward a ruddy old woman who seemed to have some mental illness. But, once again, Jesus's hands disappeared from Philly's view when he stretched them toward her. The phenomenon annoyed Philly, mostly because he didn't understand. To him it just seemed a weirder depth to an already weird experience.

Philly missed the stop he intended to use, but the next option was only slightly worse, leaving him crossing back over the North

Branch of the Chicago River. Jesus had seemed reticent once again to leave the latest object of his affection, but he also clearly enjoyed the river park they traversed, smiling effusively at children playing, and raising his face to the late afternoon sun.

Philly chuckled at Jesus's smile beamed at the woman at the hospital information desk. Philly was accumulating the impression of Jesus as a mooning romantic, which amused him—the way a father might enjoy his son's fascination with butterflies or beetles.

On the patient floor, Philly slowed as he approached the door of Grandma's room. He stopped dead still as an orderly backed out of the room rolling a bed. Philly's heart restarted when he saw that the passenger on the bed was Grandma's roommate, who lay sedately on one side, apparently recovering from some sort of surgery. As she passed, Philly smiled and nodded to the woman and the orderly. But Jesus tried to maneuver into position to touch the woman. His handicapped arms missed the chance, of course, and Philly shook his head as he resumed his pilgrimage to Grandma's bedside.

Immediately, Philly noticed the absence of the other woman in the room, a tangible vacancy, the removal of someone he hadn't even seen the last time. For Philly, this meant more room to feel his own grief. He considered how the impact of strangers nearby had stifled his emotions on his previous visit. At the foot of her bed, Philly stopped and stared at Grandma. In the low light, his eyes not yet adjusted, he couldn't see any movement—not even breathing.

Jesus turned and stepped silently to the near side of the bed. He leaned close but seemed to intentionally withhold his touch—perhaps to spare Philly his discomfort over the disappearing hands. Jesus's bold initiative spurred Philly beyond his stalled contemplation. He walked gingerly to the other side of the bed, this time forsaking the chair.

Faintly, above and beneath the sound of the heart monitor,

Philly heard Jesus humming softly to Grandma. Then Jesus stopped and looked at Philly, as if surrendering Grandma's attention to him.

Philly took his cue. He cleared his throat gently. "Grandma, I'm here. And I'm with Jesus, just like you prayed. He came to be with me like you wanted." For the first time he allowed some excitement over his unique visitation.

Jesus smiled slightly and lowered his eyes to Grandma.

Philly continued. "I didn't know what to expect. I guess I'm sort of seeing the answer to my question from the other night—about what it is you pray for when you say you pray for me. I'm seeing the result of one of your prayers." Stopping to sort through what he wanted to say, Philly found inside himself an array of unprocessed reactions to Jesus's presence. He wanted to thank Grandma, but he realized how strange her prayer had made him feel. He also bumped up against his dissatisfaction with his last conversation with Brenda. That tainted the blessing Grandma had sent him.

He didn't want to sound ungrateful, however. "Thanks, Grandma. Thanks for praying for me. I guess I'm a lot more impressed with what it means that you pray for me now."

After a pause, Jesus resumed his humming. Philly sat down in the chair and found Grandma's hand to hold through the blanket. After a minute of silence, Philly watched Jesus reach up and try to place his hand on Grandma's head. But, of course, his hand disappeared when he tried. Philly just watched, annoyed and confused, mute in his consternation.

Jesus turned to Philly. "I would like to heal your grandma so she can wake up."

Philly stared at Jesus, who had pulled his hands back. His first thought was, *Well, then why don't you?* But then he remembered that Jesus had said something about not being permitted to touch people. Philly just shook his head and furrowed his brow.

"This is your chance now, Philly. Come and touch her as I'm trying to touch her, so she can be healed."

"What?" Philly slid forward in his chair.

"Do it now." Jesus's voice intensified.

"Do what?"

"Come and touch her, as you see me touching her." Jesus motioning with his hands, as if preparing to lay them on her head again.

But Philly couldn't leap the gorge in his mind between his grandma's coma and his hands on her head. He had no idea what Jesus was wanting from him. It was like he had missed a class or something, and Jesus wasn't aware of his lack of training.

As he stared at Jesus, Philly became aware of whispering by the door, beyond the curtain that divided the beds. A moment later his ma entered the room, tiptoeing as if afraid she would wake Grandma. Behind her trailed Philly's dad.

"Ma." Philly was annoyed that she had interrupted whatever it was that Jesus was trying to tell him, and perturbed at her spoiling his quiet moment with Grandma.

"Oh, Philly." Mrs. Thompson shook her head as she assessed Grandma.

Philly took a deep breath and stood up, forgetting about Jesus momentarily. He wanted to leave as soon as gracefully possible. He could tolerate his mother in most situations. But he couldn't stay and watch his ma drag Grandma's coma into her personal drama.

Mr. Thompson stood silently at the foot of his mother's bed, looking curiously at her. "She looks better. She sorta looks happy."

Philly and his mother turned from each other to look at Grandma. Philly did see a sort of serenity in Grandma's expression that he hadn't noticed before. Then he remembered Jesus and wondered again what Jesus had been saying about touching Grandma. He also remembered Jesus humming to her.

"She just looks unconscious to me." Ma shook her head, her voice low and scolding.

Philly glanced at his mother and then back at Grandma. Apparently his ma couldn't see through the gloomy cloud she carried with her. Philly just shook his head, walked to his dad, and shook his hand. Then they both looked at Grandma, still holding hands for a moment.

Jesus took the opportunity to join them, touching both of their hands briefly as they touched each other.

Philly brightened slightly.

His dad spoke again. "I think she's gonna be all right."

Philly patted his father on the shoulder, an effortless smile on his face.

"Where are you going in such a hurry?" Ma whispered hoarsely as Philly moved toward the door.

Philly's ma stood about five foot two now, in her mid-sixties. She wore a pale copper-colored wig, painted on eyebrows, and smudgy lipstick. There in the half light, Philly saw her and took pity. He turned back. He wrapped her in a brief hug, bending at the waist so it required minimal physical contact.

"I've been here a while. I'll leave you two to talk to Grandma. We've said our piece."

Philly's ma squinted doubtfully up at her son. "We?"

"I," he corrected quickly. "I meant *I've* said *my* piece."

She furrowed her thin brown eyebrows and studied him over her gold-rimmed glasses. "Are you okay, Philly?"

"I'm fine, Ma. I'm doing really well."

"Really?"

"Yes. I gotta go. I'll bring Eileen over tomorrow night." Again, he hugged his ma.

She spoke into his shoulder. "I'll make some of that chocolate cake you two like."

"That'll be great." He backed toward the door, careful not to bump into his dad who had dutifully mounted himself on the wall. "See ya, Dad." He patted his father's shoulder again and made his escape.

Jesus walked close to Philly during the escape down the corridor. "She steps on your soul when it's out of hiding—like when you see your grandma."

Philly studied Jesus and quickly turned back to face forward, lest he be mistaken for a psychiatric patient. He responded via thoughts alone. *"I guess you could put it that way."*

"It's okay, Philly, that you feel the need to defend yourself against her. It's no shame on you."

Philly hadn't known that he needed consolation about this until that moment. He was relieved when they got on the elevator, because Jesus had, once again, struck a deep nerve with simple words. On the elevator, he had to concentrate on not welling into tears. He sniffled hard and briefly wiped his eyes as the elevator door began to open.

A kindly older woman carrying a bouquet of flowers stood waiting for the elevator when the doors slid open. She smiled sympathetically as Philly passed her.

Philly returned the smile. He walked down the marble corridor to the open lobby area and out into the early evening air. He purged his lungs of the hospital and shrugged off some of his frustration with his ma. For a moment, despite having just visited his comatose grandma, he felt lighter.

He turned his head toward Jesus. "I don't hate my ma." It felt less like a denial than a clarification, perhaps for himself.

Jesus nodded, turning his face toward the setting sun and smiling. "You're gonna be just fine, Philly."

Philly envied Jesus's effortless self-assurance. He felt its absence in himself—like a dehydrated marathon runner longing to absorb what his rigorous journey wouldn't allow just yet. As he thought through this, he knew that Jesus could hear all his frustrations and longings, even the ones unfamiliar to himself. In that knowledge, he took comfort. He smiled silently at Jesus, stepped off the curb, and headed back toward the train.

Though he could afford a cab, Philly walked past two of them. He simply wasn't the kind of guy who would drop twenty dollars on a ride home when he had his monthly pass for public transit. He suspected that Jesus preferred the train as well. It would be less disruptive for Jesus to attempt to heal a stranger on the train than an unsuspecting cabbie, Philly thought.

"Hey, what was that you were saying about me touching Grandma like you were doing?"

His comfortable companion assessed him as if guessing his weight or height. "You don't believe that God can work through you."

Philly raised his eyebrows and shrugged. Certainly what Jesus said was true. But why did he feel he needed to say it?

"As I explained before, I generally work only through people." Jesus followed Philly onto the train platform. "And I intend to work through people just like you. My healing power is available to you. When you see me reaching out to touch someone, you know that you only have to cooperate to make something happen."

To Philly, Jesus's explanation defied comprehension, like an avant-garde jazz musician describing a composition which, to Philly's untrained ear, sounded like random tones and beats. He just shook his head as he walked, feeling that understanding what Jesus was saying required some hidden knowledge that had been locked away in some great steel vault. Philly didn't know the combination. Rather than struggle directly with the implications of what Jesus said about healing power, Philly considered how this person walking with him could stay so calm and patient with him. His own level of frustration with himself seemed nearly unbearable.

"Don't curse yourself, Philly." Jesus seemed to respond to his line of thought. "That only grinds your soul to a stop and keeps you from moving forward. It's good to see your shortcomings. But whipping yourself over them doesn't benefit anyone."

Philly wished he had gone to church more, wished he understood Jesus better, wished he had some context in which to process this relationship. Heeding Jesus's advice, however, he didn't stop there, instead allowing himself to enjoy the personable company beyond his frustrations.

As they rode the train, as they walked, while waiting at Sheridan Road, and while sitting on the bus, Philly worked on communicating silently with his personal Christ. Like so much of life, he found that practicing improved his abilities. The most difficult part of this new skill was not reacting visibly when Jesus said stunning or incomprehensible things, or things that tore open some pocket of Philly's heart and revealed scraps of junk that had collected there.

While on the bus, Jesus said to Philly, "You've been living like an abandoned orphan child. The world has taught you to think of yourself as being on your own and to think of God as a neglectful father who left you alone on the playground, forgetting all about you. You're not an orphan, Philly. You belong to my Father in heaven. He loves you and really wants to be with you."

This declaration burrowed into Philly like a mouse seeking a warm nesting place. His heart lurched with the rocking bus. His mind seethed and recoiled. And he began to cry, right there on Sheridan Road in a half-full bus. Still self-conscious, he hoped people would just think he had allergies as he sniffled and rubbed his eyes. And the fight to contain his emotions became his focus, distracting him from the significance of what Jesus had said.

When Philly finished his frozen dinner that night, his phone rang. It was Brenda's ringtone. "Hi, Brenda." He tried to sound as if nothing had happened between them that day.

"Philly, I owe you an apology for the way I reacted today at lunch—and for not replying to your email."

This impressed Philly. Brenda rarely apologized for

anything. But he suspected that there had been a rise in the number of rare occurrences since Jesus showed up.

"I don't really think you do need to apologize though. I mean, it's all so weird. And I know whatever that was that Jesus said about your childhood must've been hard to take. I know he's done that to me a couple o' times." In contrast to Brenda, Philly apologized a lot. He naturally looked for a way to let someone off the hook. It all certainly would be familiar to Brenda, who had often pouted or shouted in response to Philly's past attempts on her behalf. Brenda, however, bypassed her usual impatience at Philly's apologizing.

"You're right, Philly. What you told me about my doll, Nancy, getting torn up by that monster of a dog pulled up some really sore memories. Worse than the doll ... getting trashed ... was what my father said when I told him what had happened. He was always so busy ... and didn't want to be bothered with my little-girl problems. When I cried about what Gerry Holly did to my doll, my dad just called me ... a 'cry baby.'" She cut off after that, either too angry or too sad to say more.

Philly stayed silent for a few seconds. "I'm sorry, Brenda, but I gotta say that really sucks. I would be totally pissed if my dad said something like that."

Brenda sniffed. Her voice hit low gear. "I've been mad at him for years and years over that. I never forgave him ... until now." She seemed to rest there for a second. "That's why it hit me so hard when you brought back that memory. I knew right away that I should forgive my dad. Strange that I hadn't thought of it before."

"Mm-hmm," Philly was pretty sure that the less he said the better on this unfamiliar ground.

"So, do you still see and hear him?"

"Jesus?"

"Yeah." Brenda sniffled lightly.

"Yeah. He's right here."

Seeing Jesus

Brenda waited. Philly could hear her breathing, and he waited too. Turning to check with Jesus, Philly saw his new friend make a gentle "wait and see" motion with one hand.

After several seconds, Brenda broke the silence. "Could you ask him something for me?"

"Sure." A chill shot up his back and neck.

Brenda waited a few more seconds, and Jesus spoke into the silence. "Tell her 'yes.' And that she need not worry about it anymore."

Philly cocked his head but gave it a try. "Well, he has an answer already, I guess. He says, 'Yes, and you don't need to worry about it anymore.'"

The sound of Brenda sobbing over the phone released the backlog of breath Philly had been holding. He leaned back and resisted following her into that catharsis. He listened in silence for about a minute.

Only after she heard Philly sniffle did Brenda speak again. "Are you crying, Philly?"

"Kinda."

"Do you know what my question was?"

"No. He just told me the answer. Maybe I'm not supposed to know the question."

Jesus raised his eyebrows in affirmation of this conjecture.

"Yeah, I suppose so. Is that okay?"

"Of course."

Another short silence followed. "I'm tired. I need to sleep. But we should talk about what's happening to you with all this." When Philly offered no immediate answer, she said, "See you at work tomorrow?"

"Yep, see you at work. I'll bring the coffee."

Brenda breathed a small laugh. "Thanks, Philly."

The conversation ended as it had begun for Philly—in his apartment on a windy April evening, very much alone. That is, except for Jesus.

Chapter Six

After staying up later than he'd intended, reminiscing with Jesus about his childhood, Philly did remember to make coffee for him and Brenda the next morning. His head felt detached from his body, however, both from the late night and from his expanding realization that Jesus knew everything about his past, as if Jesus had lived it himself.

Brenda looked a bit worn when she greeted Philly in front of the office, the gray sky and blustery wind doing nothing to help. She delicately removed hair from her eyes—which the wind very indelicately whipped back into her face—as she took the coffee from Philly. Holding the travel mug and standing still for a moment, she looked as if her composure might wash away under a shower of tears.

This time Philly helped Brenda to the front door, adopting the reverse role with ease. Jesus accompanied them with a proud smile.

For most of the workday, Jesus sat smiling in Philly's office, also following him to the network room several times. During one of their trips back to his office, Philly listened as Jesus explained how he wanted to use people to touch others for healing, as well as to communicate with others.

Philly forgot once again to respond silently. "I thought that sort of stuff ended after the apostles and saints all died." He spoke as he walked the smooth carpet from the elevator to his office.

Dennis bumped into Philly just then. "What did you say?" Dennis's face clouded.

"Oh, sorry. I was just, uh ... " He stopped there, not wanting to lie again. Standing there with nothing to say, he felt like a schoolboy caught drawing on the bathroom wall.

"Who were you talking to?"

Philly tried to answer. "Well, it's kinda hard to explain. I guess you could say I was thinking out loud without realizing it."

Dennis raised his eyebrows and frowned. "You should be careful about that sort of thing, Phil. It makes you look ... unprofessional."

Philly grinned weakly and nodded. "Yeah, I'll be more careful."

Dennis just nodded, clearly unmoved by Philly's commitment. He turned and headed for the elevators without another word.

Philly thumped himself on the forehead and stepped into his office, shaking his head. *I gotta be more careful, or Dennis is gonna fire me for insanity.*

Jesus answered him silently. "You don't have to worry, Philly. My Father will take care of you."

Philly scowled at Jesus. "Take care of me? How are you gonna do that if I don't have a job? Help me move back in with my parents?" This was the surliest response Philly had jabbed at Jesus since he began shadowing him. A brief guilt smothered Philly's explosion like a lead shield.

Jesus resumed his seat in the guest chair.

With deflated angst, Philly plunked into his chair. "Sorry for snapping at you like that."

Jesus smiled. "You are forgiven, Philly."

Though Dennis seemed worried that Philly's work was suffering, Jesus often helped him remember things throughout the day, which saved him time and saved the company from trouble. Philly had begun to rely on the steadying voice and timely prompting of his eternal escort.

During the day, Philly exchanged emails with Brenda. In response to Philly's simple "How are you?" she wrote:

Philly,

Thanks for asking. I'm making it through the day alright. I just keep my head in the work as much as I can and don't let my thoughts wander. I'm so tired. I think that actually makes it easier to just type and not think about anything else.
Oh well, sorry to be so gloomy.
Thanks again.
Love,
Brenda

At the end of the day, Philly walked the stairs down to Brenda's department and stopped by her cubicle just as she was shutting down her computer. This wasn't miraculous, or even much of a coincidence. He had been monitoring the files she had opened on the network and could tell when she was starting to close up for the day, based on how many files she saved and closed. Philly never told her he did stuff like that.

"Hi there."

Brenda looked up from her monitor. "Hi, Philly. All done for the day?"

"Yep. Ready for the weekend."

"Yeah, me too." Brenda pulled her purse out from under her desk and swung it over her shoulder. They said nothing as they walked together to the stairs and down to the lobby. For Philly, the tension between Jesus and Brenda seemed inescapable, but he couldn't tell how much of that was his imagination and how much Brenda really felt.

On the sidewalk in front of the building, they stopped a moment, catching their breath against a swirling wind that twirled bits of garbage and leaves around their feet. Brenda arranged a wayward lock of hair, and Philly turned his face into the wind to keep his bangs out of his eyes.

Brenda regarded Philly for a second. "Is Jesus still with you?"

Philly checked that no one overheard that question. "Yes.

He's right here."

Brenda nodded and turned her face away, into the wind. Then she aimed a tight-lipped grin at Philly. "Well, call me when he's gone, okay?"

Philly shook his head. "Why? I mean, you don't want to talk to me until he's gone?"

Brenda nodded, her lips pinned together.

"Why? I thought he told you some important stuff that was true and all." Philly regretted the whine in his voice.

Brenda drilled into Philly's eyes. "Of course it was important and true. That's just it. I can't take any more of that. It would drive me crazy. I just can't deal with it." She choked off there and looked away again.

Philly glanced at Jesus, who seemed restrained—as if held back by the wind—though his face continued to declare his love for Brenda with passionate intensity. Jesus shook his head slightly to signal for Philly to let it go.

Philly nodded at Jesus.

"You can call me anytime. If you change your mind ... Anytime." He knew he was trying too hard.

Brenda faced Philly with an expression similar to Jesus's. She patted him on the arm and turned to walk toward the train station.

Philly watched, noting that they had said goodbye without words, and wondering when he would hear from her again.

Jesus took a deep breath and stepped closer to Philly.

Philly wondered if Jesus experienced this kind of thing all the time—loving and longing to be with people who, nevertheless, held him at arm's length, afraid of him for reasons true and imagined.

"*But I thought you showed her something important about her childhood.*" Philly remembered not to move his mouth on the way to the bus stop.

Jesus monitored the people they passed. "Yes, that's true.

And that's why she wants you to stay away."

Philly shook his head. *This is one of those women things.*

Jesus responded to that thought, even if it wasn't aimed directly at him. "No, Philly, it's just a human thing. There is a large gap between believing that God is real, and even that God is engaged in your life, and choosing to cooperate with that engagement."

As he arrived at his bus stop, Philly looked hard at Jesus. For a moment, he thought that perhaps Jesus's comment applied not only to Brenda, but to him as well. But that application seemed to have no handles that Philly could grasp, and it slipped past. Before he could respond verbally, the bus arrived, bearing a huge ad that featured a barely dressed woman. All that bare skin looming up in front of him startled Philly.

Jesus, on the other hand, seemed to say something under his breath, and then he put his hand on the forehead of the woman's image before he followed Philly onto the bus.

Philly forgot the previous line of conversation. "*Why did you do that to the picture?*"

Jesus stood next to Philly, who had taken a forward-facing seat next to a young woman. "You could see the ad as just a picture of a human being," Jesus said into Philly's mind. "Or it could be a spiritual magnet, attracting lonely souls and their deepest hurts."

"*What do you mean?*" Philly asked silently but furrowed his brow despite himself.

"Look at the young woman next to you."

Philly turned briefly toward the window and stole a glance at the college-aged woman next to him. She was listening to music on white earbuds, had long, straight, golden-brown hair, large brown eyes, and full lips. Philly found her very attractive. He started to turn to Jesus before remembering not to look at his invisible friend. "*What about her?*"

"What did you notice about her?"

"*She's beautiful.*"

"What about him?" Jesus nodded to an aged man with an old-fashioned hunter's cap pulled low and a million wrinkles on his sullen face.

"*What about him?*" Philly remained silent, as far as the other passengers were concerned.

"Isn't he beautiful?"

Philly looked again, restraining himself from making a face. "*I guess, if you think of it that way.*"

"When you see the woman in the ad or the young woman next to you, you think they're attractive. That's actually a good word for what you're feeling—you're attracted to them. The attraction is the voice of a need you have—a need that was never met—a need that you press down inside to keep from going crazy."

Jesus continued a tone like Philly's favorite elementary school teacher. "You think this ideal woman might be able to fill that gap in your soul, and you look at her with longing to find out if she can. Fortunately for her," Jesus nodded toward the young woman, "you're afraid to try to find out if it's true. Otherwise you, and hundreds of other men, would be bothering her all day long, and she would be the one going crazy. In fact, she's just a person who has needs and who is not the answer to anyone's deepest longings. You turn to her, or images of women like her, because people all around you have devoted their creative energy to serving a pagan deity that broadcasts the lie that sex with a beautiful woman will bring you the fulfillment you crave. This lie is not told to your rational mind, which would figure out that it's a lie. It's told instead to a confused little boy inside you—what you think of as your emotions, and what I think of as a broken part of your soul."

This therapy session would have been hard for Philly to absorb if he were sitting anywhere. But the bus had provided perfect visual aids for the lesson, so he did absorb some of what

Jesus was saying.

"Now, quietly tell the woman next to you that God knows her desire to be honest and pure, and that he will help her tonight when she faces the uncomfortable situation she's worrying about."

Philly stared at him incredulously, ignoring how that stare would look to anyone paying attention to him.

"Go ahead. And don't worry how she responds—they're my words, not yours."

Philly shook his head. But he glanced at the young woman just as she bit her lower lip in a gesture that seemed to confirm her present worries. As if shaking free from the shell in which he traveled, Philly impulsively turned to the girl. He stopped suddenly, however, realizing that she wouldn't hear a quiet voice through the music in her earbuds.

His movement apparently caught her attention. She pulled the right earbud out with a questioning look on her face.

Jesus repeated the message and Philly relayed word-for-word.

The young woman stared at Philly, her eyes enlarged and her mouth sealed shut.

When he finished, Philly was just glad she hadn't slugged him or cursed him.

Finally, she spoke. "How did you know that?"

Philly hesitated, then made an apologetic frown. "Jesus told me to tell you."

She nodded slowly and blinked rapidly. "Thanks. That helps. It really does."

Jesus touched Philly on the shoulder, and Philly turned forward, noticing his transfer stop approaching. He looked back at the girl. "Good. Well, I gotta get off here." And he lurched to the front of the bus as it settled next to the curb. He glanced back at the girl once, and she was still watching him. He felt someone pushing him toward the door and realized that it was Jesus.

Philly followed that divine impulse and exited the bus without looking back again.

As he waited for his next bus, Philly stood perfectly still, but he thrashed around inside his head.

"Breathe, Philly."

Philly took several deep breaths to catch up. His stomach had curled into a wadded washrag, and now it began to relax. Deeper than all that, he felt a sort of tearing as the bus pulled away and the young woman left him standing there. Sweat beaded on his brow and upper lip, though the day was cool and windy.

That was wild. Philly couldn't decide yet whether he liked the experience. No one who knew him would have considered Philly an adrenaline addict, and the thrill of the supernatural interaction with the young woman had spiked his levels well beyond familiar limits.

Jesus spoke to him as Philly wound down, standing and waiting for the Sheridan bus toward home. "That was very valuable to her. And your nervousness actually made it easier for her to accept. You didn't look like you were playing mind games with her or trying to sell her something."

Philly cringed at the realization that his anxiety had been obvious to the young woman—a fact that didn't really surprise him, but which he preferred not to hear described out loud. Fortunately for him, no one else could hear Jesus.

The Sheridan Road bus trip was uneventful for Philly, who needed to decompress from his psychological sprint on the previous bus ride. He thought, somewhat idly, about picking Eileen up at the airport that evening—and whether he could tell her about Jesus's appearance. Jesus withheld comment regarding the prospects, but that didn't bother Philly. He had lost all energy for deliberation. Speculative scenario rehearsals better suited his current state.

Philly's mother called him twice that evening to make sure

he was going to pick up Eileen. He managed to repress the urge to swear at her, even after he hung up the phone the second time. Jesus's attentive look when Philly began to vent helped him to staunch his hemorrhaging temper.

"She's not saying that she doesn't trust you to do as you promised. Actually, she's feeling guilty that *she's* not going to pick up Eileen. Her phone calls make her feel that she's at least doing something."

His previous notions of Jesus and God inclined Philly to expect theological lessons and exhortations to good behavior. The sort of psychological insights he had been hearing from Jesus struck him as more personal and intimate than religious people had led him to believe.

"I wonder if they would be as surprised at what you're like as I am."

Jesus spoke aloud as far as Philly could tell. "Many of them would be. Your expectations of me were formed by the culture around you, including the religious people you know."

Philly thought about this and then wandered onto thinking about Brenda, despite the fact that she had said very little to him about her understanding of God. Perhaps he was just searching for some reassurance that Brenda would still be part of his life when this season of divine visitation ceased.

He busied himself with cleaning out the closet in his bedroom to pass the time before driving to the airport. He eventually left later than he intended, having become mired in sorting through old files and photos that he found in a moldy smelling box he pulled from behind his hats and baseball equipment on the top shelf. As he ran out the back door, he hung onto an old Kodak color photo of him and Eileen. Two small children at the zoo. Lost in his memories and leaving in such a hurry, Philly was startled when Jesus slipped into the passenger seat next to him.

"Jeez, I almost forgot you were around." He recovered from the shock and started his car. After pulling carefully out of the parking lot, he climbed out and locked the gate behind him. "Hey, it sure would have been helpful for you to get the gate," Philly teased Jesus.

"Oh, I wouldn't want to scare your neighbors." Jesus grinned.

As Philly wound his way toward O'Hare Airport, he attempted to pull Jesus into whether to tell Eileen about his revelation, though he knew to avoid pursuing the real question in his mind: *How will she react?* The reason this question preoccupied him, whereas telling his parents didn't, was Eileen's role in his life. Three years older than Philly, Eileen had often filled in where a motherly touch would have suited. And she clearly relished her role as the worldly-wise big sister. Though Philly didn't still consciously seek her approval, he felt now like that time in high school when he talked Karla Anderson into being his girlfriend. Eileen was the most natural person to tell his news. She usually kept criticism and teasing to a minimum.

"I'm assuming you think I should tell Eileen about you being with me." Philly spoke aloud to Jesus for a change.

Jesus nodded. "I know that's what you want. But you also know that neither of us can guarantee her response."

Philly shook his head. "Doesn't that bug you, that you can do all kinds of miraculous things, but you still can't get people to respond the way you want them to?"

Jesus shrugged a bit. "Bug me? No, not really. This is the way we designed you—to have your own mind, your own choices, your own way of responding to the world and to the one who created you. We never thought of you as a lot of toy soldiers for us to manipulate."

That analogy made sense to Philly. He had loved spending hours laying out a battlefield with his little plastic soldiers. The same appeal attracted him to chess, of course—the tactical and strategic art of placing his men where they would do the most good and the most damage. He had fantasized that in another generation, he might have been a great field commander or even a general. That is, if he lived in a different family in that other generation. He could never imagine a great general emerging from his passive dad and nagging ma, though he could easily imagine his family spawning a serial killer.

Eileen, the firstborn, had been more of a rebel than Philly—dying her hair purple, getting her nose pierced and such. She yelled at her parents far more than Philly ever did and, in doing so, made life a little easier for Philly, having blasted away some of their parents' rough edges. As that pioneering sibling, Eileen held a sort of gatekeeper role for Philly. Her endorsement of his experience with Jesus would enlarge the impact of that experience.

After nine in the evening, the traffic to O'Hare amounted to a few weary souls returning late from work and a handful of drinkers who had quit before they lost the ability to find their cars. Philly drove conservatively, as an occasional driver and not a hard-core commuter. On top of that, his mind still played with the pieces of his relationship with Eileen, trying to arrange them so that the outcome of his time with her would smell like victory and not reek of shame.

The highway lights created a corridor through the deepening night, a path that Philly's car seemed to follow on its own, the wide overpasses at the airport looming above him like the wings of a mother bird pulling the car into safety. With little effort he found the lane for meeting arrivals and located the terminal for the airline on which Eileen had flown. It was nine forty. He hadn't taken time to check her flight but knew of no bad weather between Chicago and New York. Eileen would only have carry-on luggage, so she should be waiting behind the yellow curb, under the artificially white lights over the island on which arriving passengers stood. He passed several who searched hopefully for a car and a face they recognized.

Philly spotted Eileen before she saw him. She stood with her arms crossed over her chest, her weight on her right foot, and her left foot propped on her high heel, the sharp toe of her stylish shoe pointing toward the sky. Then she saw him as he slowed to allow a van to withdraw from the curb. He waited for an SUV to coast slowly ahead of him, the driver apparently looking for someone he knew and wanted to take home with him.

Eileen grinned reservedly and reached down for the extended handle of the small carry-on case that stood next to her.

Swinging his door open carefully, Philly hoisted himself out of the low driver's seat. An urgent wind buffeted his face and tousled his hair. He still needed a haircut.

"Hey, how are you?" Philly grabbed a full-on hug and smiled freely at his sole sibling.

"Oh, you know. How are *you* doing?"

"I'm actually doing pretty good." He took Eileen's case from her and scooted back around to the driver's side, having forgotten to pop open the trunk. As he made the circuit, he noticed that Jesus had gotten into the back seat, solving a problem about which Philly hadn't yet begun to worry.

Eileen watched Philly moving around the car. "What's up with you?"

Philly slid into the driver's seat, and Eileen mirrored his entrance on the other side of the car. Turning the key, Philly checked the rearview mirror and seized an opening. "Why do you ask?"

Eileen shrugged. "I don't know. There's just something different about you. Are you in love or something?"

Philly laughed uncomfortably. Love was a subject he would have addressed with Eileen, and he did think of Brenda immediately when she asked. But he was pretty sure that his sister's guess had missed the mark. "Mmm, I don't think that's it."

"Is this the same car you had when I was here last?"

"Yep. It was brand new when you were here, remember?" Philly hit the gas to accelerate past slower traffic toward the highway leading into the city.

"Oh, yeah. It's nicer than I remembered."

Philly glanced over his shoulder at Jesus sitting behind Eileen. He was smiling broadly, which confirmed what Philly had begun to surmise. Eileen was detecting the presence of Jesus or, perhaps, the effect of his presence on her brother.

"How's Brenda these days?" Eileen persisted with the twenty questions.

"She's fine. I've talked to her a bit this week, but I don't think we'll be going out for a while."

"So, you're seeing her again?"

"I'd like to, but she's not so sure just now." Philly knew he was explaining without actually explaining everything. "We haven't gone out since we broke up two years ago." That concrete bit of information covered the obfuscation that preceded it. For Philly, this wasn't really calculated, just a defensive instinct to protect a vulnerable spot. He had always allowed Eileen into his relationships, but always on *his* terms and in *his* time.

Eileen nodded and seemed to relax for a moment—not a common state for her, in Philly's experience.

"You seem relaxed."

Eileen lifted her head off the headrest and considered Philly. "Yeah. I guess it's good to be home. Believe it or not, New York is way more tense and fast-paced than Chicago."

"I believe it."

As if reminded by her own comment, Eileen rubbed her neck. "Got one of those cricks in my neck."

Jesus leaned forward, his face next to Eileen's head rest. "I could heal that, you know."

Philly glanced at Jesus, whose proximity to Eileen bothered him.

"I can heal her neck pain."

Philly forced himself to respond mentally. *"Why are you saying that?"*

"Because it's true. And because I'll need your hand to help."

As Philly checked from the corner of his eye, Jesus reached around to Eileen's left shoulder, but his hand did that disappearing thing. "Now you just put your hand where my hand would be."

Philly caught the car drifting toward the next lane of the thruway and corrected a bit too abruptly.

Eileen moaned, the swerve certainly jostling her painful neck.

"Go ahead," Jesus said. "I'll watch that you don't crash."

Philly focused on the road but glanced at Eileen. *"What do I have to do?"*

"Just put your hand here and say, 'Jesus heals you.'"

Philly gripped the steering wheel extra tight and kept his eyes forward, unable to imagine himself doing and saying that. *"I can't."*

Eileen picked up the conversation again as Philly headed toward his parents' house. "Did you see Grandma today?"

Philly shook his head, "No, not today. I know Ma was there for a while tonight. I'll go see her tomorrow."

Eileen nodded slightly. "It's hard to imagine her in a coma, or even gone for good. I really miss her."

"Me too."

They drove in silence over dark streets with few other cars to slow them, only an occasional traffic light flipping from green to yellow to red. Clouds dominated the night sky, but the moon shone bright through rips in the ragged covering.

"Maybe you can come and get me for lunch tomorrow, and we can see Grandma together," Eileen said. "I want to spend some time there without Ma."

Philly nodded but kept his eyes on the road. "Sure, that would be good. But you can't tell Ma until I get there, so she doesn't have time to tag along."

Eileen knew how to maneuver around their mother, but

Philly had more recent practice at it. She didn't complain about the tactical reminder.

They turned into the neighborhood where their parents lived, not far from the tollway. Philly felt the intestinal churn of lurking gremlins from their childhood as they neared the residence that would reunite the dislocated family. After ten o'clock, he knew that their father would be in bed and their mother waiting up for them. Philly remembered the promise of chocolate cake, and his mouth started to water for that lifelong comfort food, washed down with cold milk, of course.

Jesus rode along quietly, attentive to his two fellow travelers. He followed them into the house after Philly parked in the driveway. He didn't say anything to Philly during the raucous greeting between Ma and Eileen, nor while sitting in the gray-and-yellow kitchen under the light of a single sixty-watt bulb. And, when Philly excused himself just before eleven o'clock, Jesus rose from his seat and joined Philly in hugging his mother and sister and saying goodbye.

Philly noticed an unusual expression of longing on the faces of the two women as he said goodnight.

Chapter Seven

Philly had gone to sleep thinking about the young woman on the bus and the look of discovery on her face when he delivered Jesus's message to her. In his sleep she stayed with him as he dreamed of being married to her and yet unable to touch her. Frustration mounted, as each time he even thought about touching her she disappeared, until he had to accept that, though she was his wife, he wouldn't be allowed to ever touch her. Of course, Brenda substituted for the unnamed woman on the bus at times, and other unrecognizable women also stood in for some scenes of the maddening subconscious drama. Though Jesus didn't appear in those dreams, Philly sensed his presence throughout his unrequited journey.

When he woke in the morning, his first thought formed this way: *"I think that was all Jesus's fault."* Immediately he questioned this conclusion as more of his mind engaged the waking world. That world now included Jesus sitting in the chair in the opposite corner of the room. He was petting Irving.

The cat had restrained his Saturday morning angst over the lateness of his meal while in Jesus's lap. He had never been able to do that before. Motion from the man in the bed seemed to awaken Irving's hunger, however. He jumped to the floor and circled the bed to find Philly's face. The big gray cat stood on his hind legs with his front paws on the mattress next to his master's cheeks.

Philly opened one eye and then closed it just in time to avoid the clawless paw of his apartment mate, which batted his nose and eye. This method had worked on most weekend mornings in the past, and Philly was just glad when Irving didn't resort to it any earlier than seven o'clock. Wrestling his right arm free to fend off his furry assailant, Philly opened both eyes and looked at the digital clock. It read 7:53. "That may be a record for a Saturday," Philly said aloud, employing his other hand to scratch Irving between his ears.

Philly yawned, stretched, and rolled over to see Jesus sitting and smiling, as he expected. "You're still here." It was like he was seeing an old friend who had come to visit. Philly had never had such a reliable companion—except Irving, perhaps.

After going to the bathroom, then pulling on a pair of sweatpants, Philly performed his usual Saturday schedule of tasks with Jesus as a sidekick. He turned on the public radio station and listened to the mix of human interest and news broadcasting that filled in behind his ordinary Saturday activities. Philly liked listening to the radio with Jesus even more than he liked listening on his own. The Savior would occasionally offer his own commentary to a news story.

When the report on a congressional committee meeting on budget priorities ended, Jesus said of the chairwoman of that committee, "I hope she gets some rest. She's really feeling the stress of all this, on top of the problems she's having with her daughter."

When Jesus didn't explain, Philly searched online and found stories about a drug-related arrest of the nineteen-year-old daughter. Jesus wasn't divulging confidential information. But he did turn a standard news story into a personal concern. Philly just raised his eyebrows, impressed that Jesus could see beyond the politics to the people involved. Philly would pay more attention to the news if he knew this sort of personal information about the movers and shakers.

Around eleven o'clock Eileen called to confirm their lunch date. From her hushed tone, Philly could tell that she was concealing her plans from their ma. His big sister had slipped right back into that old slotted track around which she had spun more than two decades before. In her days as the bad girl of the family, sneaking out on her mother had been a standard move.

Not long after hanging up with Eileen, he led Jesus out to the car. Philly was all cleaned up and dressed for the day, except for his neglected whiskers. Grandma wouldn't notice, he concluded when he stopped to consider whether to break his usual Saturday moratorium on shaving. Where Jesus would land on that question was apparent, wearing the standard Jesus beard that any Sunday school kid would expect.

Spending Saturday alone rarely satisfied Philly. Going to pick up his sister for lunch was a nice reprieve from lonely weekends. Making the trip with Jesus sitting in his passenger seat levitated his mood even higher. The climax of this levity came when they braked behind a car at a stop light and read the bumper sticker: "Dog is my copilot." Both Jesus and Philly laughed to the point of tears.

"You didn't arrange that, did you?" Philly wiped a tear off his cheek and sniffled.

That started both of them laughing again, though maybe for different reasons.

Eileen stood on the driveway of their parents' house talking on her cell phone. She waved to Philly as he pulled up the long concrete drive. Ending her call, Eileen dropped her phone into her small gray purse and opened the car door. Jesus vanished from Philly's view, but then waved in the rearview mirror.

"I told Ma I was going outside to make a phone call. It was the only way I could get out. She was all over me."

"You gonna call her and tell her what you're doing?" Philly was restraining a laugh.

"Yes. What are you laughing at?"

Philly backed the car down the drive, shaking his head. "It's just amazing how far we have to go to live adult lives without Ma's meddling."

She shrugged and retrieved her phone, making a call to Ma that required some terse and irascible responses. Philly could hear the plaintive tone of his mother's voice escaping the tiny

Seeing Jesus

speaker on the phone. The call ended with a primal noise from Eileen's throat—between the bulging veins on her neck.

"Looks like a two-martini lunch."

Eileen snorted. "Why are you in such a good mood?"

Philly just shook his head slightly and grinned. "I was thinking salad for lunch."

Eileen pursed her lips. "That's nice of you. I know it's not your favorite."

"Oh, I get a craving now and then. Probably just before I have a heart attack from not eating healthy enough."

"A salad sounds great."

Jesus remained attentive but silent throughout the ride to Eileen's favorite salad spot and throughout ordering and brother-sister chatting. When Eileen and Philly were fully engaged in excavating among the lettuce, arugula, carrots, and such, Jesus broke his silence.

From his place behind one of the chairs that hadn't been pulled out from the table, he sounded urgent. "You'll need to hurry, Philly. Your time with your grandma won't be what it's meant to be if you take your leisure at lunch."

This counterpoint to the mood of the morning and the light talk at lunch raised Philly's shields. He had never transitioned well between activities or attitudes.

Jesus insisted. "It will go much better for her and for you if you get there in the next twenty-five minutes."

Eileen had stopped eating. She sipped her white wine with recreational savor. Philly would have to say something to her if they were going to follow Jesus's direction. He suddenly resented Jesus there, interrupting his Saturday ease, obviously pushing some contrary agenda. He cast glances at Jesus while chewing another mouthful of lettuce, dressing dripping down his chin.

Eileen laughed. "Still a slob."

"Hey, I just dripped a little. I was never a slob." And the repartee continued, friendly and playful, and shutting Jesus out.

Philly kept his attention on his salad or on Eileen, avoiding the man across the table. But he couldn't keep that up for long. After ten minutes or more, he finally said something to Eileen. "Hey, you don't think Ma is heading for the hospital this afternoon?"

Eileen shrugged.

"'Cause I got this feeling that we should get moving—to make sure we get some time with Grandma, in case Ma's gonna show up." He suspected his tone lacked sincerity.

"You tired of the salad?"

Philly had satisfied the initial craving that had inspired this lunch destination. "I guess so."

"Well, let me catch up then and finish my wine."

Philly backed off. "Sure, take your time. Who knows when Ma will go see her, anyway?"

Jesus, who hadn't mentioned anything about Philly's ma in his warning, just looked at Philly with a pensive air and said no more.

Altogether, with Eileen finishing her meal, waiting for the check, and then for the waitress to run his credit card, as well as the drive to the hospital, Philly knew they were much later than Jesus had wanted. He felt more nervous than guilty about that, but he did avoid eye contact with Jesus during the transition from lunch to hospital.

When they arrived outside Grandma's room, Philly stopped at the sound of voices inside the half-closed door. He peeked through the opening and caught glimpses of two women in hospital scrubs working over Grandma's bed. Philly guessed what they were doing. But he couldn't tell how far along they were in the process.

"I think they're washing her up and changing her sheets and stuff. Why don't you go in and see when they'll be done?"

Eileen nodded. She might have been sensing Philly's tension, but the wine she drank at lunch certainly dulled her a bit. She slipped into the room, leaving the door mostly closed. Philly

Seeing Jesus

heard her ask the nurse how much longer they would be, after introducing herself. Though he couldn't hear the exact words, the tone of the response made it clear that he would have to wait in the hall for a bit.

He turned to look at Jesus, who was watching an elderly man walking slowly past with a woman about the same age on one arm and a mobile IV rolled along by his other hand. In these situations, Jesus seemed to Philly to look almost anxious, like a kid waiting to be offered something. Still confused about what that thing might be, Philly offered nothing.

Finally a nurse and a female orderly exited the room, pushing a cart packed with linens and supplies. When they had passed him, Philly headed boldly in. Aware of someone following him, he assumed it was Jesus. But a woman's voice just behind him made Philly whip his head around. Three young people followed him into the room—a young woman carrying flowers, a young man with a balloon, and another young man carrying an overnight bag. They were there for Grandma's roommate.

His heart sank at the loss of the quiet time with Grandma that he and Eileen had planned.

Eileen was seated on the other side of the bed. Holding Grandma's hand through the blanket, she looked up at Philly only briefly. Jesus walked next to Philly, but seemed torn between the roommate and Grandma, as if he expected little would be required of him by Philly and Eileen.

The family behind the golden curtain began to wind up their volume, even as Philly stood silently with his back to them. He wondered if he could ask them to quiet down. Eileen seemed less disturbed by the rising noise, locked in on Grandma, probably stunned by the tactile reality of her condition.

Jesus interrupted Philly's silent daze. "Your mother and father are on their way up from the parking lot."

Philly looked at him, trying to recalculate the timing of their visit against the timing that Jesus had advocated at the restaurant. He felt the oxygen-sucking impact of having ignored Jesus's earlier warning. They had missed their target by as much as half an hour, the difference between being in the room before the change of linens, which they surely could have postponed, and getting wedged in now between two other inconveniences.

Almost forgetting his grand secret for a second, Philly had to stop himself from warning Eileen of the approach of their parents. He wasn't ready to reveal his source for such intelligence. Instead, he leaned over Grandma and gave her a kiss on the forehead, then rested one hand on her shoulder for a moment.

He decided to risk talking to her in front of Eileen. "Hi, Grandma."

Eileen lifted her head but seemed unperturbed by her brother's speaking.

"Eileen's here to see you. She flew in from New York, just to see how you're doing. We had a nice lunch and then came to see you."

Eileen stepped in. "Hi, Grandma. This is Eileen. I almost forgot to talk to you, just sitting here holding your hand. I guess I was too stunned to say anything."

Philly was glad he had dislodged Eileen from her silence, knowing the circumstances for talking to Grandma would deteriorate in just a moment.

Eileen continued. "I miss you, Grandma. It's not nearly the same to come home without you here to talk to." She hesitated. "I mean to have you awake and talking to me too." Her voice quavered.

His sense of loss during his grandma's coma had lacked the scope necessary to include Eileen, because Philly had somehow forgotten how Grandma might serve a similar role in his sister's life. This moment of revelation, illuminated by Eileen's intimate tone and affectionate words, expanded Philly's appreciation of Grandma—and of Eileen. He had easily slotted Eileen into one of two places in his emotional universe—either in the space occupied by his ma, or the rebellious big sister space. In the first, Eileen nagged him about his life. In the second she yelled at her parents and gave them the finger before slamming the screen door behind her. Now Philly opened a much closer space for the sympathetic sister who missed Grandma just like him.

Even as Philly settled into the warm camaraderie with Eileen, listening to her continue to say the sort of things that he had said to Grandma, the door to the room opened and Philly heard a familiar voice.

"So, this is where you kids ran away to. I thought this might be where to find you."

Philly turned toward Ma, aware of Jesus making that same turn in sync with him. And he sighted his dad bringing up the rear, as usual. Somehow, in that moment, Philly realized that Jesus heard his ma's whining tone as clearly as he did. But Philly watched as Jesus stepped through the current of her "Why-is-the-world-so-cruel-to-me?" attitude, offering to embrace her.

As Jesus stood there ready to wrap his arms around Ma, Philly caught a glance from the Savior's eyes that said, "This is where you ought to be."

Eileen stopped talking to Grandma and straightened up in her chair—like a woman caught in the throes of lovemaking, gathering her clothes and shame around her.

Philly knew how this scene would play out—especially the way the atmosphere would change—the noxious fumes of his mother's sorry soul filling the room and banishing the very memory of the sweet communion that had hung there a moment ago.

Again, in the look on Jesus's face, Philly found the courage to confront a monster. He turned squarely toward his ma and Jesus. He nodded a greeting to his dad. Then he wrapped his arms around the aching bones of the woman that shoved him out into the world thirty-eight years before.

In his awkward arms, his round belly pressing against her

arms crossed over her chest, his ma burst into tears.

As many times as he had heard her suffering protests and sampled the aftertaste of her bitter soul, Philly had never seen her cry like this before. Had Dad? He had certainly archived many of Ma's secrets behind his JC Penny façade. To Philly, the explanation for the unique catharsis was obvious. His arms, his hands, filled in where Jesus stood, where Jesus wanted to connect with his ma. Of course she would be moved.

Eileen and her dad, however, stared as if they had just watched Ma shove her hand into her chest and produce a bloody, pulsing organ that must certainly be a living human heart. Eileen rose with questions all over her face. What had happened to Philly? And what was he doing now to Ma? She sucked an audible breath through her teeth. Then she too began to cry.

Philly, floundering as if in a deep snow drift, turned slightly to get a better look at Eileen, even as he maintained his ungainly hold on his tense little mother. He struggled with an insinuated guilt that he had violated something or someone. But he managed to remain latched to what Jesus seemed to think he should be doing. He had failed his sister and grandma by ignoring Jesus's timing for this visit. Now he was determined to hang onto something he was sure he was supposed to do, even if he couldn't explain it.

His mother focused his attention again by pulling her defensive arms free and reaching around her grownup son. Philly caught a glimpse of his dad's face just then, or at least what ought to have been his dad's face. As unfamiliar tears began to roll down his dry old cheeks, his dad looked more like Grandma than Philly had ever noticed before.

Though Jesus showed no sign of moving from his grip on the throbbing artery of one emotional trauma victim in that hospital room, Philly thought he knew better than Jesus how much his family could take. And he loosened his grip.

Instantly, Eileen, his ma, and his dad all turned toward

damage control, capturing tears and snot and apologizing for the uncharacteristic outburst.

After his ma began to fumble in her purse for tissues, the family behind the curtain began to speak up as if nothing had happened. His dad retrieved his cotton hankie from his back pocket and blew his nose. And Philly regretted releasing his mother so early.

He looked at Jesus, standing there with no hands, and wanted it all back. Philly tried several spastic moves to wrap his ma up in that healing embrace again, but she just batted his hands away and chattered at him like an angry squirrel.

Philly stood up straight and stared at Jesus, stunned by what he had just witnessed—both the power of obedience and the cost of hesitation.

He considered his ma, who was blowing her nose and turning fresh white tissues into compact wads with nervous precision. She spoke through her sniffling and throat clearing. "Must be my hormones. That doctor's not giving me the right amount of estrogen. I just know it."

Though the magic moment had disappeared, its retreat didn't return them to a familiar location. Philly watched as his dad ventured one big, gentle hand onto his wife's shoulder, and as his sister looked back at Grandma with all the love and affection that she had been pouring out before the interruption. Ma stopped muttering to herself for a moment and simply stood looking at Grandma.

Philly's dad spoke up. "She was quite a dancer when she was young." His voice gained strength as he assembled more than two or three words. "I bet you didn't know that. Folks at her Pentecostal church aren't as big on dancing these days as they used to be. And I guess the kind of dancing my ma used to do wasn't the church kind of dancing anyway."

As unfamiliar as the audible voice of God was to Philly, so too was the sound of Dad reminiscing about his mother.

"I remember at my uncle George's wedding, when I was just about nine or ten years old, how my dad was sitting with his father and a couple of his uncles. They were jawing and complaining about Eisenhower or some such thing, and Ma went up to him and just took his hand. And I guess it sort of caught him off guard, y' know, like he hadn't got his objections ready in time. And she got him to stand up. I remember the way he looked, kinda stunned at first, and then all dreamy, like he was remembering something from years before. And I thought then that this was what it looked like when someone was in love, and that my dad was remembering what it was like to be in love with my ma."

They all stared at Philly's dad as he spoke. Was Philly the only one holding his breath?

"And I watched them twirl around the room, my dad looking at her like she was Cinderella or something. And I remember how it made me feel to see them like that—in love—like in a movie." He stopped there, took a couple of deep breaths and finished. "Yeah, she was quite a dancer in those days."

Philly turned unconsciously toward Jesus. His expressive, emotionally-articulate face showed clearly that he too recalled that day, and that dance, and what it looked like for those two people to remember that they were in love.

Chapter Eight

Philly and Brenda had planned a date for Saturday night, their first in over two years. He looked at Jesus, who sat now in his parents' living room scratching their obese terrier behind the ears. Philly told himself that Brenda would be there for him in the future. Reviewing what he had seen and heard from Jesus, and what he had seen Jesus inspire in the people around him, he didn't regret having to wait for Brenda quite so much.

Eileen sashayed into the living room from the kitchen. She looked at Blacky, the terrier, perhaps noting the way he sat so intently concentrated on an empty chair. Usually the poorly disciplined dog would be jumping on her or begging someone for food.

Philly suppressed a smile, still fascinated by the selective invisibility of his guest. Blacky could clearly see him.

"Supper's almost ready." She plopped on the other end of the couch and idly lifted a news magazine from the end table there.

"Great." Philly glanced at Jesus when Eileen opened the magazine.

Jesus said, "You might want to tell them all together after supper."

Philly didn't need to ask what Jesus was talking about. He knew that Jesus was answering an earlier question which Philly had poked and flipped over more than a few times. Very briefly he anticipated losing the hidden jokes—such as the dog's unusual behavior—if he were to let his family in on it. But he tossed that aside as a distraction. *"Yeah, that could work."* Philly grinned at the dog who was enjoying the divine attention.

Eileen interrupted his thoughts. "Did you ask that girl out— what was her name?"

"Brenda." Philly resisted the annoyance of Eileen forgetting.

"Yeah. Sorry, jet lag. Well, did you ask her out?"

Philly nodded, assuming he would tell the truth, but careful about how much he carried into this *hors d'oeuvres* conversation. "Yeah, I did. I figured out that she wasn't still going out with the guy that she dumped me for."

Eileen nodded, still looking at her magazine. "Did she seem open to the possibility at least?"

Philly bypassed his usual wriggling response to this sort of inquisition, preoccupied instead with measuring his answers for honesty. "Yeah, maybe in the future. Not just now, she said."

"Did she say why?"

"Yeah, but you never know if someone is telling you everything."

"You think she still likes that other guy?"

"No, not really. I didn't get that impression."

"Maybe she just needs some time to recover."

"That sounds about right." Philly suppressed a grin at her accidental accuracy.

Dad stepped into the room. "Supper's ready, kids."

With that, Philly crossed the finish line to the obstacle course constructed by Eileen, the winner's tape trailing off his round, but hungry, torso. He had answered her, had not lied, and had not told her the whole story. That, he assumed, would happen in due time.

They followed the salty aroma of roast beef into the dining room, Blacky rising to accompany them only when Jesus did. With Jesus a step behind him, Philly tried to nonchalantly pull a chair out for him—to avoid the distraction of Jesus standing up during the meal. Having pulled out a chair at the empty place at the end of the table, he made a little noise to imply that he recognized his mindless error. Then he pulled out his own chair, which dragged on the dark gray carpet, as he surveyed the meal. The roast beef, mashed potatoes, green bean casserole, and Jell-O salad reincarnated a favorite dinner of his childhood.

His ma set the gravy dish next to Philly's plate and nodded as if to affirm his realization of where she expected him to sit.

Jesus thanked Philly for pulling out a chair, just the way a guest would thank his host under normal visibility conditions. This, however, caught Philly off guard by its normality, and he said "Mm-hmm" audibly, in response to Jesus. No one asked why he said it, however, as his reflex reply mingled with the sounds of chairs sliding on carpet, forks ringing against plates, and Dad clearing his throat.

Philly's dad generally maintained a low, rumbling base level of noise via small inarticulate hums and gentle grunts—ever since he lost much of his hearing in an accident at the plant in Waukegan, where he worked twenty years ago. Philly thought of that stream of little self-sounds as a sort of audio test pattern that Dad maintained, to make sure that his tiny hearing aids were working. His hearing loss had complicated Dad's emotional exile, which predated the industrial explosion.

For a moment, Philly entertained a feeling that he ought to offer Jesus a plate of the good meal.

Jesus smiled at the thought and replied without moving his lips. "Thanks, Philly. But I think messing with the dog is quite enough for tonight."

Philly smiled but kept his eyes on his family as he did so.

"Okay, dish up. What're you smiling at, kiddo?" Ma eyed Philly.

"Oh, there's so much to smile about."

Eileen scowled at her little brother. She dished mashed potatoes. "Philly's been acting pretty strange since he called me about picking me up at the airport."

Philly winced internally out of habit, generally reticent to bring Ma into private conversations not edited for her consumption. But he stopped himself when he factored in his plan to tell his family about his guest. He ladled gravy onto his beef and potatoes and passed it to his dad.

"You always thought I was strange." Philly passed Eileen the gravy.

"Oh, everyone thinks their little brother is strange, no matter how good he is," Ma said.

Eileen shrugged and nodded, pushing aside the green bean casserole after taking only the equivalent of half a dozen beans.

"You watching your weight, dear?" Ma was looking at Eileen's small portions.

"Always."

Ma glanced at Philly but apparently decided not to say anything more.

Philly noted the restraint and counted it a minor miracle.

"You got nothing to worry about." Dad grinned at Eileen.

Eileen seemed to allow her selection of a dinner roll to excuse her from responding to Dad. Then she looked at Blacky, sitting next to the empty chair instead of waiting beneath the table to pounce on scraps dropped, unintentionally or otherwise.

Dad had only slightly modified his subversive feeding habit when the veterinarian told him that he was killing Blacky with his kindness.

Eileen spoke up. "What's with Blacky? Did you send him to obedience school or something?"

Ma snorted. "Obedience school? That little delinquent? No, he's just as naughty as ever."

Dad had probably missed part of Eileen's question, but he appeared to figure out what they were talking about from the tone of his wife's voice. "Hey, where is my little guy?"

Philly ventured a glance at Jesus, who looked down at Blacky and made a motion for the dog to go to Dad. The chubby terrier smartly obeyed his new master and moved to the other end of the table where he sat next to Dad. But he kept turning to look at Jesus, as if checking to see if Jesus was sure that he couldn't return to his side.

Looking now at the distracted dog, Dad snuck his left hand

down from the edge of his plate with the requisite bit of beef.

Blacky checked with Jesus before snapping up the morsel and then checked again as he licked his lips.

Ma couldn't see this disciplinary breach from the other side of the table. But that would help her maintain her plausible deniability with the veterinarian.

Eileen, however, could see enough of Blacky to see his constant attention to the opposite end of the table.

By the time Philly had nearly finished his ample portions of dinner, the finer sensors in his nose began to detect that fractionally sour smell of a meal no longer fresh. When all four of them began to coast to the end of their dinner, Blacky took the chance to return to Jesus's side.

Eileen shook her head at the dog's odd devotion to an empty chair. "I think that old dog has gone crazy. Why's he so fascinated with that empty chair?"

The childhood innocence stirred by his family, along with the roast beef, must have weakened Philly's defenses. He opened the door on his big secret much less discreetly than he had intended. "Well, the trick is that it's not really empty." Immediately Philly stopped breathing, his mind rushing for an exit strategy. How could he recapture his secret after that ill-prepared introduction?

"What?" Eileen leaned toward Philly to check the contents of the chair.

Philly didn't move. Maybe they wouldn't notice him.

Ma spoke up. "Well, it looks pretty empty to me."

Eileen agreed. "I don't see anything. What are you talking about?"

Philly continued to fish for an out. Then he looked at Jesus, who just smiled back and cocked one eyebrow. For a moment, Philly thought Jesus was waiting to see how Philly could avoid answering Eileen. But then he knew, of course, that Jesus awaited the big revelation. As had happened several times now, the look on Jesus's face sent Philly full speed into certain disaster.

"Well, I didn't wanna tell you like this, 'cause you're gonna think I'm crazy. But I've been looking for a chance to tell you all about something big that's been happening to me." He sat up straighter in his chair. Good posture might add credibility.

Dad turned up his hearing aid on Philly's side, and both women stared speechlessly.

Again, Philly looked at Jesus for encouragement.

When Philly looked back at Eileen, preferring to make eye contact with her instead of Ma, he saw the confusion on her face. That stopped him again.

Jesus spoke up. "Go ahead, Philly. You can do it. I'll back you up."

That settled it.

Philly began with the story of visiting Grandma and asking her to pray. Then he told about discovering Jesus sitting on the bus, and then him following Philly wherever he went.

When Philly finished, Ma's brow was deeply furrowed, but she seemed unable to speak.

Eileen's voice was reedy in her throat. "So, you believe you're seeing Jesus sitting there in that chair?"

Philly glanced at Jesus, who still smiled gamely. "Yep. He's sitting right there. That's why Blacky's so interested in that chair."

Bringing the dog in as star witness seemed to stifle every response his family members might have been preparing during his delusional story. If Philly was delusional, then Blacky seemed to be sharing in his illness.

Dad weighed in. "What did you do to that dog?"

Philly shrugged. "I didn't do anything. Animals just like Jesus. Irving likes him better than he likes me, and I feed him."

Jesus made a motion with his hand above Blacky, and the dog barked at him.

Ma looked at the dog and then at Philly. "What *did* you do to that dog?"

Philly shook his head. "I didn't do anything. It's Jesus. I guess animals can see him, even if most people can't."

"How can you be sure you're really seeing him?" Eileen spoke with a stiff half volume, perhaps not sure what the right answer to her own question would be.

"Well, I thought I was crazy at first. But then there was this guy on the bus who *was* really crazy, and he freaked out because the voices in his head told him Jesus was there. And he kept saying 'Jesus' really strangely. And then there was Irving, who loves to be wherever Jesus is. And then I told Brenda about him, and he told me to say something to her that I didn't know about—something that happened when she was a kid, which she had never told me about. So, Brenda believed me." Then he remembered the clincher. "And when I was on the phone with you the other day," he turned toward Eileen, "he told me to ask you about your job, to prove to me that he was really there and not just in my imagination."

All his listeners stared at Blacky, now standing on his hind legs, leaning on the empty chair, acting as if someone was scratching him behind the ears.

"How could you be seeing Jesus if we can't see him?" Ma sounded like this was the clincher for her.

"That's just how Grandma prayed it, I guess."

"You leave your grandma out of this." Dad spoke more forcefully to Philly than he had in decades.

That tone sent Philly searching for a place to hide. He looked at Jesus, who stopped scratching Blacky and appeared to relax in his chair, as if to say, "This may not be going as you had hoped, but don't worry about it."

Eileen was shaking her head and huffing. "So you see Jesus now? What's he doing?"

Philly looked at his invisible friend as naturally as if he were on the phone describing someone to a person in a faraway location. "Well, he's just sitting there looking at me, a very pleasant smile on his face, as usual. He stopped scratching Blacky and seems to be waiting for us to work things out."

Jesus nodded in response to Philly's interpretation of his posture and then raised his eyebrows at Eileen.

"Now he's looking at you."

Eileen's eyes swung toward the empty chair and back to Philly, as if retreating from the urge to look at her brother's hallucination. Ma started to say something, but Eileen cut her off. "How do you know this is Jesus you're seeing?"

"I guess I just believed it when he told me. He knew things about me that no one else could know. And he's told me things about other people too, that all proved to be right. Who else could he be?" Philly had reverted to the voice he had used as a teenager when arguing with his sister. But he didn't feel so much of the churning anxiety that had frayed his teenage years. Instead, he felt genuinely sorry for Eileen and his parents.

Eileen seemed to be calculating something as Ma grabbed the floor. "Philly, you need to see someone about this. This is a serious problem. You might be really sick."

Philly welcomed the brief wind of care from his ma, who generally seemed only concerned about herself. Then he realized that her concern for him could simply be worry about how his insanity would impact her. That comforting feeling faded.

"Okay, so if Jesus is there and knows everything," Eileen said, "then have him tell you who I'm dating back in New York." The confidence on her face said that she was certain she had dashed Philly's delusion.

Philly looked at Jesus.

Ma recoiled in her seat, clearly missing the significance of the gauntlet thrown by Eileen. "Who *are* you dating?"

Philly ignored the interruption. He looked at Jesus, who smiled tilted his head.

Then Jesus answered the challenge. "She's going out with Roger Peterson, an account executive at a firm that provides communications consulting for her employer. He is forty-two years old and has a wife and two children in Paramus, New Jersey. Eileen doesn't know about the wife."

Philly locked up for a second, hanging on that last bit of information. But Eileen's insistent face provoked him to report what Jesus had said, within a few syllables of perfect accuracy.

Eileen's face lost both its harsh edge and its color. She tried to speak a few times but barely produced an entire syllable.

Ma barged in. "Eileen! Why are you going out with a married man?"

"Marge." Dad was probably not so lost as Ma.

"What?" Ma turned on her husband.

"How do you know he's married?" Eileen was leaning away from the empty chair.

The spin of revelations and questions was too much for Philly. He sat staring at Eileen for a tottering moment.

"He lied to her," Jesus said. "He told her he was recently divorced."

Philly parroted this additional information.

Eileen turned red now. Her breath surged in great puffs. She grabbed her wine glass and downed the last two inches of the smoky liquid. She looked at Philly, hysteria in her eyes. "How?" Then she just stuttered, "How ... how ... " She glared at Jesus.

From Philly's perspective, Eileen and Jesus made eye contact. But he knew his sister was getting no benefit from that one-sided encounter. She burst out crying for the second time that day. As she wept, she buried her face in a napkin and gasped for breath.

Eileen raised her head abruptly. She was ignoring her mother's efforts to calm her. "In the hospital today, was that part of this?"

As a boy, Philly often pretended not to understand a

question in order to delay his answer. Sitting there at the dinner table that evening, he genuinely missed the connection Eileen was making. Because Jesus had accompanied him for most of the past week, it took Philly a moment to catch up to Eileen. A glance at Jesus, however, reminded Philly of the connection. He looked at Ma and Dad and nodded.

Though Eileen had clearly linked her two tearful experiences together, Philly saw her confusion written in the little glyph that formed above the bridge of her nose between her carefully cropped eyebrows.

"Remember when I went over and hugged Ma?" Philly finally spoke, glancing at his mother. He preferred focusing on Eileen. His ma still seemed to be drifting far from the shore of this conversation. "Well, I hugged Ma because Jesus was hugging her and wanted me to do the same. You see, he can't really touch people directly—he wants me to do it for him." Though Philly was still working on this concept of Jesus using him to touch people, he had accumulated enough instruction from Jesus to say that much.

Eileen furrowed her brow, still wiping at tears and still ignoring her mother's weak protestations. "Why does he want you to do it for him? Why can't he just touch people himself, if he's right here?"

Philly looked at Jesus, who seemed to be ready to evaluate Philly's answer to this question, like a teacher waiting for his pupil to demonstrate that he had been listening and learning. Rather than the smart kid response, Philly opted for honesty. "You know, that part has been really hard for me to get." He turned from Eileen to Jesus again. "Apparently, this is generally how he works in the world. It's not just me. He's counting on people to do the good stuff he wants to get done."

At this, Jesus stood up from his chair. Blacky backed away to allow him space.

Eileen gasped, perhaps noting Philly's eyes following Jesus's movement in coordination with Blacky stepping back. Was she beginning to believe?

Jesus spoke to Philly. "I want to heal your dad's hearing." He arrived at the other end of table, stood with his hands ready, and waited for Philly.

Philly translated for the others at the table. "He says he wants to heal Dad's hearing." His voice cracked slightly at the thought of it.

Dad followed Philly's gaze, looking suspiciously at the space next to his chair.

Ma said, "What are you talking about?" If she got any more lost, they would have to report her to the police as a missing person.

Jesus tipped his head toward Philly. "You know I can do this, right?"

Philly nodded, still stuck in his chair.

"Come on then and put your hands over your dad's ears."

Philly explained apologetically. "He says he wants me to put my hands over Dad's ears."

"You'll do no such thing," Ma said.

"Marge. What could it hurt? You know my ma believes in this kind of thing."

The decades-old split between the sides of the family opened right there, like a crevice revealed when a violent wind tears at the accumulated brush concealing it. Though Grandma hadn't found her supernatural faith until late in her life, the Thompson family had been Protestant, and Philly's ma had been raised Catholic. Instead of deciding between them, Ma and Dad had simply agreed to dump them both when they married. And, when Grandma Thompson had found a more miraculous spiritual life, her son had listened far more sympathetically than her daughter-in-law. Maybe Dad was spiritually thirsty enough to keep alive the possibility of something more. But Philly hadn't heard him defend his mother's faith in all the intervening years—as if surrendering to Ma's suspicious disapproval.

Philly got out of his chair, keeping his eyes on Dad in case the old man changed his mind. But Dad just sat up straighter.

Jesus nodded to Philly and then reached his hands toward Mr. Thompson's ears.

Philly, standing opposite Jesus, mirrored his movement and gently touched his hands to his dad's ears. This skin-to-skin contact doubled Philly's discomfort at this strange event.

"Okay, now you say, 'Hearing, be restored.'"

Philly's stumbled forward. With his hands over his dad's ears, he said, "Hearing, be restored." He pronounced the words mechanically, with no particular conviction.

Dad reacted immediately. "Hey, that feels hot. My ears are hot."

Philly pulled his hands back, afraid he had done something wrong.

Jesus said, "That's good. That's healing power starting to work. Put your hands back."

Philly obeyed.

Again, Dad reacted. "Yeah, that feels hot, but it's not bad—just a lot hotter than normal."

Philly checked with Jesus, like a medical technician consulting the physician.

Ma broke in. "This is crazy. Philly, you stop that. This is nuts!"

Philly just glanced at Ma, then at Eileen, who had an expectant look on her face. Eileen's apparent openness intrigued Philly and boosted his faith.

Suddenly Dad shouted. "Whoa!" He reached for both his ears, fishing for his hearing aids with the tips of his thumbs and forefingers.

Jesus withdrew his hands and smiled.

Philly followed his example. Though his smile was probably not so certain.

Dad sat in his usual place at the head of the dining room table. That was the only thing that was familiar to Philly. His father held a hearing aid in each hand. Eyes wide and mouth open, wonder and awe transformed him.

"Say something," Dad said.

Eileen said, "Can you hear me?"

Dad smiled and nodded slowly. "Well, I'll be!" He chortled.

Ma said, "What are you talking about? You can't hear without your hearing aids. Nobody knows that better than me."

"I can hear *now*, Marge."

Philly gawked at Jesus. "You healed his ears?" He said it aloud.

"Who are you talking to?" Ma said.

Eileen answered in a hushed voice. "Jesus."

Dad just kept smiling.

Seeing Jesus

Chapter Nine

If Jesus healed Dad's hearing, shouldn't Philly's family change? Shouldn't they leap into new faith? Philly didn't know. But he did know his family. Even if they were supposed to be transformed, the average between what ought to be and what *was* would surely produce some kind of a muddle.

Sunday, Dad had called several of his old friends and relatives to tell them the good news about his hearing, driven on, certainly, by the wonder of clearly hearing their voices over the phone.

Eileen had left for New York that afternoon, after asking occasionally about what Jesus was doing at a given moment and hugging Philly extra long at the airport. She had already confronted her newly ex-boyfriend by phone. She had apparently inspired a dumbfounded silence from him when she detailed his real life, as if she had hired a private investigator to check him out.

Ma, on the other hand, had contacted both the priest in the local diocese and a family friend who was a psychiatrist—to attempt to dam the flood of Philly's insanity.

Philly and Jesus returned to their normal life on Monday, escaping the storm whipped by the countervailing winds at his parents' house. He did have to brave the oppressive heat of going to work without permission to talk to Brenda. And his work climate also included the suspicions of his boss—suspicions that Philly had lost his edge, distracted by personal problems.

Sitting in his office, still damp from the thin drizzle that dogged him from home to work, Philly confirmed that the shades beside his door were tightly shut. Then he consulted Jesus, who was sitting in his usual place. "You think I should go and see Ma's priest?" He kept his voice low, in case Craig or Dennis might approach his door.

Jesus smiled. "He's a sincere man and would benefit greatly from hearing what you've experienced. That is, if he were inclined to believe you."

"Shouldn't a priest believe in this sort of thing?"

"You really should read my book."

Philly tightened his brow, his hand on the computer mouse, motionless.

"If you did some reading, Philly, you'd see that religious people have often been deeply divided over what to believe about me."

Philly nodded, once again visiting foreign territory. He decided he would take Jesus's gentle rebuke seriously and get himself a Bible. He returned to the original question. "So, should I make Ma happy and visit this priest?" He clicked away some junk email as he spoke.

"Are you asking me what I want you to do?"

Philly shrugged. "Yeah, I am."

"Okay. You should see him, but not to assuage your mother's fears—it won't work for that. But visiting him will give Tim a chance to take a closer look at some things in his own life." Jesus referred to the priest by his first name, which Philly only recalled at this reminder.

"You're saying I should see the priest for *his* benefit?"

"Yes."

Philly raised his eyebrows at this concept, simultaneously noting a meeting with Craig on his calendar. They needed to discuss what to do with an accumulating pile of old computers, down to the components and accessories. Philly sent an email to Craig to arrange their meeting for the storage room instead of his office.

At ten o'clock, Philly headed for the storage room, a cup of strong coffee in one hand and his laptop in the other. He would consult the spreadsheet detailing the contents of the gray and black computers, which had once been office workhorses but now collected dust in the closet behind the room.

Craig was already there when Philly and Jesus arrived. He had the light on and a damp cotton cloth at work wiping a layer of dust off the tops of tightly stacked computers.

"Hey, good to see you already on the job." Philly smiled at Craig. Then he pointed to Craig's nose. "You got a smudge of dust right there."

Craig wiped the sleeve of his denim shirt across the bridge of his nose, erasing most of the dust. Against his dark brown skin, the light gray dust still streaked his nose and cheek.

"A bit more." Philly stepped closer but tried not to bust in on Craig's personal boundaries.

This time Craig wiped his hand over his nose and cheek, the remainder of the visible smudge disappearing. "Did I get it?"

"Yup. You allergic or something?" He heard a bit of congestion in Craig's voice.

"Yeah, probably. But I might just have a cold. I've been feeling tired and congested all weekend. Guess I didn't get enough sleep." Craig absently surveyed the shelves lining three sides of the small storage room. "Come to think of it, I moved those old boxes last week, before this started. Maybe it is allergies."

"You should wear something over your face. You could get petty cash and go to the hardware store for some of those masks painters wear."

Craig shrugged. "I should have thought of that, but the damage is already done."

Philly noticed Jesus maneuvering in close to Craig, and he anticipated the meaning of the move.

Clearly reading his thoughts, Jesus nodded at Philly.

Philly set his coffee down on an old computer desk by the door, the cup plowing a small pile of dust aside. Carrying on as if Jesus weren't there, Philly said, "Well, it looks to me like there's still plenty of dust here, and it can't be good to inhale this stuff even if you're already feeling allergic." He felt like a big brother, teaching Craig to be more responsible for his health.

Jesus, on the other hand, seemed determined to cut past responsibility to recovery. He looked at Philly expectantly.

Philly battled with the possible consequences of bringing Jesus, and healing, into his work relationships. Would it be safe? But the bright anticipation on Jesus's face, combined with the memory of the exhilaration from healing his father's ears, stirred Philly's courage.

"Uh, Craig, I know this is gonna sound strange, but, uh, well, I've been having some good results from sort of, uh, well ..." Philly trailed off, not knowing how to introduce the oddball idea.

Jesus helped out. "Just say, 'I've been seeing Jesus do some healing through me lately, and I wonder if you'd like me to try with your allergies.'"

Philly managed to untangle from his objections to these words, desperate to dispel the confused mask Craig's face now wore. "Uh, what I mean is that I've been seeing Jesus do some healing around me some lately, and I wonder if you wouldn't mind me trying to heal the allergies. It's nothing too weird or anything."

Craig elevated his eyebrows. "I didn't know you were into that kinda thing." He didn't appear to be as freaked out by the idea as Philly feared. "My mom's church does that sometimes."

Philly had to hold back a chuckle, maybe a bit delirious.

Jesus helped him again. "Just ask if you can put a hand on his shoulder for a few seconds."

Philly nodded at Jesus, before considering how odd that gesture would look to Craig. He just hoped his coworker was as open as he appeared. "Okay if I put my hand on your shoulder for a few seconds?"

"Sure, go ahead. It's worth a try. I sure would like to breathe again."

Philly reached up and gently rested his left hand on Craig's shoulder. He just realized that he was still holding his laptop in his right hand. Too late to do anything about that now.

Jesus instructed Philly. "Just say, 'Jesus heals you.'"

Philly repeated that phrase with more self-consciousness than faith. But, as soon as he said the word "you," Jesus reached up to Craig's shoulder.

Craig ducked suddenly. "Hey!" He started to shake, his eyes wide, sweat beading quickly on his forehead.

Philly pulled his hand back, afraid that he had done something wrong. He had been prepared for heat, like he felt when Jesus healed his dad. But Craig reacted as if Philly had punched him and then plugged him into a light socket.

When both Philly and Jesus had removed their hands, Craig stood still a minute with his eyes closed, his hands halfway to his face. Then he relaxed, took a deep breath through his nose, and smiled. "Hey, that worked! I feel much better." His voice sparkled with satisfaction. He studied Philly now. Then he laughed. "You look like you were expecting something else to happen."

Philly let his eyes shift to Jesus and back. "I guess I didn't know *what* to expect. So, you really feel better?"

"Yeah, I feel great!" Craig laughed some more. "Wow, that's fantastic! Where did you learn to do that?"

Philly shrugged, smiling slightly. "I'm just learning now. I'm just kinda figuring out what God wants to happen, and I try to go along with it."

Craig nodded, but tapered his laughter. "But *how* do you figure that out?"

Again, Philly looked at Jesus. "Well, it's kind of like I can see Jesus and can see what he wants."

As he said this, Dennis appeared in the storeroom door. He arrived just in time to hear half of that last answer from Philly. "What are you guys doing in here? I heard you all the way out in the hall."

Philly spun around and felt his face flush. Craig looked at his

Seeing Jesus

boss's boss with his smile frozen in place.

Jesus rescued Philly. "Just tell him your business here and let him figure out the rest."

Philly started with a stammer but rallied to explain their task of deciding what to do with the old computers in storage.

Dennis assessed the two of them. Craig's smile had faded to a minor grin. Dennis seemed to be considering a more direct question about what he overheard, but just nodded and vacated the doorway.

Philly waited a few seconds and then turned back to the shelves full of computers. "Well, back to business." He avoided commenting on his boss to his subordinate, knowing that was inappropriate and not knowing what to say anyway.

But Craig addressed the awkwardness. "I hope you're not gonna get in trouble."

"Oh, don't worry about it. I'm just glad you're feeling better." Philly opened his laptop and set it on a bit of open shelf at eye level, noticing his hands shaking.

Once Craig's attention turned back to the computer hardware, Philly spoke to Jesus internally. "*I'm not gonna get in trouble, am I?*"

Jesus replied in kind, not moving his lips. "You shouldn't worry about that. Just do what you know is right and let the consequences take care of themselves."

This answer seemed to imply that he might, indeed, hear more from Dennis regarding more unprofessional behavior.

Philly strained his attention back to leading Craig through assessing the hardware, determining what to recycle, what to offer to employees, and what to keep. After fifteen minutes, a handful of complaints in his email about a slow internet connection pulled Philly away. By then he was confident that Craig could finish the sorting process.

On the way back to his office, Philly saw Brenda briefly. She looked at him, smiled mutely, and immediately resumed her course. For just one second Philly regretted Jesus's presence with him, feeling the accumulation of his boss's suspicions, Brenda's leave of absence, and his mother's witch-hunt.

"It will always cost you something to be with me." Jesus spoke into Philly's head.

Philly glanced briefly at him, careful not to be caught looking at thin air. Then a question occurred to him. *"How long can you stay with me like this?"*

"How long *can* I is a different question than how long *will* I stay like this."

Philly stepped around his desk and checked his internet connection, resorting to a testing website to acquire objective data regarding available bandwidth. "Slow" was subjective, and the causes of genuine internet slowdowns usually passed quicker than springtime in Chicago.

As he began to burrow into the task at hand, Philly paused to note how easily he could duck from the stinging prospect of Jesus's departure. But he did have to focus now, to check the available speed of the office internet connection, to test a backup connection, and to open a network administration application to find who might be using up the available data pipeline to the wide world. Grateful that all this work had become reflex, Philly looked up to see Jesus smiling at him during each hourglass moment provided by his finite desktop computer.

After one of those glances, Jesus said, "Dennis is coming."

At Jesus's warning, Philly locked his gaze onto his computer screens, defending against Dennis catching his enamored stare at his empty guest chair. The door stood open ten inches, and Jesus's warning proved timely.

Dennis knocked and pushed the door open simultaneously. "You looking into the complaints about the internet?"

Philly looked up. "Yeah. Someone is downloading some large files up in the drafting department, it looks like. I'll figure out who it is and give them a call in a few seconds."

Dennis nodded, apparently satisfied that Philly was back at work and acting normal again. When he turned to leave, Dennis pulled the door closed, though it didn't latch.

Philly looked over at Jesus and spoke in a whisper. "Thanks."

When Philly hung up the phone call to the drafting department, Jesus offered this insight into Philly's earlier question. "In a way, you're working with a disadvantage now, with me visibly and audibly present outside of your mind."

Philly scowled at Jesus.

"You see, most people who talk to me while they work, such as your grandma, for example, can do it without a temptation to look at their guest chair or to speak out loud." He grinned. "Having me outside and visible like this strains you more than it will when I'm only with you internally."

Philly had finally begun to accommodate himself to Jesus beside him. Jesus *inside* him tested his mental flexibility like the next level of a stretch once he had made the first press to lengthen a hamstring or back muscle. Again, he had to fight against the frustration that he needed to continue working and couldn't just flop down under a tree somewhere to consider the wisdom Jesus tossed to him. He assumed it was wisdom, anyway, given the source and the fact that he couldn't comprehend most of it.

The end of that workday arrived after Craig checked in to clarify what to do with a few odd hardware items and to say his allergies were still cleared up.

Philly smiled at the cheerful way Craig accepted the healing. He did wonder whether Craig would think differently when his friends scrutinized the story. Philly still wasn't fully confident that Craig's curb appeal carried very far inside. But maybe all that recursive thinking originated in Philly's guarded relationship with Dennis, and not in Philly's relationship with his agreeable assistant.

As he headed for the front door, Philly realized he was a couple minutes early. Whether he had genuinely forgotten his ban or was mulling a revolt against it, he didn't know himself, but he took two steps toward Brenda's department before stopping himself and reversing back to the glass doors and the flash of bright sunshine outside. Jesus hadn't made the brief detour. He had continued toward the outside, as if he knew all along that Philly wouldn't follow that urge to see Brenda. Philly followed Jesus through the doors, though *he* actually had to *open* them to pass outside.

Jesus looked back over his shoulder. "She'll be here."

Philly nodded in reply and then shot an apologetic look at the architect who had exited the building with him, unsure whether the older man had noticed him nodding to his imaginary friend. The architects generally regarded the computer guys as an alien race anyway, so Philly wasted no more energy worrying about the impression he had left.

As he walked to the bus stop with Jesus, his phone rang. Philly answered the generic ringtone of an unrecognized number. "Hello."

"Philly? This is Dad."

The voice sounded similar to his father's, as if Philly were hearing a different version of his dad, like Dad 2.0.

"Dad?" He didn't stop his voice from arching.

"Yeah, I got a new cell phone."

"Dad, you got yourself a cell phone?"

"Yeah, your mother thinks I'm crazy, of course. But it's about time I got one of these things. It's not one of those fancy ones with movies and stuff on 'em, just a freebie that comes with the contract, y' know."

"Okay." Philly picked up his pace from the diminishing stagger he had fallen into.

"I can hear now, of course, so this all works much better than it did before. I can hear you real clear."

"Yeah, I guess that would make a big difference." Elements formerly rooted in Philly's brain had broken loose and now floated uncontrollably up and away from the planet on which he had once lived.

"So, here's the real thing I wanted to call you about. I thought you'd understand." Dad was stretching his newly won record for longest initiated phone conversation in his son's adult life. "I called the pension board from the plant, and the new company that owns them now, and I told them that my ears had been healed, so they could adjust my disability and retirement benefits."

Philly stopped in the middle of the wide, gray sidewalk. His bus neared the stop, but he had ended his approach twenty feet short. "You told them you were healed?"

"Yeah." Dad laughed. "I had to explain it to six different people and to three of 'em twice." He sounded giddy.

Philly briefly considered whether his dad was drunk so early in the day, but then looked at Jesus, who was gesturing toward the bus. Philly took off at a slow trot and hopped on just in front of the clamping doors. He fumbled for his pass, ran it through the scanner, and then stumbled toward an empty seat as the bus lurched away from the curb.

"What did they say?" Philly spoke as he tried to pocket his wallet and sit down.

"They said they didn't have any way to process a claim like mine, and I should just leave things the way they are. One guy said I probably should have gotten disability earlier anyway, so I deserved to keep getting it." Dad's voice bounced with amusement.

"Man, Dad, that was gutsy. I can't believe you did that. What did Ma say?"

Dad snorted a laugh. "She couldn't speak. Can you imagine that? She couldn't speak. She took some aspirins and went to bed. I'll tell her to stop worrying when she wakes up from her nap."

Jesus spoke up, as if he were hearing the entire conversation.

"Tell him to go ahead and talk to her now. She's not asleep, and she really would like to hear that everything is okay."

Philly started to report these instructions and worried that the woman seated next to him might be tuned in to his conversation. "Uh, my friend says you should go ahead and tell her now."

"Your friend?" Dad said.

"You know, the one who helped you with your hearing."

"Oh, you mean Jesus?"

"Yeah. He says she's not asleep and needs to hear the news right away."

"He can do that? I mean he can see her or something?"

Philly could tell that his dad had opened the back door and entered the house. Apparently he had been calling from the driveway, just like Eileen and Philly did with their cell phones. Philly waited a moment as his dad walked without talking.

"Hey, he's right—she's awake." He spoke in a hushed tone. "Okay, talk to you later. And thank your friend for the advice." His dad chuckled.

"Okay, bye Dad." Philly tapped "End Call" on his phone and slipped it into his pocket, sleepwalker fashion.

"It wasn't a nutty thing to do, Philly. It was honest and trusting and the right thing for your dad to do."

Philly stopped himself from speaking aloud, still constrained enough to care what people would think if he started shouting at his invisible Jesus seated across the aisle. "*He could have lost his income.*" He tried adding stern overtones to silent words.

"Yes, that was a possible outcome of his actions." Jesus sounded like a therapist speaking gentle correction.

Philly shook his head and then froze, fully aware of the people around him. "*He needs that pension to live on—for him and Ma to live on.*"

"Do you really think I don't know everything about every dollar and penny that passes through their hands?" Jesus wasn't matching Philly's level of perturbation.

Philly filtered those words and then responded internally. *"I guess I never thought about it. Like, you have time to think about everyone's money issues?"*

"Two thousand seven hundred and twenty-three dollars and seventy-two cents."

"What?"

"That's how much money you have in your main checking account at this moment."

Philly glanced at Jesus, pulled his phone out again, and opened the app for his bank account. He logged in and viewed the list of accounts. There, in his main checking account, was $2723.72.

"I can do these psychic tricks all day and all night." Jesus gave Philly his cheesiest grin. "But the real question you have to answer is, 'Why do I care?' not 'What do I know?'"

Philly tried those questions on. "Why does Jesus care?" Not "What does Jesus know?" He seemed to know everything. But comprehending what Jesus was saying about money felt like trying to play chess on a curving and meandering landscape instead of the flat, black and white eight-by-eight checkerboard. *"I don't know what you're saying to me."*

"Go and see that priest your mother wants you to see. You'll learn some things there that will help."

Philly looked straight ahead as the bus picked up speed. At least here was something concrete he could do. Even if it was bound to be uncomfortable.

Hopefully Jesus would be there to help.

Chapter Ten

Tim Amundsen, forty years old, barely over five and a half feet tall, dark conservative-cut hair and clerical garb, sat behind his neat maple desk looking at Philly. "So, Phillip, what brings you to see me?"

Philly looked for a simple but genuine answer. "Uh ... well, it was my ma's idea. I think she's hoping you can sort of straighten me out or something."

"Yes, I got a call from your mother, Margaret, about meeting with you. But I couldn't understand her concern. Can you tell me what she's worried about?"

Philly decided not to say that she was worried about *everything*. "I think she's afraid that I'm hallucinating or delusional. You see, I let her know a couple of days ago that ... " Here he had to push through a stiff gate toward vulnerability. Glancing at Jesus, sitting in the chair next to him, Philly continued. "I told her that I've been seeing and hearing Jesus for the last week."

"Seeing and hearing Jesus? What do you mean by that?"

"Well, it's pretty simple, really. I see Jesus sitting right here next to me, and I can hear him when he talks to me. But no one else is able to see him or hear him."

Father Tim glanced at the empty chair. "Are you seeing him right now?"

Philly looked at Jesus, who lifted his hands from his lap in a gesture that said, "Here I am." He smiled broadly.

"Yeah, he's sitting right here, smiling at me."

"Smiling at you? Does he always smile at you?"

Philly nodded. "Most of the time he's smiling, unless he's telling me something serious."

"What sort of things does he tell you?" The priest adjusted himself in his chair.

"He gives me advice sometimes, or teaches me things, or sometimes he tells me things that I should say to other people." Philly's throat tightened as he detected growing tension in the priest.

"Why do you think you can see him but no one else can? Why is he just appearing to you?"

"He says it's because my grandma prayed for me. You see, she's in a coma, and I was talking to her—telling her how much I missed her—and I asked her to pray for me, if she could hear me. And she did pray and asked Jesus to come be with me while she's not able to talk to me."

"Do I know your grandmother?" Maybe Father Tim was thinking she might be a saintly member of his congregation.

"Uh, no, I don't think so. She goes to a different kind of church." Philly had grown up with the contrast between Catholic and Pentecostal, much of which consisted of the contrast between his grandma and his ma. The detailed theology and practice of the two had entered discussions very rarely during his childhood.

Father Tim nodded. He seemed less nervous, but still unconvinced. "So, your mother wanted you to see me so that I could convince you that you're not really seeing and hearing Jesus?"

"Yeah, I guess so. She got really upset when my dad's ears got healed. After that she was pretty freaked out."

"Your father's ears got healed? Tell me about that."

"Well, Jesus said he wanted to heal my dad's ears. Dad lost most of his hearing in an explosion at work about twenty-five years ago. So, Jesus stepped up to my dad and told me to put my hands on Dad's ears. When I did, they got really hot. And then he grabbed his hearing aids out and said he could hear. And I know he can hear, because he called me on his cell phone the other day. He could never talk on the phone before and didn't even have a cell phone until now."

Father Tim seemed to wait for this tide of information to

wash over him. "So, was it you who healed your dad's ears, or Jesus?"

"Well, I'm sure I could never do anything like that by myself. But Jesus insists that I have to put my hands where he wants to heal someone. When he does it by himself, it looks to me like his hands just disappear." Philly was feeling a relieved lightness from telling all of this to the priest, even if he wasn't sure Father Tim was believing him.

"Do you consider yourself a particularly holy person?"

"Holy? No, not particularly."

"Many a great saint has lived a long and torturous life of self-denial and devotion, and yet has never seen nor heard the Lord—or even one of his angels." The priest spoke in a firm and pedantic voice. "I don't understand why you would receive such a remarkable visitation."

Philly looked over at Jesus, whose face shone damp with tears as he faced Father Tim. He looked about like a jilted lover. Instead of his usual self-conscious glance away, Philly stared. "*Why are you crying?*" He didn't say that aloud.

Jesus turned from Father Tim to Philly. "I've longed to meet with many of the saints of whom he speaks, but many of them missed my invitation because of their religious busyness." Then he smiled slightly. "To others I *have* appeared in many forms, physically or spiritually, and he doesn't know about all of those intimate times with my friends."

Father Tim seemed to grow impatient with Philly staring so intensely at the empty chair. "You're acting as if you see Jesus now. Is he communicating with you?"

Philly looked back at Father Tim. For the first time, he was more interested in what Jesus was saying and doing than in protecting his self-image. Without responding to Father Tim, he looked back at Jesus. "What do you want me to tell him?" This time he did speak aloud.

"Tell him that I have loved him all his life and have tried to communicate with him ever since he was seven years old, sitting in his grandfather's apple tree, wondering if I was real."

Philly turned to Father Tim. "Jesus says he has loved you all your life and has tried to communicate with you many times since you were seven years old, sitting in your grandpa's apple tree, wondering if Jesus was real." He said it plainly, with little emotion.

"My grandpa's apple tree?" A haunted look captured his face.

"Well, technically he said, 'your grandfather's apple tree.' I messed that up a little." Here Philly was, apologizing again.

Father Tim's face flushed. "What do you know about my childhood? Have ... have you been talking to ... to ... Father O'Neal about me? Who are you?"

Jesus intervened again. "Tell him that Father O'Neal doesn't know about the time Tim was eight years old and, seeing a dead cat in the road, tried to raise him from the dead."

Philly passed on that message, being more careful to use the exact words Jesus used.

Again, Father Tim stared with his mouth cocked open. "What is this? Are you some kind of psychic?"

Philly shook his head. "I'm just a guy that gets to see and hear Jesus. I don't know anything about saints and being holy. I don't know anything about psychics either. But my grandma must have prayed for me, in her coma, and then this happened. I'm pretty sure it's not because I'm anything special."

Jesus beamed at Philly.

"Well, tell me this. If you and Jesus can heal people, then why is your grandma still in a coma?"

Philly snapped his head toward Jesus. A dozen questions filled his mind all at once. They coalesced into one. *Are we gonna heal Grandma?* He kept the words internal this time.

Jesus smiled more broadly and nodded.

"Okay." Philly turned to Father Tim. "Hey, thanks for your help. I'm going with Jesus now to heal Grandma. Thanks so much!" Philly stood up and stretched his hand toward Father Tim.

The priest stood too and mechanically reached his own hand across the desk.

Jesus had stood up with Philly and reached over to touch Father Tim when Philly shook his hand. At that moment, the priest began to tremble like someone on an old vibrating bed.

Philly let go of Father Tim's hand and stared.

Father Tim tried to speak. "Wha-ha-ha-hat ... i-i-isss ... th-th-thissss?"

Philly answered without consulting Jesus. "That's Jesus. He touched you."

Jesus had begun to walk toward the door. Philly turned to follow him, glancing back at Father Tim. "I'm pretty sure it'll be okay. He'd never do anything to hurt you."

As he reached the office door, he was grateful that Jesus had never done that tremor thing to him.

"Don't knock it until you've tried it." Jesus responded to that thought, laughing out loud—at least as far as Philly was concerned.

Philly follow Jesus out of the office, out of the rectory, and onto the street with his mouth halfway open. He closed it when he got to his car. "Can we really go and heal Grandma now?"

"Yes, we can."

Philly considered Jesus, standing there on the sidewalk in the sunshine, comparing him to the picture in the stained-glass window of the church next to the rectory. Not a bad likeness, he thought.

Jesus looked at the window and grinned, then climbed into the car.

As Jesus slid into the passenger seat, a disturbing question occurred to Philly. "If we heal Grandma, does that mean you leave?"

Jesus looked at Philly like a father satisfied with his son. "I will be *leaving*, but not right away." He added an ironic emphasis to the word "leaving."

Philly started the car, attempting only briefly to discern the source of that irony, but not asking about it. Instead, he focused on the prospect of waking Grandma from her coma. "You tried to get me to do this the last time we were there."

"Yes. But you weren't ready to do your part yet."

Philly nodded, stopping at a light and idly watching a woman pushing a stroller over the crosswalk in front of them.

"Do you know her and the baby?" He nodded toward the pedestrians.

Jesus smiled, watching the small, dark-skinned woman maneuver the big blue stroller up the slight ramp on the other side of the street. "Yes, of course. But she doesn't know me." His face clouded slightly at this last note.

Philly watched this reaction on Jesus's face and then heard a honk behind him. The light had changed. He pressed the accelerator and surged across the intersection apologetically. "You must go through that a lot—people that you know, but who don't recognize you." He tried to imagine the emotional weight of such persistent rejection.

"I don't suffer from the same pain of rejection that you do." Jesus responded to both the spoken question and the unspoken thought. "For you, there's the fear that you're being rejected because you're unlovable. That is the source of the pain you feel at emotional or relational rejection. For me, however, the pain of her rejection is the pain of her loneliness, her fear, and her sadness—not mine." He was watching Philly. "I feel genuine emotional anguish, but never for my own sake. I have all that I'll ever need. But so many people have little of what they really need. I'm content, yet I grieve the profound lack of contentment of most of the people that I love." Jesus gazed out the windshield again. "You won't fully understand these things, Philly. But it's good for you to keep trying."

Philly accepted this reassurance and challenge like a Christmas sweater from a dear relative. The discomfort of the fit did nothing to dampen the warmth of the love with which it was given.

Within fifteen minutes, Philly pulled his car into the hospital parking lot. The western sun tinted the clear spring day a gentle orange as evening approached. For a confused moment, Philly considered whether it was a good idea to visit Grandma around supper, forgetting that her only nourishment came through plastic tubes.

Jesus put his hand on Philly's back briefly as he accompanied him toward the hospital entryway. He seemed to be pushing him through the stream of panic that had risen in Philly's head. Jesus's touch tranquilized that panic into a sort of anticipation and expectation.

Entering the shady garage marked for staff, Philly noticed a tall nurse heading toward the automatic sliding doors ahead of him. In the wide marble lobby, the mix of artificial and natural light accentuated the curves of that nurse's body, which captivated Philly. He watched her walking ahead of him for a few seconds and then slowed suddenly, nearly stopping to smack himself in the forehead. *What am I doing? I'll ruin everything, thinking like that.*

Jesus looked at Philly with his head tilted slightly. He didn't look as disappointed as Philly was. Nor as fearful of spoiling their mission.

Philly tightened his brow.

Jesus answered Philly's questioning look with a question of his own. "Did you think that you were going to heal your grandma by your holiness?"

There was that word again. "Holy." Philly resumed his march toward Grandma's room, but more slowly and absent the feminine distraction. *"Of course not,"* he said internally. *"I don't even know what 'holy' really means."*

"'Holy' means you're sold out completely—all in."

This explanation baffled Philly for its incongruity with the way he perceived religious people using the word. Instead of solving that riddle, however, Philly returned to focusing on the task at hand. In the elevator, Philly saw his reflection in each of the shiny metal walls and doors, alongside Jesus's multiple images. Philly marveled that he not only saw Jesus but saw his reflection. Something about that seemed extra fascinating.

Exiting the elevator on Grandma's floor, Philly hesitated a second when he saw his parents leaving her room.

Jesus saw that hesitation. "Don't worry, they're not staying. We'll have Grandma all to ourselves."

Once again, Philly surfed forward on the swell of Jesus's encouragement. He smiled at his ma and dad as they approached.

Dad looked happy to see him. Ma looked concerned. She seemed worried about something she saw in his face.

"How ya doin' Philly?" Dad offered his hand and patted Philly's shoulder. Philly noted the extra physical contact that accompanied his father's greeting.

So used to Jesus's presence, Philly felt a momentary discomfort that Ma and Dad didn't greet his friend. But he pulled past that and turned his thoughts toward Grandma. "Any change in her condition?"

Ma shook her head, donning her most mournful veil. "She's the same—not really there, not even like she's sleeping." She nearly moaned.

Philly nodded, touching the juxtaposition between Ma's moroseness and his own hope that Grandma was going to wake up in a few minutes. He actually had to suppress a giggle. Congratulating himself for resisting that urge, he expected he had avoided horrifying his ma and prompting her to make a call to the psych ward.

Once again Jesus put a hand on Philly's back, reconnecting him to their goal.

Philly stiffly hugged his ma. "Okay, well, you two have a good evening. It was good to see you both." One brief, awkward dance later, Philly had extricated himself from his ma, waved goodbye to his dad, and scooted down the hall.

As he approached the door of Grandma's room, a nurse brushed past him on her way out. Not until she had excused herself and made half a dozen paces from the room did Philly recognize the nurse he had ogled in the lobby. Jesus's touch on his back assuaged Philly's need to reiterate his penitence. Instead he threw his weight toward pressing into Grandma's hospital room.

The bed next to her lay empty, the sheets stripped and the patient apparently checked out. Jesus was right—they would have the room to themselves. Despite that observation, Philly felt a presence in the room beyond his grandma's. It was as if he needed to lean forward to reach her bedside. He glanced at Jesus but saw no evidence that he felt any resistance. Philly allowed his concern to slow him.

"Don't worry. We can do this. And no one can stop us." Jesus didn't waver at all.

Philly sucked in a deep breath. Jesus seemed to confirm that sense of opposition in the room, but he wasn't intimidated by whatever was behind it. Even as Philly locked onto Jesus's confidence, his body seemed to drift beyond his control, like a boat given too much slack from its anchor.

Jesus circled the bed and stood next to Grandma's pillow, on her left.

Philly adjusted his course and edged into the space opposite Jesus, to her right. As Jesus reached out, Philly followed, allowing the pull of Jesus's will to draw him forward. They stood there across from each other, looking down at Grandma. Both were silent for a moment, hands gently on her forehead.

Jesus instructed Philly. "You say, 'Wake up, Grandma.'"

Philly looked at Jesus and thanked God that no one was there to see him. Clearing his throat in case verbal clarity mattered, Philly said, "Grandma, wake up."

For a second or two nothing seemed to happen, and then Grandma's color visibly darkened, from pale paper to warm skin. A chill ran down Philly's spine at the sight of this change. But she didn't move. He looked at Jesus. "What now?"

"Just wait."

Philly looked at Grandma and then back at Jesus. When he returned his attention to Grandma, Philly's brain flailed for an explanation. *Why does Grandma look so strange?* Then he realized that he wasn't used to her opening her eyes in that hospital bed. Nor was he used to seeing her without her glasses.

Grandma turned her head toward Jesus and smiled. She turned and looked at Philly and smiled again. Then she started to chuckle.

Could Grandma see Jesus? She seemed to look right at him. She did that before she made eye contact with her grandson. Philly loosed some hysteria-tinted laughter, like what Jesus had caused before. He started to remove his hands from Grandma's head, but Jesus lowered his forehead toward her to stop him from pulling away. When Philly resettled his hands on Grandma's head, he saw her color improve another shade. It occurred to him then that healing someone in a coma could be complicated. Not only did she have to overcome the original cause of the coma, but she also had to recover from the effects of being incapacitated for a long time. Grandma hadn't eaten anything for many days now, for one thing.

Grandma slowly reached up to Philly's right hand with her own and then turned back to Jesus, trying to reach his hand as well. When she held both of their hands, she closed her eyes and seemed to have completed some sort of power circuit. She started to vibrate slightly. Philly thought of Father Tim. But Grandma's vibration was less violent. It seemed to soothe her in some way.

"Grandma?" Philly finally spoke once the vibration had stopped.

She opened her eyes, her smile turned more playful and vivacious. No longer the passive patient, she now looked the part of the spry grandma Philly had known all his life.

"You're awake."

Grandma nodded. "Yes, I'm awake." Her voice was faint and the tubes in her nose weren't helping. "How long was I asleep?"

Philly looked at Jesus, who allowed him to answer.

"You were in a coma for over a week."

"Oh." She paused slightly. "I knew it was something." She surveyed the plain walls of the hospital room. She looked at Jesus for a few moments. "How is it that you're here like this?"

Again, Jesus allowed Philly to answer the question.

"The first time I visited you here, I talked to you. And I didn't really know what to say, so I just said how much I missed you, and then I asked you to pray for me while you were away—so I wouldn't miss you so much." He couldn't stop his voice from quaking. "The next day, I met Jesus on the bus on the way to work, and he told me that you did pray for me. And he's been with me while you were in the coma. But no one else could see him until now." Philly's voice trailed at the end as he approached that final oddity.

Grandma turned from Philly to Jesus again. She studied his face with a sunny smile in her eyes and on her lips. "I remember praying now. It was so good of you to come to Philly like that. Thank you."

Jesus smiled warmly. "You asked for something that I just couldn't refuse."

She seemed to know what Jesus meant, slowly closing her eyes and nodding very gently. She turned her smile on Philly again. It was the same welcoming smile he had always known from her. But now he suspected her welcome also included accepting him into her communion with this Jesus that she knew so much better than he did.

She seemed to grow tired of rolling her head left and right to look from one to the other. She tried to sit up, releasing their hands and pushing against the sheets.

Philly looked for the bed controls. He found no remote but discovered buttons on the side of the bed. He managed to raise the head of the bed eventually, taking care to leave slack in all the tubes still attached to Grandma.

Just as they finished rearranging her pillows, that same attractive nurse poked her head in the door.

She hung there for a moment and then stepped into the room. "Mrs. Thompson?" Her voice faltered. "How are you feeling?" She hit a slight squeak.

Seeing the nurse's face for the first time, Philly had to hurdle over his own disorientation. He was trying not to stare at the beautiful woman about his own age. Trying to tell himself to cool down, to not notice how attractive she was. This wasn't the time. Somewhere in his adjustments, he realized that the nurse was the only person in the room who couldn't see all the others present. What to say to her totally eluded him.

Grandma answered her. "I'm feeling quite well, in fact. But I am really very hungry. Am I allowed to eat?"

The nurse nodded. Her name tag said Theresa. She allowed her eyes to dance from Grandma to Philly. Those big green eyes were asking a question. Her full lips stood open half an inch. The question on those lips seemed stifled for the moment. Did Philly know that question? Was she asking him?

There was something about food being offered. Philly answered. "Uh ... Nothing for me, thanks."

Jesus laughed.

Theresa bypassed Philly's odd reply and clearly didn't hear Jesus. "When did she wake up?"

Glad for a direct question, Philly said, "A couple of minutes before you looked in."

Theresa still looked at the pair, as if waiting for more of an explanation.

Jesus said, "Why don't you tell her?"

"Well, what would you like to eat?" Theresa asked Grandma.

Grandma looked at Jesus, then at Philly, and then answered Theresa. "I could eat anything you're willing to bring me. Soup and crackers would be nice."

"You mind instant soup?" Theresa seemed to welcome the familiar task of arranging for food. Her pace picked up and her voice became firmer.

"That would be fine. I'm so hungry that it will taste wonderful, I'm sure."

"Tell her," Jesus said again.

Grandma consulted Jesus and then Philly.

Philly cleared his throat. "Well, you might be wondering how Grandma suddenly woke up."

Theresa stopped her busy little movements around the medical equipment and focused on Philly. "Yes, I'm really surprised to see her awake."

"Well, I sort of prayed for her to get well. I mean, I sort of woke her up." He hesitated, wondering how to say it without sounding like he was bragging. He looked at Jesus. "Jesus did it."

Theresa stood perfectly still, except for her eyes. She batted long, dark lashes and explored the two visible people in the room. She even seemed to cast a query at the place where Jesus stood. "That sounds like a miracle to me."

Philly smiled.

"That's exactly what it is. Jesus and my grandson came to wake me up, and it's a miracle!" Grandma laughed, and the sound of it evoked giggling children at play.

Everyone else in the room laughed as well.

Theresa approached Grandma and took her hand, holding it for a moment as she contemplated the older woman's cheerful eyes. "That's wonderful. Well, I'm glad to meet you finally." Again, she ventured a brief look toward Jesus.

"She believes," Jesus said.

That left Philly wondering what to say. Grandma seemed just as bereft as him.

Theresa ended the awkward moment for them. "Well, I'll see about that soup and some crackers for starters. But first I'll arrange to get the feeding tube removed."

"Thanks," said Philly.

"Thank you," said Grandma.

"I love you, Theresa," said Jesus.

Chapter Eleven

Philly held his cell phone away from his ear to diminish the blast from his father shouting on the other end.

"Oh my." Grandma laughed from her place propped in the bed.

Philly tried to resume the conversation, the phone against his cheek. "Do you want to talk to her?" His question intersected with more shouts.

"Talk to her?" Dad dropped his volume just a bit. "Of course I want to talk to her."

Just before he handed the phone to Grandma, Philly heard his ma say, "You don't mean to tell me she's really out of the coma?"

"Yes, Marge. Listen for yourself."

"Hello, Dale." Grandma held Philly's phone.

Philly heard his father's voice, greeting and then breaking down into inarticulate blubbering. Philly looked at Jesus, raising his eyebrows at the sound of his dad coming loose from the brackets that had held his emotions in place for as long as Philly could remember.

"Well, dear, I'm so happy to hear you too. Though for me it just feels like a long sleep. I hardly remember the stroke at all." Grandma spoke right through the tumult.

Ma's voice crept out from the muffled background of the cell phone signal. "Can she speak? How can she speak? She had a stroke! How can she speak?"

"She's healed, Marge. She's really healed!" Philly heard his dad though Grandma still held the phone to her ear. Her hearing hadn't been good the last few years, so the raucous voices probably didn't bother her. She seemed to be enjoying the sound of her boy celebrating.

Theresa returned with a tray and a doctor in tow. Philly took the phone back gently and said to Dad, "Okay, the doctor just arrived, so I'll hang up for now. You guys could come over, of course."

Grandma chuckled at the suggestion of a growing party, as well as the approaching food tray.

"Mrs. Thompson, I'm Dr. Blassini. I couldn't believe what the nurse was telling me, so I had to come and see for myself."

"You didn't expect me to wake up?" Grandma said.

The doctor sobered. "No, ma'am, I really didn't expect you to wake up."

This was news to Philly. He hadn't talked to the doctor himself, but he was sure that Ma would have told him if she had heard that they didn't expect Grandma to recover.

"You mind?" The doctor pulled a small flashlight from his pocket and gestured his request to trade places with Philly.

Philly backed out and rounded the bed to the other side, to stand with Jesus.

The doctor did a brief examination of Grandma's reflexes, sensation in her extremities, and ability to move both her feet and hands. He looked in her eyes a second time. "I'm glad I saw this for myself, because I wouldn't have believed it if someone else had told me."

Theresa rolled her eyes a bit, having certainly been the one who gave the doctor the good news. She slid the tray next to the bed, nearly bumping the doctor out of the way. "Mrs. Thompson is understandably hungry."

The doctor laughed. "I'll bet you are. It's been over a week since you've eaten." He looked at Philly. "You should give us a minute while I pull her feeding tube out."

Philly grimaced slightly and headed for the other side of the room. He took the opportunity to call Eileen and give her the news, uncertain whether Ma and Dad would have had the presence of mind to call her. Philly got the answering machine at

Eileen's apartment, left a brief, cryptic message, and then tried her cell phone.

"Hello, Philly."

"Hey, Eileen. Good news! Grandma's awake."

"What? She's out of the coma?"

"Yep."

"When?"

"About twenty minutes ago." Just then he noticed that Jesus had stayed with Grandma and had not accompanied him to the other side of the room. The past week of Jesus following him almost everywhere had led Philly to expect him to stay close. Again he considered the possibility that his time with Jesus was coming to an end.

"She just woke up? How is she?"

"Actually, Jesus and I came here tonight to wake her up. It's a long story. But she's wide awake and talking and laughing. The doctor's taking out her feeding tube now so she can eat some soup and crackers. She's really hungry."

"Can she feed herself? Did the stroke leave any other issues?"

"She's fine. Both hands, both feet, feeling and movement—the doctor just checked it all out. He said he wouldn't have believed it if he hadn't seen for himself. He said he hadn't expected Grandma to recover at all."

"Philly, it's a miracle!"

"Yeah. That's what they're calling it."

Philly's ma and dad arrived within fifteen minutes, just after Grandma finished her soup and crackers and a box of apple juice. She greeted her son and daughter-in-law like they had just returned from a long trip.

The party in Grandma's room, including visits from half a dozen nurses and four doctors, had to end at nine o'clock due to other patients on the floor. Grandma agreed to stay overnight on condition that they remove the IV tubes, which a medical technician did after Ma and Dad had gone home.

Philly, the last to leave, hesitated at the door when he noticed again that Jesus lagged behind. He had to force himself to step outside the room at the risk of finding that Jesus would no longer accompany him. But, as soon as he stepped into the hallway, Jesus appeared beside him, ready to go home.

"*For a minute there I thought you were going to stay with Grandma.*" Philly communicated silently as they ambled down the hall.

"I did." Jesus offered a sly smile, looking straight ahead.

Philly slowed down. "*No, I mean that you would stay the night with her and not come with me.*"

Jesus nodded. "I know what you meant. I'm coming with you, *and* I'm staying with Grandma tonight."

Still walking slower and forgetting not to look at Jesus, Philly managed not to speak aloud. "*Are you serious?*" The look on Jesus's face, though cheerful, convinced Philly that he had understood correctly. "*You're with both of us now, even when we're separate?*"

"I am."

Philly picked up his pace. "*Cool!*"

The next morning, Philly commuted to work as usual but called his grandma's hospital room as soon as he sat down at his desk. "How are you feeling?"

"I'm fine, Philly. I'm ready to go home. I wanna get outta here before they think of doing any tests on me. Your dad is coming to get me in about an hour."

"That's great. The doctors agreed to this?"

"I didn't give 'em much choice in the matter." Grandma's voice rose, a hint of restrained laughter.

Philly chuckled and then considered Jesus in his guest chair. "Did Jesus stay with you?"

"Yes, he did. I can still see him now. What a wonderful blessing for both of us. He told me last night that he was still visible to you at the same time. Isn't that marvelous?"

Philly snorted an airy laugh. "Yes, it is."

When he said goodbye and hung up the phone, Philly looked at Jesus. Once again, he absorbed the warm comfort of his new companion. He savored the friendly wisdom simply waiting to be tapped and the constant love he had only to observe to know was real. Never in all his life had Philly enjoyed something so much. *Better than Christmas*, he thought. With this cheerful thought still hanging sweetly in his mind, Philly heard a knock at his door.

"Come in." He said it almost playfully.

Craig opened the door. Behind him stood Allyson Elders, a young woman who worked as a designer, producing digital drawings for the architects. Philly had never held an actual conversation with Allyson, and her presence in his office surprised him. Craig ushered her in and closed the door behind them. That last move cemented a feeling in Philly that a storm front was approaching. He would either have to yield to its force or get up and run for cover. He stayed in his chair.

"What's this about?"

Craig motioned to the guest chair next to Jesus for Allyson. And he sat down on Jesus, as far as Philly was concerned.

But Jesus popped from the chair to the narrow space next to it, wedged against a file cabinet and still apparently pleased at the company.

"Well," Craig said, "I was telling Allyson about my allergies and the way you ... ah ... healed me."

Allyson nodded, regarding Philly like a zoo patron observing one of her favorite animals. She had very large eyes in her narrow face, anyway. They were supersized just now.

Philly looked only briefly at Allyson, shy of all strangers, but particularly disturbed by the expectant expression in the young woman's eyes.

"It came up because I've been working with the helpdesk on getting her a more ergonomic setup at her desk. She has shoulder pain and pain in her mouse hand. I don't know if it's okay, just now stopping to think about that, but I thought maybe you would see if you could do anything for her. She's pretty worried about losing her job, the way things are going now." Craig settling on a small sideways grin that might be both an appeal and an apology.

Jesus broke into Philly's hesitation, stepping around Craig and placing himself in front of Allyson. "I want to show her how much I love her."

Though Philly was beginning to understand what it meant to cooperate with Jesus's healing agenda, he found the Savior's declaration disorienting. All he managed in response was to think "*How?*"

"*You* tell her."

Philly stood up from his chair, adjusted his pants, tucked in his shirt, and straightened his hair. He stared at Jesus as he did this. When he checked in with Allyson and Craig, they seemed nervous about how nervous *he* obviously was. He considered how his visitors must have strained their own comfort limits by even coming here to ask.

"Sorry about my hesitation." He cleared his throat, then focused on Allyson. "I don't know if you'll understand this, but Jesus is telling me to let you know something—besides just healing you." Philly's throat was slightly clogged. "He said he wants you to know how much he loves you." His voice came out squashed, the last word cut off.

Allyson crinkled her brow and then glanced at Jesus. She had certainly noticed Philly staring at that spot. "You hear Jesus speaking to you?"

Suddenly Philly remembered that he hadn't introduced Craig to his escort when he healed him the other day. But, instead of expounding the entire story, he opted for obscuring the details. "Well, I try to listen for his instructions, 'cause it's really him that does the healing, of course." Philly snuck a brief consult with Jesus to see if he was getting himself into trouble.

Instead of a rebuke, all Philly saw on the face of Jesus was the same enraptured fascination that Brenda had inspired—in fact, the same look of unquestioning love Philly had seen aimed at himself.

Overwhelmed with the profundity of those loving eyes, Philly tripped ahead. He blurted what he saw. "I wish you could see his face when he looks at you."

Allyson and Craig both followed Philly's gaze. Then they turned questioning eyes back toward him.

"*You* do the look," Jesus said.

"What?" Philly said aloud.

Craig was staring at his boss, his eyes so wide that Philly could see white all around his dark brown irises.

"You look at her with the love that you see in my eyes," Jesus said.

To obey Jesus, the introspective shroud that Philly wore every day—mending it and securing it in place between him and the searching eyes of other souls—would have to drop to the floor, leaving him naked. Very briefly, Philly scowled at the thought that Jesus was trying to excuse himself from healing Allyson by asking too much of Philly. But the purity of the Lord's loving gaze trounced that distracting thought.

Jesus seemed to recognize Philly's limits and moved on. "Ask her to stand up, and you take her hands in yours."

Philly stood in front of Allyson. She was nearly as tall as him, slightly taller than Craig. "Okay, could you stand up please, Allyson?"

Craig followed when Allyson rose to her feet. Because of the tight space, Philly now stood nearly toe-to-toe with the hesitant young woman. Her discomfort was about as obvious as Philly's own.

Again, Jesus kept the process moving. "Ask for her hands."

"Can I take your hands?"

Allyson mechanically complied.

Philly briefly sensed a shift in Craig's face. Was he jealous of this contact between Philly and Allyson? Were these two a couple? He resisted being distracted by Craig's mood shift.

Jesus continued. "Tell her I love her passionately with all my heart."

Again, Philly hesitated, longing for the good old days of simple physical healings. "Uh ... I ... uh, I mean, Jesus says to tell you that he, uh, loves you passionately with all of his heart." He repeated the message dutifully, conscious of how much of Jesus's passion he had left out of his voice.

Allyson's lower lip began to quiver slightly. In a breath of time, her face changed from a young woman at work to a small child lost for love.

Jesus now had a hand on her cheek, staring at her like an infatuated schoolboy.

His contact with her hands was crawly for Philly. The intense emotional contorting of Allyson's face was even worse. But laying all of this on Jesus made it tolerable. Philly began to feel warmth flowing through his hands into Allyson's.

Craig watched wide-eyed. And Philly saw no more of those jealous side-glances that he imagined he had seen a moment ago. Was Craig feeling something in the room? Philly and Allyson were both clearly connected with Jesus now.

Jesus nodded toward Craig. "Have him put his hand on her sore shoulder."

Philly motioned with his head toward her shoulder and spoke quietly. "Go ahead and put your hand on her shoulder while Jesus heals it."

At that, Jesus followed Craig's hand, reaching across Allyson to just touch the peak of her shoulder where Craig's left hand now rested. As their hands converged, Craig pursed his lips and widened his eyes.

Philly, now the veteran of three successful healings, said, "That heat is healing power."

Craig nodded.

Allyson appeared wrapped up in both the emotional miracle and the warm relief for her shoulder pain. Philly and Craig just watched in silence. Allyson's face was wet with tears and as peaceful as a baby dreaming of milk.

The entire process of Allyson's healing took just a few minutes. That slim passage of time, however, was full of too much for Philly to process, even after he was left alone.

He chuckled to himself several times during the day, recalling the intimate and intimidating experience. He was relieved that his soul-to-soul contact with two people he hardly knew hadn't ended in humiliation.

Philly wondered if he should have said anything to Craig and Allyson about keeping the healing a secret between them. He was still worried that this Jesus stuff might affect his employment.

At the end of the day, Philly left the office a bit late, hoping to catch the bus that followed his usual ride. The scent of recent rain filled Philly's nose as he stepped out of the building, but that refreshment turned a bit sour when he spotted Brenda scampering toward her train. Impulsively, he reached for his phone and glanced over his shoulder at Jesus, who smiled at his intention. As he walked to the bus stop, Philly called Brenda's cell phone, determined to leave a message if she decided not to pick up. He wanted to give her the news of his grandma's recovery, and to keep the door open between them. When Brenda picked up, Philly hesitated out of surprise.

"Philly?"

"Yeah. Hey, how are you?"

"I'm fine. Do you have something to tell me?"

So focused on his agenda, Philly first missed the implication of that question, then recalled that Brenda was awaiting news that Jesus had gone away. Philly surged past that realization. "Yeah. I wanted to tell you that Grandma is awake from her coma, and she went home from the hospital today."

Brenda said nothing. Philly could hear her breathing

vigorously as she walked.

"Jesus healed her, so she just woke up and has no symptoms from the stroke."

This seemed to only extend Brenda's silence. Finally she spoke breathlessly. "That's amazing. I'm happy for you." But her voice betrayed feelings other than simple happiness.

The bus approached, and Philly joined the line of people waiting to board. He could see that it was full. "Well, I just wanted to let you know. My bus is here, and I don't want to talk in the crowd inside there."

"Okay. Well, have a good night," Brenda's tone remained brassy.

"Yeah, you too. Good night." He reached for his bus pass and hung up. Glancing at Jesus, he thought, *"She's still waiting for you to go away."* He slipped his phone into his pants pocket.

Jesus nodded, speaking silently. "What if I never go away?"

Philly missed the second step and grazed his shin on it. He staggered forward, failing at his attempt to recover his balance and his dignity. The bright yellow steel railing saved him from physical injury, and he ran his pass through the card reader using his other hand, with his head barely as high as the bus driver's. He grinned self-consciously at the driver, stood up straight, and wedged his way into the packed passengers.

Jesus followed closely. "I've told you that the way you see and hear me is unusual, and you know that you won't always see me as you do now. But that doesn't mean that I'll ever leave you."

Philly nodded very slightly and thought in return, *"Yeah, I think that will be okay with Brenda. At least I hope that will be okay with her."*

"What if it's not?"

Philly paused to consider what sort of question Jesus was posing. He doubted that he would ask a mere hypothetical question, after rejecting Philly's own hypothetical explorations.

Jesus interrupted his calculations. "The reason I raise the

issue is so that you will give some thought to calling a phone number that Grandma has for you."

Philly connected the clues and remembered another time when Grandma gave him a phone number to call. She and one of her cronies from church had tried to match Philly up with that other woman's granddaughter. The girl, a full ten years younger than Philly, had stunned him with her childlike enthusiasm, leaving him feeling like one of those huge elephant seals parked on a beach with small birds flitting about him. Paula Bingham, the blind date, was one of those little birds—flighty, chirping, and too quick for Philly even to focus on. The theory that opposites attract suffered a monumental setback on their first date.

Returning to the present, Philly thought, *"Where could Grandma get a woman's phone number so soon after leaving the hospital?"*

"She didn't even have to leave the hospital."

Philly's inner libidinous teenager emerged momentarily. *"Wait, someone from the hospital?"*

"I just want you to consider the possibility."

Philly got nothing more out of his companion on that subject, but he called Grandma at home after finishing his frozen dinner. "How are you, Grandma?"

"Oh, I'm doing great, Philly. Ya know, Jesus told me who was calling, sorta like the caller ID you have on your phone." She laughed.

Philly laughed lightly. "Yeah, I think he does stuff like that just for fun." He surveyed Jesus where he stood in the doorway between the kitchen and the living room, holding Irving. "Irving really likes him, over here."

"Do you suppose that they just become one Jesus when you and I get together?"

Jesus nodded the answer.

"Mm-hmm."

"Oh, he says he does." Grandma apparently got the same

answer at her house. She chuckled. "He has to keep reminding me to do things. I just want to sit and talk to him all the time."

In that confession, and with the loving tone in her voice, Philly guessed that Grandma enjoyed the visit from Jesus even more than he had. But then, she'd loved him forever.

The Jesus in the doorway smiled like a groom watching his bride walk down the aisle. Philly assumed that Jesus's thoughts about Grandma inspired that look.

"Oh, Philly. Jesus just reminded me. That pretty nurse at the hospital, Theresa, wanted me to ask if you'd call her some time. She said she wanted to know more about the healing you did, if you don't mind talking about it."

Grandma's explanation of Theresa's interest veered from what Philly thought he had heard Jesus saying about a woman he should consider calling. He thought Jesus was talking about a potential girlfriend and not merely a religious seeker. On the other hand, Philly had certainly liked what he saw of the tall, shapely nurse. He stopped himself there and looked at Jesus. Philly answered Grandma. "Sure, I'd be glad to talk to her. She seemed like a nice person."

"Yes, she did seem nice—and very good looking too, didn't you think?"

Philly suspected Jesus of telling his thoughts to his grandma, but Jesus shook his head resolutely. "You don't have to be God to recognize a man who's attracted to a woman." Jesus lowered his eyes as he stroked the big cat.

"Yes, Grandma, she was very good looking."

"That's good, 'cause I think she's interested in more than just the story of my healing."

"Did Jesus tell you that?"

"No. I could just tell. A woman knows these things."

"Yeah, is that so?"

"Yes. Would you like to come over for dinner tomorrow night? Your dad took me to the grocery store on the way home, and I got a wonderful roasting chicken."

"Wow, that sounds great. But are you really up to cooking a big meal?"

"Up to it? I'm feeling wonderful—never better. I want to put some of this new energy to good use. I'm even going to ladies' Bible study tomorrow morning, to tell them all about my healing and Jesus being with me. That should be a hoot." Her laugh was very nearly a literal hoot.

Philly had no idea what she meant by that last comment. His idea of a ladies' Bible study was more of a snore than a hoot. But then he had no idea what such a meeting was really like. He had never been to a Bible study of any kind.

"You'll have to tell me all about it tomorrow night. What can I bring to dinner?"

"Oh, maybe some white wine would be nice. That is, unless I can get Jesus to make some out of water." Here she cackled uproariously.

Philly and Jesus laughed with her.

The next day back at work, passing through the lobby, Philly thought he received a strange, searching look from one of the designers and perhaps another from the receptionist. The latter said, "Good morning, Phil," for the first time he could remember.

In the elevator, alone with Jesus for the trip to the third floor, Philly asked without speaking. *"Is there something going on here that I should know about?"*

Jesus smiled into the blurry reflection on the elevator doors. "Allyson and Craig have been talking to a few of their friends and coworkers."

An expanding bubble of fear began to rise from his gut to his head as Philly stepped off the elevator and walked to his office. Safely planted in his chair, the next shoe dropped when Philly opened his email. He found the following note from one of the computer-aided design techs that sat near Allyson:

Phil,

I heard from Allyson what you did for her hand and shoulder pain.

Would it be asking too much for me to stop by and see if you can do something about my neck pain?

Thanks,
Ben

Philly noted that this third potential beneficiary of Jesus's healing touch at work was also African American, though the racial mix in the company skewed heavily toward European Americans. The voluntary segregation of relationships in the office explained the small trend, and the significance for Philly was more of a curiosity than anything weightier. He had few friends of any color in the office. Opening his life to Craig and his acquaintances made as much sense as anything.

The anxiety launched by that email arose from Philly's fear that Dennis would hear about his new ministry. He knew his boss wouldn't be sympathetic. That anxiety ballooned even more when he found two more healing requests from employees that had never spoken to him without a computer-related motivation.

Even as he hung precariously on the hook of his deepest fears, Philly read the next healing request in his email:

Dear Phillip,

I don't think we've ever talked much, and I hope you don't mind me contacting you about this now, but I heard from Craig, your assistant, that you have found a way to heal people of different kinds of health problems. I was diagnosed with breast cancer a few weeks ago. The doctor says it's pretty far along, and my biopsy showed that it's a very aggressive type of cancer. I'm not ashamed to admit that I really am scared. The prognosis doesn't look good for me. So, really I'm begging you to give me a few moments of your time. This is a matter of life and death. I

would really, really appreciate it if you would at least give it a try. I know there's no guarantee. I'm just looking for a chance.
Thanks so much,
Anna Beth Miller

Dangling just short of panic, Philly looked at Jesus. For the first time, the peace and confidence on Jesus's face aggravated him. *"How can you just sit there smiling? This is getting out of hand. This girl is dying and thinks I can help her. And everyone seems to know what we've been doing with the healing stuff."* Philly's anxiety dispersed toward the end of his minor mental tirade.

Jesus's tranquil eyes softened slightly to include a patient compassion as he listened to his scolding.

Philly grabbed his forehead with both hands and said aloud, "Oh, I'm sorry. This is really stressing me out."

"Why?"

Philly raised his eyebrows and looked at Jesus. *"I know you're not worried. But you gotta understand why I'm worried."*

Jesus smiled and answered telepathically. "When God asks you a question, it's not because we don't know the answer. Ask yourself, Philly, why are you stressed? Is your old life so precious that it's not worth risking any of it to save someone else's life?"

Philly just stared, trying to find a place of safety against the invading force scaling the walls, collapsing the gate, and overwhelming his defenses.

"I didn't just come into your life to keep you company while your grandma was in a coma. I came to capture you."

Planting both feet on the ground, Philly slowly rotated to face Jesus more squarely. He sat looking at those eyes, ingesting what he had just heard. Of course, he had known for some days now that this encounter with Jesus would impact him far beyond the duration of his visible and audible presence. But Philly hadn't ventured into assessing *how* it would impact him. Certainly, he had already seen several people around him palpably affected, and he would scarcely see his dad, his grandma, or even Craig again without a reminder of what he had seen Jesus do.

"*Capture me?*" Philly thought in response.

Jesus stood and stepped close to Philly. He leaned down slightly and took Philly's face in his hands. In that gesture and that loving attention, Jesus seemed older and more fatherly than Philly had noticed before. Indeed, he received that touch—and the winning, inescapable gaze—like a shot glass of pure love, ninety proof.

For the first time, Jesus's presence in Philly's office directly interfered with his work. Philly dove into those eyes and began to weep uncontrollably. Part of him wanted to lock his door, but he couldn't move. His will and desire had finally latched onto an object for which he had been longing all his life. Other, lesser, wants and fears bled away under the captivating draw of that kindly face and those powerful hands.

Later, when his face had finally dried and Philly could feel the responsibility of work asserting itself again, he woke his computer from its screen saver and discovered that he had lost twenty-five minutes. If the clock said it had been four hours, he would have believed it. He also would have accepted evidence that only a few minutes had passed.

The intoxication of that deeper link with Jesus faded enough to allow Philly to return to his duties but remained strong enough that he accepted all four of the healing requests now in his inbox. He invited each to his office during lunch, after only briefly considering how to fulfill their requests. He glanced at Jesus before hitting "send" each time and saw only affirmation there.

When the morning had nearly passed, via sundry tasks, the buzz from Jesus's touch had faded. Philly began to second-guess the wisdom of trying to heal all those people, especially at work. At least he had thought to schedule it during lunch, as some small protection of his job. He checked the weather online to see if he could take his little congregation outside. The internet told him what his windowless office couldn't—that it was in the upper fifties outside and partly cloudy. He decided that the walk to Washington Square Park wasn't too much to require of people desperately seeking healing.

Ben Rogers, then Anna Beth Miller, and finally Darcy Chalmers and Sandy Kowalski—accompanied by Allyson and Craig—gathered outside Philly's office. He told himself that it might look like a bunch of friends going out to lunch, as he had seen others do in the office. Anyone who knew Philly, however, would have had difficulty believing that explanation—although perhaps not more difficulty than believing the real reason for this odd coalition.

On the way out of the office, Craig eased Philly's self-consciousness by walking next to him—opposite from Jesus, who, of course, seemed nearly ecstatic at the reason for this convoy.

Philly's fears were confirmed when the website and social media administrator stood in the lobby staring at Philly and his entourage. Allen Breen would very likely mention this to Dennis. Philly briefly wondered if he had enough cash on him to offer Allen a sufficient bribe.

Craig just said hi to Allen and smiled, apparently amused at the dumbstruck gape of Allen's mouth.

Out in the partly sunny fresh air, Philly breathed easier, feeling he had escaped the gauntlet—at least for now. He was determined that they would not all return to the office together in the same conspicuous configuration. These thoughts, boosted by the spring weather, relaxed Philly as much as anyone could expect of him in company with so many imperfect strangers. Though he could identify each of the supplicants, his past relationship with all of them had constructed no facilities in which to hold the activity at hand. He was grateful for his positive experiences with Allyson and Craig. And he adjusted from resenting their addition to the size of this group to gratitude for their support. At this moment, Jesus seemed less like a supporting companion and more of a rogue force of nature. Washington Square Park began to loom in Philly's thinking as the place where miracles would certainly occur, as if the park had become magical. Yet he knew that the miracles actually accompanied him on his walk, as they turned on Chicago Avenue, off of LaSalle.

When he saw a sign about a Bible Institute of some kind, Philly wondered what the people there would think of this mission. He assumed they would be happy about it but wasn't sure about that. It was just one more reminder of how unprepared he was for this whole experience with Jesus.

Heading north on Clark Street, the caravan had stretched out to nearly a whole block, the seven fully visible people walking in groups of two or three. That these other folks had previous personal connections with each other added some organic comfort. The fact that Philly was the least connected of them all simply perpetuated life as usual, a little piece of familiarity in the heart of this peculiar event.

Tulips bloomed and daffodils swayed in the persistent breeze, beneath trees seriously contemplating unfurling leaves in the near future. Philly felt a fleeting regret that Brenda wasn't with him as he walked beside the low, wrought-iron fence into the park. He assessed the sparse population of walkers, runners, and strollers passing through, and located a vacant spot under a tree. He wished for leaves and their shade to conceal the weird little meeting, but pushed all regrets to the background, latching onto Jesus and what he had in mind.

With Jesus next to him, Philly faced the other six mortals, who formed a rough semicircle. Ben Rogers was a lanky young man with golden-brown skin and brown hair braided in cornrows. He stood half a head taller than the rest of the group. Allyson and Craig stood with Ben. Anna Beth Miller stood back a bit, a bump on the semicircle. Her artificially black hair hung down her pale young cheeks, her head slightly bowed—as if she were praying or struggling with some deep fear. Next to Anna Beth stood Darcy and Sandy, two administrative staff members, both in their late thirties or early forties, both slightly overweight like Philly, clearly leaning on each other for support.

Philly decided he wanted to heal Anna Beth first, yielding to a compulsion to relieve her of her understandable anxiety.

Jesus, on the other hand, motioned toward Ben. "We should start with him."

Philly had already stepped toward Anna Beth and didn't want to embarrass himself even more by backtracking as if uncertain about what he was doing.

Jesus reiterated his strategy. "This will work best if we start with Ben."

Philly, who assumed it was all the same really, allowed his nerves to overrule his invisible friend.

He motioned for Anna Beth to step into the circle. She obeyed hesitantly. She probably weighed less than a hundred pounds, and Philly loomed over her. He felt sorry for her, and that trumped everything else.

Jesus stayed off to Philly's right, within arm's length of Ben. But he kept his hands at his sides, apparently allowing Philly to lead on.

The others shifted and glanced at each other uncomfortably as Philly hesitated, looking off to his right again and again. Ben raised his hands slightly as if asking what Philly wanted him to do.

Philly tried to save himself by uttering a strange prayer. "Jesus," he glanced to his right, "please come here and touch this girl to heal her of her cancer."

Several things happened at once. Anna Beth cowered at the mention of her cancer. At the same time, Jesus walked over to where Philly stood. And the rest of the observers turned toward Anna Beth, who was probably the only person there shyer than

Philly.

"You're scaring her," Jesus said.

Philly froze. He looked at Anna Beth, saw her cringing, and then dropped his hand, which had been gently resting on her forehead.

"Tell Anna Beth to relax and that you will get back to her."

Philly followed Jesus's instructions and then stepped with him toward where Ben stood waiting.

Anna Beth's posture eased slightly, and she stepped back out of the circle.

Philly spoke to Ben. "You have neck pain?"

Ben nodded gingerly and put his right hand to his neck. "The doctors are afraid to do anything because of the way my discs are inflamed."

Jesus stepped right up to Ben and put his hand near his neck, ready for Philly to follow.

Philly reached up toward the left side of Ben's neck, opposite Jesus, and hesitated, wondering whether he should touch exactly where Jesus did.

But Jesus reassured him. "No, you're fine where you are. Just say, 'In the name of Jesus, be healed.'"

Philly repeated that line with his hand gently touching Ben's neck. For a moment nothing seemed to happen, and Philly noticed a young woman running past who slowed to check out the odd activity under the trees. He focused back on Ben, who suddenly startled.

"Hey. Hey, that feels good. It feels good. I mean, damn, the pain is gone! Oh, sorry."

Philly brushed aside the errant curse.

Jesus removed his hand, nodding at a job well done.

Philly thought, "*Who's next?*"

Jesus tipped his head toward Allyson.

Philly stared at Jesus to confirm where he thought he was looking.

"She has another issue. Ask her about her lower abdomen."

Philly walked gingerly up to Allyson. "Uh, do you have a problem in your lower abdomen?" He put his hand on his own belly.

Allyson's eyebrows shot up. She looked at Craig and then back at Philly. "Yes." She hung there for a second. "It's a woman thing."

Jesus said, "Have Anna Beth put her hand on Allyson's belly, and I'll heal it."

Philly looked at Anna Beth, who had faded back behind the others. "Would you be willing to put your hand on Allyson's belly?" He indicated the place again with his hand on his own stomach.

Anna Beth looked as surprised as Allyson had, but then she seemed to brighten at the invitation. "Okay." She checked with Allyson for permission.

Allyson nodded, perhaps relieved that she didn't need to say more about the nature of the problem, or that Philly wouldn't be touching her in a sensitive place.

Anna Beth stood beside Allyson and gently placed her right hand just above Allyson's belt line.

Allyson put her own hand a bit lower and to the right. "It's here."

Apparently assuming she should put her hand as close as possible to the problem, Anna Beth followed Allyson's direction. The strangeness of everything that had happened since she showed up at Philly's office door probably blurred the question of the appropriateness of where Anna Beth now rested her hand. But before anyone had time to focus on that question, Allyson said "Oh."

Philly could see that this exclamation corresponded exactly to when Jesus placed his hand on the sore spot. He also saw how Anna Beth's face lit up as she cooperated with Jesus's invisible touch.

Then Allyson began to bend in half, groaning slightly. Anna Beth tried to maintain her touch, but finally gave up as Allison's upper torso reached parallel to the ground. Just as Philly, and probably Anna Beth, stopped breathing, Allyson unleashed a hearty laugh.

Relieved laughter spread around the little group. Philly smiled at Jesus, who had also released his touch and stood watching Allyson.

Jesus directed Philly to move on. "Now you can ask Anna Beth if she's ready."

Philly nodded. When Allyson's laughter began to diminish, Philly spoke up. "Are you ready now, Anna Beth?"

She appeared about half ready to say "yes."

Jesus offered some help. "Tell her that we don't have to touch the area where the cancer is—just a hand on her shoulder will do."

Philly offered this proposal, and Anna Beth nodded.

Jesus responded to her acceptance by moving in close and placing his hand on her left shoulder.

Philly mirrored him on the opposite shoulder.

Anna Beth studied Philly briefly and then closed her eyes like someone savoring a new taste. After a moment, she opened her eyes and glanced down at her chest, as if checking something.

Philly kept looking at Jesus, determined not to screw this up. But Anna Beth's frequent visual checks of her breast strained Philly's determination. He got the impression that she was checking to see if someone were touching her where he never would have touched her. Philly lost his distracting concerns, however, when he saw the Savior's curved lips and smile-creased eyes.

Anna Beth started to weep. She didn't open her eyes but lifted her hands to clasp them in the center of her chest. Philly got the impression of someone wrapped in a loving embrace.

Philly could hear both Darcy and Sandy crying softly behind

him. He assumed that Anna Beth's emotional experience had arched over to them. But whispers and exclamations mixed in with those soft sniffles, as Darcy and Sandy pulled Allyson into what was happening to them. Philly wanted to turn to see what it was, but forced himself to remain as Jesus was, still devoted to Anna Beth.

Though the significance of the moment surely inflated the amount of time in Philly's experience, Jesus must have healed Anna Beth in two or three minutes. When he released his hold on her shoulder, Philly turned to find smiles on all the faces around Darcy and Sandy.

"I'm healed!" Darcy said, a bubbly bounce in her voice. She twisted her torso left and right. "I can do that without any pain at all. That would have hurt like mad a few minutes ago."

Sandy laughed and indicated the base of her throat. "I had a growth right in here. It pressed on my esophagus and made it hard to swallow. I was supposed to go in and get a biopsy to see whether it was cancer." She chirped a laugh. "But now it's gone!"

Philly looked over at Jesus for an explanation. Jesus smiled knowingly but said nothing.

Craig saw Philly's attention turn to that empty space near Anna Beth once more. "Do you see something there, Phil? Do you literally see Jesus?"

Philly nodded. "You believe me?"

"I guess I just knew. I guess it just explains the miracles."

Philly nodded more vigorously. "That's for sure. I know I can't heal anybody."

Allyson got Philly's attention and pointed over his shoulder. Philly turned with everyone else in the group and saw a short blonde woman holding a toddler. She looked like she would back off at the least resistance but ventured forward still.

"I'm sorry to interrupt you, but I was wondering ... I thought I heard someone say something about healing. Is that what you were doing?"

Philly glanced at Jesus again and then nodded to the woman.

She continued. "I'm sorry, I hope I'm not butting in, but I wonder if you could do something for my little boy here. His name is Kyle, and he has severe allergies. He's allergic to lots of foods and things in the air."

For Philly, the answer walked toward the mother and her son in the form of a Middle Eastern man from outer space.

He spoke to the mother. "It's no problem. Jesus is coming to heal him right now." And, while Philly stood where he was, Jesus reach up to Kyle and tapped him on the head.

"You are well, Kyle," Jesus said.

Philly smiled. "Jesus just touched him."

Kyle leaned his head away from his mother, took a deep breath, and shouted. "Yes! Mommy, I feel good! Mommy, Jesus healed me!"

Now everyone laughed or cried.

Chapter Twelve

To his amazement, Philly arrived back in his office less than an hour from when he left. He sat down at his desk, logged in to his computer, and thought, "*I got away with it.*" He checked with Jesus, not sure if he needed to repent from this thought. But Jesus seemed noncommittal on the point, his pacific smile undisturbed.

But at two thirty, Dennis called Philly and asked him to come to his office. Philly hung up the phone and looked at Jesus, a wave of numbness preventing him from screaming in panic.

Jesus pursed his lips and squinted at Philly, losing his usual carefree smile.

Philly's adrenal glands hit overdrive when this subtle sign from Jesus confirmed his fear. "Am I going to be fired?"

"Not yet."

"Not *yet*?"

"Let's go see Dennis." Jesus stood and motioned to the door.

Philly rose from his chair, considered sitting back down and properly logging off his computer, but lost his determination when he considered that he was usually the one to terminate employees from computer access. He wondered who would block his access. He locked the computer instead.

Jesus interrupted his panicked speculations. "Let's see Dennis first, before you worry about that sorta thing."

Philly nodded, feeling a slim influx of hope—enough to get him out the door and to the elevator.

As he waited for the elevator, a middle-aged Pakistani man from Allyson's department approached. "Hey, Phil, I wonder if I could talk to you about something in private when you get back to your office?"

Philly stared at him until the elevator arrived with a high

metallic "ting." They stepped onto the elevator together.

Jesus helped Philly out of his stall. "Tell him not this afternoon. Something has just come up."

Philly repeated this somewhat robotically, unable to slip free from the weight of impending doom.

"Okay, I understand." The man exited on the fourth floor. Philly said goodbye and stayed on for the ride to the fifth.

In executive territory, on the fifth floor, Philly had always carried himself like a large man in the porcelain-and-glass-knickknack aisle of a gift shop. This time was different. Now he felt like that same large man after having stumbled through a display of hand-blown glass figurines.

At Dennis's office, Philly knocked on the half-opened door. Dennis motioned him in and pointed to a guest chair as the COO's voice followed the low beep of the intercom on his phone. Dennis picked up the phone quickly as Philly stepped in, to prevent Philly from hearing what came next.

Careful not to look expectantly at Dennis, Philly closed the door behind him and glanced around the office, nonchalantly including Jesus in the course of his survey. He was glad Jesus was there, though he doubted he would provide any substantial help in this situation.

Dennis listened to his boss on the phone, made one low comment, listened some more and then said okay and goodbye. He hung up the phone and nodded to Philly.

Philly had sat in the chair on the left, leaving the one next to him for Jesus.

"We'll wait a minute. Mr. Hazelton will be joining us in a moment."

Philly nodded. Mr. Hazelton was Dennis's boss, the Chief Operations Officer of the firm. Philly's fear said, "I told you so."

Dennis shuffled through some papers, looked at his computer screen, and clicked something. Clearly Dennis had been instructed not to say anything until his boss arrived. "We'll just wait until he gets here." He glanced from his computer screen to Philly and then back.

After a few hundred more heart beats for Philly, Mr. Hazelton entered, closing the door behind him. Philly stood, Jesus moved, and Mr. Hazelton took Jesus's seat.

"Go ahead and have a seat, Phil."

When Philly sat down, he could feel Jesus standing behind him with his hands on his shoulders. He welcomed the palpable support.

"Do you know why we've called you here?" Dennis said.

Philly glanced at Mr. Hazelton. "I have an idea, but I'm not sure what you've heard, exactly."

"Well, let's start with that," Mr. Hazelton said. "Go ahead, Dennis."

"Frankly, I was shocked at what we heard, but at the same time I see it fitting in with some behaviors that have been concerning me lately." Dennis inhaled as if preparing for an operatic aria. "You've seemed distracted a lot lately, and I attributed that to your grandmother being in the hospital." He hesitated. "How is she, by the way?"

Philly cleared his throat. "Oh, she's doing fine. She went home from the hospital yesterday, fully recovered." He tried to keep his voice clear and steady.

Dennis furrowed his brow. "Oh, I'm glad to hear that. I guess she wasn't as ill as they thought?"

Though that sounded like a question, Philly doubted he was expected to answer.

Dennis continued. "Whatever the reason for your distraction, *and* some odd behavior, I was shocked to get half a dozen emails this afternoon about your activities over the lunch hour. Frankly, I don't even know how to describe this." He halted, looking at his computer monitor again. "Here, let me read what Ginny Abbot, up in Design, wrote me:

Dennis,

A couple of the people in my department are telling their friends and coworkers that they have been miraculously healed of some serious health conditions, and that it happened over lunch. The stories are really disrupting work up here, but I'm writing you because, according to them, your network administrator was the one that convinced them they had been healed—at some kind of gathering they had outside the office over lunch today. I don't know what to make of all this, and I'm having a hard time cutting off the conversations raging up here.

Just thought you should know,

Ginny

Dennis glanced at Mr. Hazelton and then settled his eyes on Philly. "One of the other emails said that you claimed you could talk to Jesus and could see and hear him." Dennis's face was pinched, his mouth puckered, and brows knit.

Silence followed. But Philly couldn't tell whether he was expected to answer, since this time Dennis's statement sounded nothing like a question. Philly glanced to his right, at Mr. Hazelton, and Jesus squeezed his shoulders.

"They're really confused about what to do with all this, Philly. You need to help them out." Jesus patted him.

He had said a lot of strange things to Philly, but this one was near the top of that list. *"Me, help them?"*

"Yes. Tell them the whole story about your grandma."

If he hadn't been desperately worried about losing his job, Philly never would have considered telling his boss, and his boss's boss, about his Jesus experience. But the pressure of their silence squirted the words out of him.

Again, he cleared his throat, really wishing he had some water. "I'd like to tell you what's been happening for me lately, with my grandma and all."

Mr. Hazelton seemed to relax more. "Okay, go ahead."

Dennis didn't look so relaxed, but Philly knew the shape of the firm's hierarchy. He forged ahead, beginning with Grandma's coma, including his first visit to her, then the strange appearance of Jesus, and, finally, Grandma's healing. When he finished describing his grandmother's full, miraculous recovery, he stopped and raised his eyebrows, inviting their response.

Dennis and his boss exchanged one look, and then Mr. Hazelton took over. "Okay, Phil. Let's just set aside religious notions that we may or may not share."

Philly could tell, of course, that they definitely did *not* share his view of his experience.

Mr. Hazelton continued. "Let's just look at this in terms of your work here for the firm and the impact of this sort of talk on the workplace. You see, we want everyone to feel comfortable at work, free to believe whatever they want, and free to practice their religion on their own time. You can understand that, I'm sure."

Philly nodded.

"Right. And we value your contribution to the firm. Dennis and I were just talking today about how smoothly things have been running lately under your management of the network."

The way he said this implied that they had just coincidentally been speaking about him in glowing terms. But Philly knew that any such conversation corresponded to their damage control efforts that afternoon. He thought this as he listened— self-consciously trying not to appear self-conscious.

"So, what we're after here is an agreement that we all want your work here to continue, for you to be free to practice your beliefs outside the office as you see fit, and for that practice not to interfere with your work."

Philly's spirits rose on a wave of relief. They had not called him there to fire him, just to get him to conform to their expectations for workplace behavior. His account of Grandma's coma and healing had established his religious faith, perhaps. But it had also wedged that faith between Philly and his two bosses.

Jesus squeezed Philly's shoulders again, and Philly relaxed a bit more.

"I understand what you're saying." Philly sat up straighter in his chair. "I'll be careful to do that, to make sure nothing from my personal life hinders my work."

Mr. Hazelton smiled and reached out his hand. As they shook hands he said, "I knew you would be agreeable. And now we just have to wait for the rumors to blow over. I figure by Monday they'll die down." He adjusted his eyes from Philly to Dennis, then back again. "Any chance you could take tomorrow off, just to take a low profile?"

Philly thought about it.

Jesus patted him gently on the right shoulder. "That should be no problem."

Repeating Jesus's phrase verbatim, Philly was still calculating vacation time and wondering what he would do with the day off.

"Great," Mr. Hazelton said. "I think that will help."

"Make sure you let Craig know," Dennis said.

Philly nodded in reply. They all stood up and completed the handshaking ritual, which declared peace between their tribes. Then Philly left the bosses together to debrief.

As he headed for the elevator with Jesus, Philly realized that letting Craig know about his spontaneous vacation would cover his work responsibilities and also send the message through the grapevine that Philly had not been fired. He decided to be frank with Craig and to ask him to help restrain the groundswell of healing petitions.

Philly wrapped up his work for the day with the Friday off in mind. That unplanned break felt something like finding a shiny penny on the ground—completely unexpected, untarnished, and attractive to the eye, yet he couldn't think of anything useful he could do with that new treasure.

Jesus interrupted this thinking. "You will find something very pleasant and important to do tomorrow. Your grandma has a phone number for you, remember?"

With the queue of people seeking healing and then the prospect of losing his job, on top of Grandma's rise from her coma, Philly forgave himself for forgetting about Theresa. But Jesus's reminder intrigued him now.

That evening, Philly arrived at Grandma's red brick ranch home on the northwest side of Chicago, carrying a bottle of white wine. He tried to leave outside his lingering fear that he might learn to know unemployment as a personal tragedy and not just a statistic on the news.

"Philly!" Grandma greeted him, taking his face in her hands and kissing her grandson.

Philly hugged Grandma gently and then noticed Jesus standing in the kitchen behind her. He turned to look for the Jesus that had been following him to the house and found no one there. Grandma's Jesus smiled and waved when Philly looked back at him. Of course it was the same Jesus. But Philly had to adjust, yet again, to the rules of the game.

"How ya feelin' Grandma?" Philly asked mostly out of habit.

Grandma took the cold bottle of wine from Philly. "Oh, I'm just great. I feel wonderful, and with hardly any sleep. I stayed up late talking to Jesus and totally lost track of the time. It's so marvelous to have him where I can see and hear him."

Philly nodded. He knew exactly what she meant. "So how was your ladies' prayer group? I bet they were surprised to see you." He removed his jacket and headed for the coat closet.

Grandma started to laugh as she put the wine in the fridge. "Oh, that was a doozy. What a meeting!" As she continued to chuckle, Jesus seemed to catch the infectious laugh.

Philly assessed the two of them. "What's so funny about a ladies' prayer meeting?"

"Oh well, you know that Jesus went to the meeting with me.

I mean, so that I could see and hear him real clearly. I know he's always been at our prayer meetings, but sometimes it's easier to believe that than other times. This morning was the best ever." She was still edging her words with chuckles.

"What happened?" Philly pulled up a stool at the kitchen breakfast counter and turned toward Grandma, who stood leaning back against the kitchen sink.

"Well, the girls were just floored when they saw me walk in, and they talked all at once and hugged me and all. It was just about to turn into a real party when I started to tell them about how I woke up from the coma." Here Grandma started cackling heartily. "And then ... oh, shoot ... and then they really were floored ... literally." She was wiping tears.

Philly shook his head, still missing the funny part. "What do you mean?"

Grandma wiped the back of a hand across one cheek and wound her laughter down. "Oh, well, when I told them about seeing and hearing Jesus, and getting healed when you and Jesus touched me, they all started praising him. Then he got all full of joy and started going around touching the ladies. I didn't do a thing, except watch him and praise him as he went around touching those ladies, and them falling down crying and laughing on the carpet. It was just wonderful to see." Her tears flowed more freely.

Something in that story caught Philly's attention. "Wait." He turned to Jesus. "I thought you could only touch someone through other people, not directly by yourself." He had been wondering about the unusual way little Kyle had been healed at the park.

Jesus nodded. "Generally that's how it works. But today, with all the ladies glad to be touched by me, and your grandma wanting me to do it, I had permission to touch them directly."

"Permission?" Philly had a hard time seeing that word as appropriate for the Son of God.

"Oh yes. I need your permission to do anything in your life. When it comes to your own life, you rule. You govern yourself, and you get to choose whether you receive anything I have to offer."

Explained that way, Philly could connect the notion of giving Jesus permission with his experiences. Then he turned back to the story of the prayer meeting. "So, what happened to the ladies?"

Grandma stepped back in. "Oh, they had the most wonderful encounters, and I don't know what all. I got some of their testimonies before we had to break it up, but not all of 'em." Her eyes ventured into their corners. "Maude Barr was healed of her bursitis right there on the floor. No more pain in her joints at all. And Gladys Raider was rolling around full of joy, completely done with years and years of depression and anxiety. She was a sight to see. And I could just tell that she was really changed. What a blessing!"

For Philly, this account by Grandma constituted the most extensive use of religious language he had ever heard from her. She had always seemed aware that Philly and his family didn't go to church. What little he had heard of the ways and means of her Pentecostal prayer meetings had been like stories from the other side of the world, carefully translated into his mother tongue. But Grandma's sensate experience of Jesus, and recognition of this same experience working in Philly, seemed to have loosened her restraint. Philly had been warmed by the power of Jesus's touch, so he could do some of his own translating now. Though he wasn't comfortable with any of it yet, Philly could run this holy rolling account through the grid of what he had witnessed in Father Tim's office, what he had felt flowing through him in Washington Square Park, as well as the time Jesus sat on the floor with him as he wept buckets after they first met.

"That sounds great." He suspected he sounded less than convinced.

Jesus and Grandma both laughed, confirming that impression.

"Oh, let's get that dinner on the table. You okay with eating here at the counter?"

"Sure, Grandma, this is fine." Philly swung his stool around ninety degrees and patted the white countertop. Then he noticed the small slip of paper with a name and phone number, printed in unfamiliar and artistic handwriting. The name was Theresa Bailey.

As Grandma pulled the roast chicken out of the oven, Philly held up the slip of paper. "Is this the phone number you were supposed to give me?"

Grandma glanced at Philly and then reached for a step stool. "Yes, that's Theresa, the nurse from the hospital. Such a lovely girl." She spoke while focusing on some dish on the top cupboard shelf.

Philly rose quickly from his stool and stepped up next to Grandma. "Why don't you let me get that for you?" He touched her shoulder before she scaled the little step stool.

Grandma looked at her grandson towering over her, his shoulder as high as her head. "Oh, of course. I was just doing what I always do when I'm here alone. But sure, you go ahead and reach that white bowl there for me, if you would."

Philly pulled the bowl down from its perch, seven feet from the floor. As he handed it to Grandma, he looked at Jesus. "You don't let her climb around lifting things off top shelves, do you?"

Jesus smiled. "Don't worry, Philly. I've been taking care of your grandma for longer than you've been alive. You also need to adjust your expectations a bit, to account for the healing we gave her. She's quite well, and she's always careful about climbing."

Feeling rebuked by Jesus, Philly nodded sheepishly. "She's my only grandma."

Grandma patted Philly on the shoulder and made appreciative cooing noises. "You two both take very good care of me."

That evening, Philly and Grandma enjoyed a savory hot meal together. It reminded Philly of how plastic his frozen dinners tasted.

The two of them slipped into their old patterns of conversation, Grandma asking about every part of Philly's life, and Philly checking for anything Grandma needed done around the house. Beyond Irving, Grandma was the only one Philly had ever taken care of in any significant way. Her interaction with his daily experience, along with opportunities to meet some of her needs, supplied his life with more meaning and purpose than simply working and paying bills and trying to find a steady girlfriend.

When they finished eating and began clearing away dishes, Grandma introduced a tenuous and solemn tone. "Philly, there's something Jesus and I want to talk to you about."

Philly drank the last ounce of wine from his glass and set it next to the sink. "Wow, Grandma, that sounds sort of scary. What is it?"

Grandma pursed her thin lips and looked sympathetically at Philly. "Let's sit down in the living room. Should I make us some coffee first?"

Philly nodded, not so anxious to hear the bad news, and glad for some of Grandma's home-brewed coffee. It brought back memories of the first time he was allowed to drink a cup of cream-and-sugar-fortified coffee, spoiled by his grandmother at eleven years old.

As Grandma prepared the coffee, Jesus led Philly into the living room. Grandma scooted into the room after them and set down a plate of store-bought cookies—Philly's favorite. He was glad to see that she hadn't baked him cookies on top of making supper.

Within a few minutes, Grandma was sitting in her favorite chair, next to the window, with a cup of coffee held in her lap and a tentative smile on her face.

Philly dove into the cookies, which he especially loved with coffee. Grandma remembered that sort of thing.

Jesus began the discussion. "Philly, we talked before about an end to this opportunity for you to see and hear me."

Taking a deep breath, Philly released his anxiety, relieved that this discussion wasn't about something new. He had understood that Jesus would leave him, and expected it to be soon, with Grandma's recovery. He hadn't yet captured his own feelings on that pending departure, torn between the attraction of life back to normal and the loss of his caring companion. But he knew it was coming.

Jesus continued. "I told your grandma today that I plan to change the way I'm with you at the end of this weekend. I wanted to let you know in advance, so you can make the most of the time remaining."

Philly looked at Grandma, a sort of sad satisfaction coloring her visage. Turning back to Jesus, Philly thought about how best to use their remaining time, but only spun toward unseen options and then back to his only hope for useful direction. "Well, I have tomorrow off, of course, so I'm really free to do whatever you want me to. Maybe I should follow *you* around, for a change."

Jesus beamed, and Grandma put a voice to his smile. "That's the best idea I've ever heard. But why do you have the day off tomorrow?"

Philly told her the story of his day at work, including flashbacks to the previous healings and his ongoing tensions with his boss.

"Oh my." Grandma set her coffee on a coaster that Philly had made at camp when he was thirteen, the wood-and-cork craft still sitting in a place of honor. "I guess you're feeling lucky they just asked you to take the one day off."

Philly nodded. He didn't want to worry Grandma about his circumstances, so he kept his anxiety about the future of his job silent. He looked at Jesus, who redirected the conversation.

"If you're serious about following my lead these next few

days, I would suggest that you give Theresa a call."

Philly stopped chewing. He swallowed after a searching pause. "Really? You want *that* to be part of what we do during your last three days here?"

With patience on his face, as usual, Jesus corrected Philly. "I'm not leaving you after three days, just going into stealth mode."

Smiling at the techie reference, Philly restated his inquiry. "You want me to get together with Theresa? Is this you setting me up with a woman?"

Grandma laughed.

Jesus smiled broadly. "Don't assume you know my agenda for your meeting with Theresa."

But Philly thought he detected an ironic tone to that correction.

Jesus chuckled. "I will never tell you directly to date or marry a particular woman. But, if you're asking me what to do, I say calling Theresa is a good idea. I would like to be visible to you when you get together with her."

That was all straightforward, yet still left room for mystery, which was okay with Philly.

Grandma interjected here. "So, my dear, I think you had better go and make a phone call."

Philly studied his darling old Grandma for a second. "Are you telling me to go home?"

Grandma grinned. "Just this once."

Seeing Jesus

Chapter Thirteen

Philly called Theresa as soon as he and Jesus reached his apartment. He worried that nearly nine o'clock on a Thursday night might be too late or that Theresa might be working. But Jesus had suggested he call her that evening, and Philly didn't expect Jesus to lead him into a dead end.

Theresa sounded guarded when she answered the phone—as if expecting a telemarketing spiel. She didn't recognize Philly's number, of course. "Hello, this is Theresa."

"Uh, Theresa, this is Phil Thompson." After a second of silence he added, "I met you in my grandma's hospital room the other day."

"Oh, Phil!" Theresa sounded relieved. "Your grandma kept calling you, 'Philly,' I think. That threw me off for a second. Oh, I'm so glad you called me."

The melody of her recognition injected hope into a place in Philly's heart that seemed to startle awake. Then, as fast as that note hit a crescendo, something inside him countered with disclaimers and lowering of expectations. Unfortunately, this all slowed Philly's reaction, and Theresa's enthusiasm met silence.

"Phil?"

"Uh, you can call me Philly, if you like."

"Okay." The slight elongation of that word implied uncertainty.

"Well, I was wondering if you'd like to get together sometime." Philly's words accelerated from a slow start.

"I would like that."

Jesus mouthed the word "tomorrow," and Philly stuck with his plan to follow Jesus's lead.

"What are you doing tomorrow? I have the day off."

"Oh, I do too. Hey, that's a nice coincidence."

"Yeah." Philly couldn't pretend to be as surprised as Theresa. He was still monitoring Jesus's face. "You wanna meet for lunch?"

"Sure, that would be fine."

"You want me to pick you up, or should we meet somewhere?"

"I live in Lincolnwood." Theresa seemed to leave him the initiative. Maybe she was compensating for being the one who started all this.

"Okay." Philly was familiar with that small suburb just north of the city. "Give me your address, and I'll come pick you up. What kind of food do you like?"

"Oh, just about anything." She told him her address.

Philly wrote down the address and then saw Jesus mouthing the word, "time." Maybe Theresa assumed that Philly was getting to that detail, but he and Jesus both knew that he had forgotten.

"So, is noon good for you?"

Jesus smiled at Philly's smooth recovery.

Theresa agreed to Philly picking her up at noon.

He planned to take her to an eclectic restaurant not far from her place where she could order from a variety of ethnic foods. A safe place for a first date. Philly was assuming that this *was* a first date. But he reserved the possibility that Jesus was doing more than teasing him when he cautioned about assuming the nature of the meeting.

After they said goodbye, and Philly took a deep breath, Jesus lowered his head sympathetically. "You don't have to carry all that baggage around with you, you know."

Philly scowled. "What baggage?"

"All of those years of expecting to be misunderstood and rejected, just because your ma and dad said they didn't understand you."

Philly didn't go to sleep that night until well past eleven, staying up to slog and slash through some emotional history, with an expert guide. Several times during the two-hour conversation, Philly felt as if major internal organs were swapping places inside him, or that burrowing animals were trying to emerge from his gut into the fresh air. Still, he didn't cry nearly as much as he had that first night with Jesus. Tears apparently weren't essential to the new reconstruction project inside him.

That night, Philly slept more soundly than he ever remembered. When he awoke in the morning, he recalled nothing after laying his head on his pillow and saying goodnight to Jesus. He slept until nearly nine—a record in his adult life. Philly rolled to a sitting position, looking over his shoulder at Jesus holding Irving in his lap. He wondered if Jesus had fed the cat to keep him from waking Philly up at the usual time. The lingering weight of sleep prevented him from pursuing that question, and he had more urgent business in the bathroom.

A free Friday might have looked a lot like a Saturday for Philly, but he had promised that this one would follow Jesus's agenda. Jesus suggested he take a shower and get dressed right away. Sensing that this promised some unusual activity, Philly complied and asked no questions.

All cleaned up, and fueled with coffee and toast, Philly looked at Jesus. "Well, what next?" His tone lacked the whiny protestation it would have carried two weeks ago. But Jesus could certainly tell that Philly wasn't necessarily looking forward to what lay ahead.

"I think you should go and knock on Mrs. Kelly's door downstairs and ask her if she needs help with anything."

Philly stared at Jesus. He couldn't remember the last time he had spoken to old Mrs. Kelly. He *knew* that he had never knocked on her door. And he had never randomly offered to help her with anything. But he did remember coming up the back stairs once, a couple years ago, and finding her struggling to get her groceries up to her second-floor porch. He had lent a hand without even bothering to offer that time. That memory included the relieved and grateful look on her face, which silenced some of the complaining parts of Philly's mind.

He led Jesus down the back stairs. Knocking at the front door would be too creepy, somehow. He knocked on the screen door.

Mrs. Kelly, an octogenarian with very poor hearing, stood by her kitchen counter and looked around, as if to detect the source of an alien noise.

Philly knocked louder, hoping she would recognize him right away and not be frightened by his strange encroachment into her quiet little world.

This time she looked at the back door and then startled—before relaxing into a relieved grin. She stepped laboriously across her linoleum tiles to the back door, fumbling with the lock and the doorknob simultaneously. "Yes?" She swung the door a few inches, banging it into the toe of her right foot. Fortunately, her sensible shoes took the blow. She showed no sign of even feeling that bump.

"Hi, Mrs. Kelly. It's Phillip from upstairs."

She nodded, clearly having no difficulty recognizing him.

"I have the day off, and it occurred to me to ask if you might need help with anything around your apartment?"

Mrs. Kelly nodded slowly, as if absorbing the offer, then she smiled more broadly. She stepped back and swung the door the rest of the way, motioning for Philly to come in. "God does answer prayer." She sounded like she was talking to herself.

Philly returned her grin and cocked his head in question. He could just see Jesus out of the corner of his left eye. At least some of his awkwardness was vanishing like water down the shower drain. He stepped into the kitchen, ignoring an acidic smell that seemed to linger in the air over the stove. The kitchen wasn't as clean as Philly's, and he was no great housekeeper.

"What can I do for you?"

Motioning with her right hand, Mrs. Kelly turned and led the way to a large box on the floor next to her refrigerator. The box bore the name of a food manufacturer on the bright blue label. "Soymilk" appeared on all three sides Philly could see.

"My grandson arranged for this to be delivered here, and I got the girl across the hall to carry it upstairs for me. But now I'm having a devil of a time trying to get the thing open."

Philly nodded. He spoke loudly. "I know what you mean. I often get packages at work that make me wonder how they expect us to open this stuff. I've even thought, 'what would an older person do if they had to open it?'"

"I guess they'd just have to pray for help to come."

He paused. "So, really? You prayed for some help to arrive, and I just showed up at your door?"

Mrs. Kelly nodded. "I can't say it works every time, but it seems like it sure did this time." She tilted her head up at Philly as if to see what he thought about that.

So he told her that he had decided to do a little experiment today, to do whatever he thought he heard Jesus telling him to do, and that the first order of business was to come downstairs and offer Mrs. Kelly some help. When he finished his account, he worried that he might have said too much. Mrs. Kelly's eyes had welled up, and she put her hands over her mouth, speechless.

Philly watched the compact old woman for a moment to make sure she was okay. "Where do you keep a sharp knife? Or scissors?"

In about a minute, Philly had cut through the excessive layers of packing tape, the heavily glued box, and the hard plastic wrap around the soy milk boxes themselves. The work was a strain to a man in his thirties. He didn't doubt that his neighbor needed his help. In a minute more, he had lifted each box to the cupboard Mrs. Kelly indicated.

With tears still brimming in her pale gray eyes, Mrs. Kelly thanked Philly, told him there was nothing else right now, and escorted him to the back door. They exchanged pleasantries and smiles, and Philly encouraged her to ask him for help any time. He left her his cell phone number.

On his way back upstairs, Philly stepped lightly, just like Jesus, who jostled him at the third-floor landing.

Philly looked at the Savior's jolly grin, feeling it mirrored on his own face. "That was cool. What a great start." Maybe this weekend with Jesus could be a fun adventure. He was ready for his next divinely directed good deed.

But Jesus surprised him again. "Just relax and clean up a bit here."

After pausing to adjust his aim, Philly guessed that relaxing and cleaning up "a bit," wasn't supposed to be an apartment overhaul. Instead, he put on some favorite music, straightened up a little, petted Irving, changed the towel in Irving's cat basket, and sat for a while talking about this and that with Jesus. He then trimmed his sideburns in preparation for his lunch date.

At eleven thirty Jesus said, "Okay, I want you to be early at Theresa's house."

Philly nodded, did some primping in front of the mirror, checked his breath, swished some mouthwash, and tied his shoes.

When Philly looked in the mirror one last time, Jesus imitated his hair adjustment. "Maybe she'll have a friend for me."

Surrendering his frustration at his need for a haircut, Philly laughed all the way down the back stairs, thinking about a double date with Jesus.

Though Philly had assumed that Theresa lived in an apartment like he did, the address she gave was a red brick ranch-style house something like Grandma's. That started him wondering about this woman of whom he knew so little.

Philly rang the doorbell a full ten minutes early. Should he apologize about being early? Maybe he could just blame Jesus.

Jesus replied telepathically. "It's not something you'll have to apologize for."

Theresa opened the front door, holding her phone in her hand. "Philly, come on in. I'm just finishing up a call with my mother."

They exchanged smiles, and she returned to her phone conversation, stepping away from the door and heading for her kitchen.

Philly stood by the door, next to a mirror-and-hat-rack combination. He saw Jesus standing next to him looking in the mirror as well. But his attention turned to the tone of Theresa's conversation with her mother. He caught the words, "Yes, he is a bit early ... No, I think that's a *good* thing, Ma."

Though he missed the exact words after that, he could hear Theresa disentangling herself from her mother in a way that sounded familiar. Theresa did it very deftly, from what he could hear, assuming her mother was as much like Philly's as it sounded.

After Theresa said goodbye, she returned to the living room and apologized. "Oh, I'm sorry. Come on in and have a seat. I'll pull together a couple of things and we can go."

Philly nodded, smiled, and perched himself on the edge of the couch. As he sat there, a tiger-striped cat rounded the corner of the couch, regarded Philly, and then meowed at Jesus. Philly had to repress laughter. He looked at Jesus, who clearly didn't intend to pick up Theresa's cat. Philly dared him to do it, in a swift, silent banter back and forth. Jesus laughed openly. He didn't have to hold back. Theresa couldn't hear him.

As they drove to the restaurant, Philly asked about Theresa's day off, which led to questions about her work. She explained that she had worked as a nurse for twelve years, ever since she completed her schooling at Loyola University in Chicago.

For the first half of that career, she had been married to a man who worked in the same hospital she did, a man who also found a new love of his life in that hospital. Divorced five years ago, she had made only tentative steps into dating, including joining a church in the near suburbs. Though she hadn't dated much there, she did meet Jesus in a way that recalled early childhood experiences at a friend's Sunday school when she was ten years old.

This part of her story led back to the event that brought them together. The story of Philly healing his grandmother had captivated Theresa for several reasons. Like most people, she had no personal exposure to miraculous healings. Further, she had long wondered why she'd heard so little about the healing work that Jesus did in the Bible. But mostly she pondered the pain and suffering of people she met through her work, regretting her own powerlessness to relieve them and baffled that God didn't use his power to do so.

When Theresa asked Philly whether he had seen other healings besides his grandma's, he told her about some of his experiences, lingering especially on the group in Washington Square Park. Philly didn't know whether he intended his expansive account to impress Theresa, or whether he merely needed to revisit that event for himself. He did, however, leave out the repercussions at work caused by the lunchtime healings. He was trying to stay positive for this first meeting.

After ordering nearly identical meals, down to the iced tea to drink, Philly and Theresa settled into an awkward silence, waiting for their food. For the first time, they faced each other for more than a passing second. One good look at Theresa's slender, smiling face flipped something inside Philly, like a flash of joy popping out from under a dull stone. Instinctively he pulled back, remembering Brenda in that moment, mostly because she was the last person that had inspired such romance.

Theresa seemed to notice the change on Philly's face and to guess the source of that hesitation. "Do you mind me asking if you have a girlfriend?"

Philly smiled shyly for a half a breath and then snorted. "I don't really know." He shrugged an apology. "I was starting to get back with a woman that I used to date, when she learned about what was happening to me ... " Here Philly stalled. He had driven right into a corner. Disarmed by the look in Theresa's bright green eyes, he had forgotten to protect his big secret.

This was typical. He often got carried away by the charm of the moment, his brain trailing along behind his mouth. In these situations, he often simply sputtered out every bit of truth at hand, whether advantageous or not. He sighed softly and looked at Jesus.

Jesus nodded for Philly to go ahead and tell her.

Theresa looked curiously at Philly and even glanced in the direction of Jesus.

Philly stepped it up. "You see, there's something I haven't told you about the healing stuff that's been happening." Then he unpacked the whole story of Jesus appearing to him. When he rounded the corner to the story of Brenda and the things Jesus told her, Theresa sat entranced.

"Can you see him now?" She leaned forward and kept her volume low.

Philly and Theresa both glanced toward the chair to his right—where Jesus sat smiling. Philly nodded. "And I know what he would want me to tell you."

Theresa sat literally breathless.

"He really loves you a lot."

Theresa shivered visibly. Where this exchange would have gone next had to remain a mystery, as the server brought their drinks to the table.

Philly thanked the server, and Theresa managed a faint echo of that thanks.

She looked toward Jesus again. "He *is* here." She said it with a kind of awestruck certainty.

Philly smiled and looked from Theresa to Jesus. Right from the start, this experience was different than with Brenda. Theresa's breathless fascination warmed Philly.

This returned them to the scene in Grandma's hospital room where Theresa had first noticed both Philly and Grandma looking to the side of her bed where Jesus stood. By the time they had finished weaving together their two individual experiences of that event, their chicken sandwiches arrived.

Theresa didn't seem to notice her sandwich. Philly was hungry and wanted to attack the aromatic food sitting fifteen inches from his chin. But he held back to allow Theresa some space.

"Go ahead and eat." Jesus spoke to Philly and motioned to Theresa.

Philly passed the message on. "Jesus says to go ahead and eat."

Theresa started to giggle, a hiccupy laughter. "Tell him thanks for the food."

Philly laughed now. "He can hear you, ya know." He stifled his laughter when he noticed people at the next table taking an interest in their strange behavior.

Theresa covered her mouth with one hand, glanced around at their fellow diners, and tamped down her mirth.

Philly lifted half of his sandwich and took a bite. Theresa followed his example, though more delicately. Her restraint reminded Philly to be careful. He checked his chin for drips with the cloth napkin from his lap.

After chewing and swallowing, Theresa picked up a loose end of Philly's story. "So, your former girlfriend said not to call her again until Jesus left? Did she mean until you couldn't see him anymore?"

Philly sat holding his sandwich in two hands. Frozen. Theresa's intuitive understanding of his Jesus experience shocked him. Maybe that was the difference between Philly's lack of church and Theresa's Bible-study-trained mind.

He set down his sandwich and took a quick sip of tea. "I'm pretty sure she meant not to call until he's no longer visible to me. I don't think she has any idea that Jesus will stay with me even when he's not visible. I know I didn't understand that at first." Philly kept his voice down, aware of how bizarre the conversation was.

Theresa had already turned her voice down, but mostly it seemed a reflection of reverence and awe. "Have you been a church-going person most of your life?"

Philly shook his head as he chewed his food. "No, I didn't meet Jesus in church—I met him on a CTA bus." He grinned and took another bite.

Again, Theresa laughed. "I guess that's sort of what I thought. You don't talk like a church person, which is funny 'cause you seem to be having a more real experience of Jesus than the people I go to church with."

This raised the issue for the first time, in Philly's mind, that maybe he should be thinking about going to church. With a swallow and another drink of iced tea, he responded more to his thoughts than Theresa's observation. He glanced at Jesus. "I should think about going to church, shouldn't I?"

Jesus smiled and nodded. He raised his eyebrows and looked at Theresa, redirecting Philly's attention.

Philly grinned at the angelic look on Theresa's face. An attractive woman by most people's standards—by Philly's standards for sure—Theresa glowed as she watched him casually interacting with Jesus. And she not only seemed to understand and believe, but she even admired his experience. He caught himself staring at Theresa, his sandwich neglected.

Theresa looked up from her plate and returned Philly's gaze for a moment, shrinking from his obvious admiration. "What are you looking at?"

Philly woke from his trance. "Just looking at you and liking what I see."

In the history of Philly's interactions with women from high school to the present, he had never said so smoothly exactly what he wanted to say until that moment and that one short sentence.

Theresa breathed a self-conscious laugh. "Are you always such a smooth talker?"

Philly shook his head. "Never."

After a brief check-in from their server, Theresa changed the mood. Maybe all that warmth jogged a need for confession.

"I told you I was married once. We divorced five years ago because he cheated on me."

She had included this fact already in the brief history she gave him in the car. Restating the point now seemed to offer Philly the chance to enter or turn away.

"Are you over it?" Philly picked up the last bit of sandwich and delicately bit off half.

Theresa sipped her tea and seemed to check her emotional inventory. "I'm *getting* over it." She nodded pensively. "I suppose asking your grandma to give you my phone number is a good sign that I really am getting over it." She smiled again, this time not so shyly.

When they finished eating, finding more casual conversation topics, they rose from the table. Philly left cash to cover the food and tip. Theresa appeared to note the large tip. But Philly didn't do it to impress her. He always tipped well, to be sure he pleased at least one person on a given day.

Outside, the sun had withdrawn under the approach of rain clouds carried by a rising wind. Philly, Jesus, and Theresa walked to Philly's car. On the way, Philly sent a silent question to Jesus. "Should I tell her about my plan to follow you today and your idea for me to meet with her?"

"There's no reason not to."

Philly knew of one reason, but apparently it didn't worry Jesus that such a revelation might intensify their relationship at such an early stage. In the car, out of the wind, Philly took shelter in Jesus's permission.

"Jesus said it's okay for me to tell you something about our meeting today."

Theresa perked up at that prelude, watching Philly carefully as he explained the news that Jesus would go invisible after this weekend, and his determination to follow Jesus's lead for these remaining days. She raised her eyebrows and then nearly cried when he told her that meeting with her was part of Jesus's plan for the day.

Then she did something no one else had tried. She turned to the back seat, apparently assuming Jesus was sitting there. And she addressed him directly. "Why did you want us to meet today?"

Jesus replied directly and Philly translated. "Because I wanted to be visible to Philly when you two met."

"Why?"

"Because, when you asked me to help you get over your former husband's betrayal, you asked me to bring you someone that you could trust, someone who has a faith that you could grow with."

Philly had done dozens of difficult things on Jesus's behalf over the past several days. Repeating this answer word-for-word was another.

But Theresa didn't seem to notice that Philly's translation basically recommended himself to her. She was too busy bursting into tears.

The outburst unsettled Philly but didn't panic him. A glance at Jesus, along with Theresa's body language, told him that the words he had relayed landed deep in her heart, and that her tears sprang from Jesus tapping something she recognized. He assumed that the tears weren't really about him.

Looking back at Jesus for direction, Philly caught a nod and heard him speak over the tears and sobs. "Go ahead and put a hand on her shoulder. Even in receiving good news she can use a comforting hand."

Philly gently rested his right hand on Theresa's near

shoulder.

Jesus leaned forward, placing his hand on Philly's elbow, which now pointed toward the middle of Jesus's chest. No electricity jolted or buzzed through that touch. But Philly did feel a warm flow from Jesus, through him, to Theresa.

Theresa looked at Philly and smiled through her tears and running makeup. "This is a lot for a first date." She blurted the words, half-laughing now.

Philly laughed too.

Jesus was smiling. "I didn't have much time—and a lot to cover."

Philly repeated this for Theresa.

She reached up and held Philly's hand on her shoulder. "Mission accomplished, I'd say."

"Yep," Jesus said.

And Philly laughed again.

Chapter Fourteen

After they walked and talked in a park along the canal that marked the border between two suburbs, Philly dropped Theresa off at her house later that afternoon—under Jesus's advice. The sudden depth of their connection left Philly floundering about what to do next. Jesus advised some time apart to allow it all to soak in. The brand-new couple parted with a hug and brief kisses on the cheek, after a stuttering on-and-off effort by both of them. Having avoided banging heads and obtaining the desired contact, the first date ended.

Jesus had offered to stay in the car, but Philly insisted he accompany them to the porch, though he had no particular reason in mind. These eight days with Jesus had bonded Philly to his constant companion, the man who would be the perfect foil for any personality. With Jesus at his side, Philly was beginning to feel as if he could do anything.

As the pioneering drops of a substantial rainstorm began to spatter the two men, Philly said, "So what do we do now? Conquer a castle? Slay a dragon?" He laughed as he unlocked the passenger door for Jesus. Grinning about his date with Theresa and the prospect of two more days with Jesus, Philly watched Jesus open the car door.

Not until Jesus had closed the passenger door did Philly reach the driver's side of the car and glance back at Theresa's house. There he just glimpsed her dim image in the picture window, still watching him. He thought he saw her eyes staring wide, like a nocturnal animal. He was pretty sure she had seen Jesus open and close the door with his invisible hands.

"Why did you do that?" Philly slipped into the driver's seat, still in good spirits.

Jesus answered Philly with a wink and then a glance back at

Theresa's window. "She'll be okay, my friend. And the more she trusts you, the better."

As he started the car, Philly sobered at the thought of someone truly trusting him. He briefly diverted a mental stream toward Brenda and her trust issues, then returned to the present. He nodded and looked at Theresa's house one last time before checking for traffic and pulling away from the curb.

"To answer your first question," Jesus said, "let's go back to your place for a while. We can deal with the dragon later tonight."

Laughing at the joke for just a second, Philly lost his humorous momentum with the thought that Jesus might be serious about the dragon—in some metaphorical sense, he assumed.

Jesus just smiled.

As they drove, Jesus started to talk to Philly about his days playing chess in school and in youth tournaments. Philly's passenger asked the questions as one who had been there and who simply wanted to revisit the memory with him. The driver tripped into the topic, kicking a toe against a dark object in his mind and then regaining his balance with some effort. Jesus reminisced like a proud coach, even remembering the names of the other players in the key tournaments. That detail ignited an old set of feelings for Philly—sympathy for his opponents, the numerous defeated challengers.

When he had parked his car and closed the gate, Philly followed Jesus up the sidewalk through the slackening rain.

Glancing casually over his shoulder, Jesus said, "Let's play some chess."

Philly asked Jesus to repeat that, though he had heard it clearly enough.

"Come on, you afraid I can beat you?" Jesus said it like a posturing teenager.

"Afraid? I'm absolutely sure you can beat me, all things considered." He paused to note that he had spoken aloud, reminding himself not to do that. Then he stumbled down that memory corridor that Jesus had swept him into. How long had it been since he played chess?

In the apartment, Irving greeted his two favorite people with unending purrs and incessant rubbing against their legs. Philly slipped his jacket off and hung it on the back of a kitchen chair to dry.

Jesus, magically dry, picked Irving up without hesitation. "It's in the back of your bedroom closet at the top—in that green shoe box." Jesus spoke of Philly's favorite chess set.

Though he still had half a dozen sets, only one was his favorite, and he only thought of using that one to play anybody—if he could be persuaded to play anybody. Philly's dad had bought him this blond-and-brown wooden set with a matching wooden case that folded out to double as the board. It just fit into a large shoe box when folded shut. The smooth wooden pieces nestled inside, cushioned in green velvet. On that birthday, his tenth, Philly felt as if his father understood him, even sympathized. After all, his mother generally purchased the birthday and Christmas gifts. That his dad had made the effort and had so deftly succeeded in getting him a perfect gift, stuck with Philly. That rich experience had, however, faded under that other memory—the one of his parents both confessing that their son was an alien to them. That one happened only two months after receiving the perfect gift.

"The rook still your favorite piece?"

Philly made a dull affirming noise.

"I like the king the best."

Philly came out of the bedroom with the big shoe box and frowned at Jesus. "The king? Are you kidding?"

"Would I kid you?"

Philly knew he would.

"I'll tell you what—I will only capture your pieces with the king. You play by the normal rules, and I'll only capture with the king."

Though he had not played in decades, Philly's brain shifted

into chess mode like a key in a lock. The mental click started him mapping ways to capture pieces with the king and ways to take advantage of Jesus's offered limitation. The trick would be fascinating to see. Any success at such a crippled strategy would have to be a trick.

"You're not gonna mess with my mind or anything to keep me from winning, are you?"

"You mean like a Vulcan mind meld, or a Jedi trick?"

Philly smirked. "Just trying to figure out my opponent."

Sitting at the small kitchen table, the afternoon sun occasionally angling onto the yellow wall behind Jesus, they sat across the chess board from each other. Even as they did, Philly approached the situation on several levels. Most obviously, he touched chess pieces for the first time since his preadolescence, using a chess board that he had saved for twenty-eight years.

As a chess challenge, he contemplated the modified rules of the game proposed by Jesus and tracked down the most elegant way to win. More deeply, he knew that Jesus had proposed this match to fix something in his soul related to the loss of his passion for the game. And he even spun through questions and scenarios regarding a contest between himself and the reigning God of the universe. This multi-storied thinking revived a joy that had hatched and died before Philly had fully expressed it. That joy showed signs of restoration in the fifteen-minute chess match that followed.

The revival of his childhood chess experience couldn't have happened before the visit from Jesus. Philly had consciously refused to engage that part of his brain with that part of his past. Now he had spilled out of his boxed-and-sealed life into an infinite existence that he glimpsed through the words and touches of Jesus.

Loose in the fields of that childhood experience, Philly began to find feelings long forgotten. The severe handicap that Jesus imposed on himself, for example, recalled Philly's social challenge of facing someone he knew he could easily beat. He had only to decide *how* to win. As they played, however, Philly could recognize the brilliance of his supernatural opponent. The king-only capture rule would have disarmed a world-class supercomputer against Philly. But winning wasn't enough. Philly wanted to win elegantly. He needed to win beautifully.

Rather than exploit the obvious opportunity to simply capture Jesus's pieces with impunity, since his king was unable to protect most of the board, Philly worked more directly to attack his opponent's strength. He focused on that small realm where the chess king can protect the pieces directly surrounding it. Philly moved carefully, and he knew that Jesus took more time on his moves than he needed. That lengthened the game beyond the time required for the inevitable slaughter that would result from Jesus's self-restriction.

Even in the midst of the strategic and tactical flow, Philly looked at Jesus and loved him for what he was doing. Though Philly had never received psychotherapy and hadn't even studied introductory psychology in school, he recognized a healing process. The tactile memory of that chess set, the thought process that awoke over the sixty-four squares and thirty-two pieces, knocked years of crust from one of his deepest cuts. His hands began to shake as he approached checkmate. Fragments of his mind willed him on. Stored grief seemed to resist more powerfully than his opponent could.

Jesus watched Philly more than the board. And the expression on his face, which Philly glimpsed on and off, grew more and more compassionate.

Finally, as Philly placed his last piece in position to end the match, his breath lurched in gasps. Gasps compounded to sobs when he met the eyes of his opponent and witnessed the trail of twin tears down the sides of Jesus's face and into his beard. The perfection of his opponent, as both a chess master and a friend, launched Philly's grieving soul into open catharsis. He rocked forward in his chair, grabbing his face and sagging toward the floor.

Jesus caught him before he hit the linoleum and laid Philly gently on his side.

Curled in a fetal position, Philly released mournful groans and breathless sobs such as he had experienced only once before, and that less than two weeks ago.

How innocent for one friend to challenge another to a game of chess. Yet Philly's life seemed to totter over the fulcrum of that game. His ability to extend himself beyond just protecting himself, into an adventure that touched the outside world with beauty and grace, had died when he shoved his chess sets into boxes and vowed never to play again. He lost some of his ability to triumph over challenges. He lost the joy of the gifts evident on the chess board. He had surrendered to the expressionless anonymity of the mundane. He sank with an anchor hooked to him by his parents, the shame of their lives drowning their only son.

Jesus sat cross-legged on the kitchen floor next to Philly as the last light of day faded amber and red after the emigrating storm. He placed one hand on Philly's shoulder and with the other stroked his hair like a mother consoling her child late on a nightmare-disrupted night. Without spoken words, the Savior communicated liberation and inspiration to Philly's raw heart.

Philly welcomed the breaking. He tasted a hint of what freedom would mean for his life from that day forward. This renewal took just hours to begin but would certainly take the rest of his life to comprehend.

When he could press himself up to a sitting position, Philly met Irving's eyes first. The cat sat statuesque, coolly observing his master's resurrection. Irving acted as though he had seen resurrection a hundred times, yet he apparently still felt compelled to watch. Philly laughed at the cat's aloof interest and then hugged Jesus for a full minute, still there on the floor.

After several minutes of clean up—of the kitchen floor and

Seeing Jesus

his own face—Philly stood in his entryway looking at Jesus, feeling a surprising physical hunger.

"I think we should go out and get a good meal," Jesus said.

Philly tipped his head at the use of "we" in that sentence. But he had no objection to the proposal. Immediately he thought of a small restaurant two blocks away.

But Jesus had other plans. "How about that little steak place on Fullerton that you like so much?"

No longer a rookie at listening to Jesus, Philly could tell that this suggestion represented more than a dining option. He could tell that, for him, following Jesus would mean going to *that* restaurant right then.

"How do you know I don't just like the food there?" Jesus responded to Philly's thoughts again.

Philly squinted at his visitor.

Jesus smiled in return. "I might one day direct you to a restaurant just because I think you'll like it." And the sincerity on his face convinced Philly that this too was true.

The restaurant to which Jesus referred huddled in the commercial section of Fullerton Avenue, not far from Wrigley Field. It ran the full depth of a building, but was only about twelve feet wide, except where the kitchen sat beside the back section of tables. Brenda had heard of the place from a cousin of hers, and Philly loved the food and the atmosphere. He had seen other people from work there on occasion and assumed Brenda had been spreading the word.

One detail Philly had dropped from consideration, as he and Jesus drove to this dining establishment, was that it was Friday night. One generally needed a reservation to eat at that popular little place.

Against all reason, Philly approached the hostess with Jesus just behind him. "I don't suppose you have a table for one available."

The dark-haired girl, whose eyes looked black in the low

light, regarded Philly like he was an ignorant tourist, but only for a moment. She diverted her eyes to the reservation book and just shook her head.

Philly glanced at Jesus but gained no insight there. Jesus seemed to be waiting for something to happen.

Philly thanked the hostess and turned to walk out, but he stopped abruptly. There stood Allen Breen, with his hands in his pockets and a droopy look on his face. On second impression, Philly could tell that Allen had been drinking already.

Allen recognized Philly and spoke first. "Hey, Phil! What are you doing here, man? That's a hell of a coincidence, I'd say. I was just thinkin' about you, wondering if the guys upstairs had fired you for real."

The topic of his employment prospects had dropped down Philly's list of pressing concerns during the day, but that fearful feeling in his gut rose from its slumber with Allen's words. "No. They just gave me a warning and told me to take the day off."

To Philly's surprise, Allen looked relieved. Allen had seen Philly and friends heading out for their lunchtime healing service and had probably mentioned it to Dennis. But he apparently had no intention of getting Philly into trouble.

"So, you'll never guess what happened to me." Allen punched Philly gently in the shoulder and shook his head slowly. "I got stood up tonight. Was supposed to meet that girl from accounting—you know, the redhead, Wanda—whatever her name is. Waited for her at the bar next door and she was a no-show. Not even a blow off text message. Left me hangin' in the wind."

"Bummer." Philly made an attempt at sympathy.

"I gotta eat anyway though." He cast about as if checking if Philly was alone. "Why don't you join me, huh? I hate to eat in a restaurant alone, ya' know."

Once again, Philly's brain weighed the extent of Jesus's intervention in these circumstances. Had he locked Wanda in a closet somewhere, to leave Allen alone and vulnerable?

In response to that thought, Jesus laughed out loud.

But Philly seized Allen's offer, such as it was. "Sure, I was hopin' to get in here without a reservation. But you know how impossible that is on a Friday. Lead the way."

"Right-o. Here I am to rescue you from another hot date with a Big Mac and fries, right?"

The hostess, who had certainly missed the exchange, looked suspiciously at Philly as if trying to figure out how he got invited onto Allen's table reservation. Philly just flashed a fake smile and followed Allen and a waitress to the table.

Jesus distracted Philly's attention along the way by touching each person that Philly brushed past through the length of that narrow restaurant. Philly even accommodated his obsessive friend by intentionally brushing against a few extra people without being too obvious about it.

The waitress chirped a surprised little sound when Jesus touched her shoulder simultaneous with Philly squeezing past her.

Allen laughed, probably assuming Philly had groped the girl.

For her part, the waitress turned to look at the corner of the room with a thoughtful air. Philly could only guess what Jesus had started in her.

The visible men both sat down and ordered drinks, Philly sticking with iced tea instead of beer or wine.

He lifted the menus and passed one to Allen.

Allen Breen still looked a bit of a boy, though he was nearly as old as Philly. His golden hair and even lighter eyelashes reminded Philly of the kid that played Tom Sawyer in an old movie made before he was born. Allen spoke with the remnant of a Boston accent, acquired during his boyhood in suburban Massachusetts. Philly had talked baseball with Allen before, there being no rivalry at all between the Cubs and the Red Sox. Allen liked to win the favor of Cubs fans by telling them that it was their turn to break the curse and win a World Series, now that his Red Sox had broken free.

Allen looked hard at Philly now. "There's something going on with you. I heard weird rumors at work. But I can tell by lookin' at you that there's somethin' ... different."

Philly nodded. He checked briefly with Jesus, who stood behind Allen, against the dark umber wall. Philly had never liked Allen. Allen reminded him of bullies in school, never showing any sympathy for other people. Drunk, Allen seemed less guarded and slower to take a poke.

"I've really had a kind of spiritual conversion, I guess you'd say." Though he wouldn't tell him the whole story, as he did Theresa, Philly knew he was here to talk to Allen. "My grandma's coma was the thing that started me thinking, and it was her prayers that really turned me around. I didn't used to think about God at all and didn't really know much about Jesus. But my grandma has always been the best person in my life, and she prays and stuff, so I decided to give it a try. And I guess I got a super-sized dose of whatever it was that kept my grandma going to church, 'cause some pretty unbelievable things started happening to me."

Allen stared at Philly as he spoke, broken from his bleary concentration only by the waitress arriving with his scotch on the rocks. He let his drink sit for the moment.

In a slightly hushed tone Allen said, "So, is it true that you healed a bunch of people, like a TV preacher?"

Philly drank some tea, his mouth extremely dry. "I don't know anything about TV preachers, but I know my grandma got out of her coma, and my dad is no longer using his hearing aids."

Allen's blond eyebrows shot up. "Wait, you did some kind of healing thing on your family, not just at work?"

"Ha. Yeah. I had no intention of doing that stuff at work. People just started asking, after I helped Craig and one of his friends. I mean, it was definitely God that helped them, 'cause, of course, I can't heal anybody."

A sort of grimace twisted Allen's slackened face. He ran his fingers through his hair and rubbed his eyes. "Hey, I'm not feeling so good all o' sudden."

Jesus leaned toward Philly. "He's got something interfering with him, sort of like that man on the bus last week with bees buzzing around his head. You need to tell that thing to stop messing with him right now. Just say, 'spirit of confusion, leave Allen alone.'"

Philly nodded, glanced around to see if anyone else could hear. He tipped forward and spoke quietly but firmly toward Allen, repeating Jesus's phrase.

Allen sat up and belched. He covered his mouth. "Oh. Sorry, man. Something really weird just happened to me. One minute you were, like, talking from the other end of a long tunnel, and then boom, you're back. Did you do something?"

Looking up at Jesus for more instructions, Philly saw him nod. "I just told some interference to cut it out. There's a kind of spiritual fight going on around you right now, I think."

Jesus proudly nodded his approval of that summary.

Allen, on the other hand, returned to staring at Philly as if he were watching the first baby dinosaur hatch from a hundred-million-year-old egg. Again, he found a break from his contemplations when the waitress arrived to take their orders. Fortunately, they both ate there frequently and knew what they wanted, despite taking little time to look at the menu that night. When the waitress walked away, Allen stared at her backside and leered.

"Nice ass," he said, too loud. A woman at a nearby table glared at him. Allen just smirked in return.

Again, Philly looked for help from Jesus.

"Just get him to talk about himself for a while, so you two can get something to eat before you do any more."

Do any more? Philly hit his iced tea again before speaking aloud. "So, Allen, is your family still living near Boston?"

Allen started a looping explanation of the migration of much of his family to Florida or Texas, and his sister's job in Toronto, and his own ideas about his future. Then he said, "Yeah, I don't really miss living there, ya' know. But, with my folks down in Boca Raton, I miss visiting the old neighborhood."

"Did you go to public school?"

Allen took a swig of his whisky and looked down the length of the restaurant, as if his childhood lay at the other end. "Nah. My ma and her family were Catholic, and they made me go to Catholic school. I hated it. It was supposed to get me all converted and into the Church. But it did just the opposite. I never wanna set foot in a church as long as I live."

Philly thought he noticed a lack of feeling in Allen's rejection of his mother's faith. "What was so bad about it?"

Their salads arrived, just in time for Allen to recount the horrors of Catholic school with ranch dressing in the corners of his mouth and gales of crunching obstructing some of his words.

More than the annoyance of hearing Allen talk with his mouth full, Philly kept feeling that Allen was leaving something out, such as the sort of event that would cause the toxic disdain he was emitting.

Jesus answered this observation. "He remembers that event, but he's able to talk around it, as if it didn't happen to him."

Philly thought, "*What happened?*"

"He has to tell you. I won't override his ability to decide who he tells."

But Philly knew enough to guess the sort of trauma Allen held back from his catalog of injustice and humiliation. Exactly what it was didn't really matter to Philly, now that he knew what Jesus had in mind—slaying the dragon from Allen's past. He didn't need to know that dragon's name.

Refocused on Allen, Philly could see that the account of Catholic school had worn Allen out. He hung over his salad plate, as if too exhausted to consume the remainder of the lettuce and purple cabbage. He set down his salad fork and grabbed his napkin from his lap. Somehow, in the motion of wiping his mouth,

Philly saw a change pass over Allen, a sort of cloud that darkened his face subtly and only briefly.

Jesus explained. "His internal enemy is moving and wants to humiliate Allen in front of the people in this restaurant. You have to tell it to keep quiet. Just say it like you did before but address your command to the raging spirit."

Anxiety sucked away Philly's breath, much as it did when he made a dangerous lane change on the tollway. Adrenaline assisted his execution of Jesus's instructions, however. "You raging spirit in Allen, you keep quiet and don't humiliate Allen here, in Jesus's name." Philly added that last part from something he had heard his grandma pray once.

Jesus clearly approved, and Allen breathed easier. This time, however, he seemed more conscious of what Philly had done, despite the high alcohol content of his blood. "You're here to help me, aren't you?" His voice sounded more ominous and mystical than the Allen Breen that Philly knew—the web administrator and office wise guy.

"Yes, Allen. More importantly, Jesus is here to help you." Philly snorted a small laugh. He tried to imagine what he would have thought of all this two weeks ago.

The main course arrived. Philly looked appreciatively at the Brazilian-style steak still sizzling on his hot dinner plate.

Allen dug into his American ribeye, ravenous and sullen. He seemed to shelter himself in the task of eating. And he neglected his alcohol intake for a time.

The steak tasted as good as Philly remembered, and he thoroughly enjoyed it. He did wish he had red wine with it but thought better of that. He wanted to encourage Allen toward sobriety. Jesus grinned at Philly's decision, again blanketing him with that proud father look, which made Philly smile as he chewed his steak.

Allen sat back for a moment. "You like your steak?"

"Mm-hmm." Philly nodded at Allen.

Again, Allen seemed to flux from one mode to another, almost changing colors. But this time he brightened slightly.

Philly crunched crisp, spicy potato wedges. "How's *your* steak?"

Allen nodded and grunted.

The waitress checked in on them. "How's your food?"

Philly said, "Great, as always. Thanks."

Allen ogled the girl and managed to grunt again, "Uh-huh."

"Can I get you another drink?" She bowed slightly toward Allen.

Philly shook his head, and Allen seemed to remember some resolve to sober up. "No thanks, just more water."

The waitress grinned slightly, which looked to Philly like approval. Though he knew the staff here generally pushed the drinks in hopes of enlarging the tip, no one wanted a sloppy drunk in the restaurant.

Philly managed to enjoy his meal to the finish, even as Allen clearly struggled for control of his faculties. Finally, as Philly chewed his last bite of steak, Jesus called the match.

"Get the check when she comes by in a few seconds. He's not going to last much longer."

Philly flagged the waitress immediately and asked for the check.

Allen growled.

That guttural response tipped the tables for Philly. He had been relying on Jesus to manage Allen and his discontented spiritual accompaniment. Now, Jesus's slightly raised eyebrows and laser focus seemed to say, "Get ready for a fight."

What kind of fight?

Allen dropped his knife and fork. His eyes screamed for help, but his lips remained locked together.

"Tell the perverted spirit to stay still and quiet," Jesus instructed.

Allen opened his mouth and made a hollow sound when

Jesus said this. It was like a meow emanating from inside a wooden box. The enemy apparently heard the words before Philly repeated them.

But Philly obeyed anyway, finishing just before the waitress got close enough to hear what he was saying. Looking up at her, Philly could see her brow deeply furrowed. "I'm getting him out of here as soon as possible."

The waitress nodded. She took Philly's debit card from him and hurried toward the register.

"What do you think you're doing, punk?" Allen spoke in a voice that sounded something like Mick Jagger.

"Tell the confusing spirit to stay still and quiet."

Again, the effect seemed to start before Philly spoke, but he said simply, "Confusing spirit, you stay quiet and still." Internally, Philly was asking, "*How many of these are there?*"

Jesus tipped his head slightly. "A few."

Philly took a deep breath and then checked with Allen. "How ya' doin' there, man?"

Allen shook his head slightly. "I feel really weird." As soon as he said that, he stood up suddenly and looked around, as if in urgent need of an exit or a bathroom. The back door, marked Emergency Fire Exit, seemed to catch his attention.

"Stop him."

Philly stood up and grabbed Allen's wrist before he turned all the way around. Allen looked back at Philly's hand there and then at Philly's face. He seemed surprised to find someone with him.

The waitress arrived with Philly's card and the signing copy of the receipt.

Philly juggled, his head going in three directions and his hands needing to cooperate. He looked at Jesus. "*Help.*"

Jesus did help, putting his hand where Philly touched Allen. A shudder started at that spot and flowed up to Allen's shoulders and down his back, causing him to slump back into his seat.

Seeing Jesus

Philly grabbed the check, took a look at the bill, and just added twenty dollars for the tip, scrawling his signature as quickly as possible.

"Help me get him out?" Philly spoke aloud to Jesus.

The waitress misunderstood. "Sure." She circled around behind Allen.

The proximity of the attractive young woman distracted Allen as Philly ushered him toward the front door, still holding his wrist. Several patrons turned their eyes toward the strange manner of their exit.

When they all stood on the sidewalk out front, Philly breathed easier.

"Is he gonna be okay?"

"Yeah, I got it from here. Thanks so much."

Just as the young woman stepped back inside, Allen whirled around and vomited against the building, his head waist high.

Philly recoiled, repressing the urge to follow suit. Jesus reached up and steadied Philly, who welcomed the comforting relief of that touch as he held onto his expensive supper. It was too late for Allen.

As soon as he finished, Philly hooked Allen's left arm and towed him toward his own car, praying silently that Jesus would keep Allen from performing a second act on the upholstery.

But Allen broke away and staggering into a narrow alley. Initially, Philly thought he was going to vomit again. But Allen ramped to escape speed, only to skid to a stop next to a dumpster, his way blocked by a delivery van.

Philly followed, Jesus urging him on.

"You need to take charge of this now, Philly. This is your dragon." Jesus spoke as if thrilled at the approaching battle.

"How?" Philly said.

"You speak for me, that's how."

"Go ahead." Philly stepped in front of Allen, who had begun pacing back and forth like a lion at the zoo.

"Tell the spirit of perversion to grab hold of all the others and get out of Allen."

Philly repeated Jesus's command, trying not to sound shrill.

Allen stood still and opened his mouth wider than Philly had ever seen done by anyone.

Jesus said, "Stop that and come out immediately."

Philly repeated Jesus's words.

Allen collapsed onto the worn red bricks and patchy asphalt at his feet.

"More games," Jesus said. "You have to get Allen to cooperate. Ask him if he wants the demons to leave."

Philly knelt next to Allen. "Allen. Allen, listen to me. You gotta tell me if you wanna get rid of these things inside you."

Allen looked up at Philly like a kid caught playing dead, then his appearance turned more normal and an expression of fear took over. "Yes. Please, help me get 'em out."

Philly didn't even wait for Jesus this time. "Okay, demons, all of you have to go now. Jesus says so."

With that, Allen belched and then dropped his head back to the ground, panting as if he had just finished running hard.

Philly looked at Jesus for an interpretation.

Jesus nodded.

Just then, the delivery man returned to his van, which was parked facing away from Allen and Philly. When the engine started and exhaust puffed out of the tail pipe, Allen tried to roll to his feet.

Philly assisted with two hands and a bit of grunting. He stood Allen against the brick wall of the restaurant. Allen continued panting, his eyes closed.

When he opened his eyes, Allen looked a question at Philly. "They're gone."

Allen nodded. "I feel empty and alone."

Philly looked at Jesus again.

"Let's take him to your grandma's house. She can pray for

him, and you two can spend the night there."

Philly wondered why he couldn't just pray for Allen, or pray adequately, if that was the issue.

Jesus answered the silent question. "You can't do everything, my friend. I designed it that way. Later you'll have others to help you in a situation like this. But for now, you just have Grandma."

Later?

Philly led Allen to his car after stopping to check that Allen had parked where he could leave his car overnight. Allen followed like a stray dog that he had given food, making no objections to Philly's plans.

Grandma welcomed the two men at her door, though it was nearly ten o'clock—late for her. Jesus had clearly warned her of the approaching guests.

In her kitchen, Grandma gave Allen and Philly milk and cake, and then she prayed for Allen's recovery and ultimate redemption, including forgiving the priest that harmed him as a child.

Allen accepted her prayers subserviently, free of his usual spite and bravado.

After she showed Allen the bathroom and where he could sleep, Allen thanked Grandma. "I really appreciate you helping me out. This is a life saver for me. Thanks."

Grandma surprised Philly by giving her guest a hug and a kiss on the cheek. "You are quite welcome. I love to do Jesus's work with him. It's grand."

Philly chuckled at Grandma and said goodnight to Allen, who shook his hand vigorously.

"You're the best, Phil. You're the best."

Philly laughed again and patted Allen on the back as he drifted into the guest room. Jesus clapped Philly on the back at that point and got a big hug from both Grandma and Philly, in turn. The three of them quietly moved into the living room to let

Seeing Jesus

Allen get to sleep.

"Have you done this sort of thing before?" Philly sat on the couch, across from Grandma.

She shook her head. "Not exactly. We pray for people at church and in prayer meetings. But I never hosted a deliverance survivor in my house like this."

"Deliverance?"

Grandma grinned. "That's what we call it when someone gets free from bad spirits."

Philly nodded but furrowed his brow. "I thought that was an exorcism."

"We try to avoid using that word." Jesus apparently referred to himself and Grandma.

"Deliverance." Philly tried the term out for himself. "Well, it wasn't too bad with you standing right there."

Jesus nodded and chuckled.

Just what he was chuckling about, Philly was too tired to investigate. He went down to the basement to sleep after Jesus reassured him that there would be no problem with Allen the rest of the night.

After hugging and kissing Philly, Grandma sat back down to read in her favorite chair.

Chapter Fifteen

The next morning, over a breakfast of pancakes and sausage, Philly listened to Grandma instructing Allen on how to truly recover from the horrors of his childhood.

Allen listened quietly, nodding, his eyes sincere and childlike.

Philly liked this new Allen. And he could see where Grandma's long experience had equipped her for this moment. He also guessed that her matronly manners helped Allen to trust her.

At ten o'clock Philly dropped Allen off at his car, reiterating Grandma's encouragement for church attendance and counseling.

Alone in the car with Jesus at last, Philly said, "I'm glad you didn't really warn me about all that. I would've run the other way screaming."

Jesus laughed. "I know. But you handled it very well. I'm proud of you."

Jesus's simple expression of pleasure with Philly's performance oozed onto his soul like warm honey. Jesus let Philly absorb his praise for a few blocks as they drove toward home.

When they stopped at a traffic light, Jesus said, "You should call Theresa."

Philly had been thinking of doing that, and Jesus's suggestion tipped him off the fence. He found her number and hit the button to dial before the light turned green. Philly put his phone on speaker so he could set it down while he drove.

"Hello." Theresa's voice was muted.

"Did I catch you at a bad time?" Philly glanced at Jesus in the passenger seat.

"No. Actually I just went on break. I'm working seven to three today. How are you and Jesus doing?" Her voice rose as she seemed to be walking.

Philly breathed a soft laugh. "We're great. He's the one that told me I should call you now. I guess he knew you were on break."

"Wow. That sure is handy, to only call when it's a good time."

"Yeah, I'm getting spoiled. Do you want to have dinner tonight?" He only consulted Jesus as an afterthought. But he could see that his passenger approved of the offer.

"Of course—I'd love to. Why don't I cook for you?"

Philly could see Jesus shaking his head out of the corner of his eye.

"You're working. I'll take you out. We can find a quiet place to eat so you don't have to do any more work tonight."

"Oh, you're so considerate. But I do want to cook for you some time."

They arranged for Philly to pick her up and said endearing goodbyes before ending the call. Philly turned briefly and smiled at Jesus.

"Pretty proud of yourself, huh?"

Philly laughed. "Actually, just really grateful to you."

Jesus smiled.

"So, what's next?" Philly asked just before he reached the corner where he planned to turn north, toward his place.

"Go ahead and turn here. But I want you to keep going up to a church in Rogers Park. I want you to meet someone."

Within ten minutes, Philly was parked under a budding cottonwood tree on the far north side of the city. Across the street stood a traditional old church building with a nontraditional name on its sign. Philly didn't recognize the brand, but trusted Jesus on this visit. He hauled himself out of the car and onto the street.

As he walked toward the front door of the church building, he saw a man about twenty years older than himself walking up to the front of the church and glancing around. As Philly stepped up on the curb, the man stopped and watched him approaching. This made Philly feel self-conscious, but also somehow welcomed.

When he approached the bottom of the stairs, the man spoke first. "I know this is gonna sound strange, but are you the guy that Jesus told to come here and meet me?"

Philly paused, feeling Jesus close beside him. He resisted glancing at him. "Uh, yeah, actually. How did you know?"

"I thought I heard him telling me to get over to the church building 'cause he was bringing a guy over to meet me here." He seemed to change gears. "I'm Dave Michaels, the pastor of the church." He extended his hand as Philly stepped up the two stairs to the little porch.

When Philly took Dave's hand, Jesus reached in, and both Philly and Dave jolted at a sort of electrical spark. They both laughed.

"I'm Phillip Thompson."

"Come on in, Phillip. Can I make you some coffee? I didn't get my fix yet this morning."

Philly laughed a bit nervously. "Yeah, that would be great."

Dave lead the way through a utilitarian-looking building, missing some of the décor and ambiance that Philly associated with church. But that only made it more comfortable for him.

The pastor stopped in a little reception area between a few offices and grabbed a Pyrex coffee pot to fill at the water cooler there.

"Caffeinated?"

"Please."

"Do I call you Phillip or Phil?"

"Philly," he said without thinking. "It's the nickname my dad gave me when I was a kid." He hesitated slightly. "And it's what Jesus calls me."

Dave nodded, grinning as he set up the coffee. When the coffee began to drip, Dave led Philly to his office and offered him a chair. He wore jeans and an old sweater over a faded button-down shirt and seemed quite comfortable with a guest in his office. Dave's hair was nearly uniformly gray, and his face had the lines of a man who had lost some weight not too long ago. But mostly Philly noticed his lively and curious blue eyes. They reminded him somehow of Jesus's darker eyes.

After arranging things to make it a bit tidier, including clearing a second chair for himself, Dave looked toward the door and sniffed. "Smells just about ready."

"Smells good." Philly settled into a chair.

Dave headed for the door, talking as he went. "A friend of mine sent that coffee to me from Africa, where he's teaching at a seminary and living with his family. They grow great coffee over there, apparently, but we don't see much of it over here." After a minute or two, Dave returned with two cups on a tray that included creamer and sweeteners. He set the tray on the front of his desk, where he had cleared a spot earlier. Then he pulled up that other comfortable armchair to sit facing Philly. "So, why did Jesus want you to come see me?"

Philly fixed his coffee with a little real sugar and a pile of powdered creamer.

Jesus helped Philly. "Tell him your story first."

Gripping his cup, Philly slid back in his chair. "Well, let me tell you the story of the last couple of weeks."

Dave settled his elbows on the arms of his chair and nodded.

As they sipped their coffee, Philly attempted to wrap up the days since Grandma's stroke into a coherent narrative. Not a practiced storyteller, he nevertheless felt like he managed to get enough out in ten minutes to give Dave the general idea.

"Man, that's fantastic!" Dave seemed to be holding back a hard chuckle. "Oh, man, that's a great story. What we'd call 'a real *God* story' around here. Do you have any idea how fortunate you are?"

Philly sat speechless for a moment, stunned by Dave's ready

acceptance of his claims. "Yes, I think I do. Jesus has told me over and over how unusual my experience is."

Dave nodded. "You seem surprised at my response."

"You could tell that, huh?" Philly snickered at himself. "Not everyone believes me, including religious people."

"Hmmm. Maybe *especially* religious people. I find religion to be more of a hindrance than a help a lot of the time."

Again, Philly stalled at this pastor's response.

Dave explained. "You see, religion is often just a way for people to try to control God. And, since God is God, it tends to get in the way of an actual relationship."

Philly nodded, trying to catch up. "I'm not a church person. A lot of this is new to me."

Dave set down his coffee. "That may be why Jesus chose you to see and hear him."

Philly shook his head. "Have you ever seen and heard him?"

Dave smiled. "No. I wish I had. But I have a strong feeling that you really do see him. And man, I am so jealous."

Philly looked over at Jesus, who had taken the seat behind the desk, putting his feet up. He seemed to be admiring Dave with an intoxicating smile. Philly couldn't resist telling him. "He's looking at you now with such a proud look on his face. I can really tell he loves you a ton." A flood of emotions rose with his words.

Dave craned his neck toward the chair, following Philly's gaze. He blinked twice, and then popped a quick sob for one intense moment, tears literally spraying from his eyes for just seconds.

Philly watched Jesus while Dave strained to get control of himself, crying and laughing at the same time. Jesus just beamed from behind the desk.

After a couple of minutes of sniffling, blowing, laughing, and wiping tears, Dave sat back in his chair. "Oh, man. You have no idea how timely that was for me." He shook his head. "It's a complicated story, but you should just know—that hit the spot." And he laughed, relief and joy spilling out of him. Philly would have said Dave was pretty relaxed already, but his host seemed to rest easier.

"He's done that sort thing to me a few times in the last couple of weeks." Philly offered that in case Dave needed cover for breaking into tears.

He didn't seem to feel the need but nodded at Philly's statement. Instead of asking for more of the story, however, Dave appeared to hear a different direction from some inner voice. "You know, Philly, I feel like I should really emphasize that not all Christians are gonna accept your story. I might even say that you should be careful who you tell. There are some churches that will just brand you a kook and show you the door if you tell them about seeing Jesus and anything about healing." Dave assessed Philly, pausing as if to listen again to that inner voice. "Have you given some thought to attending church?"

Grimacing an admission, Philly grabbed for what lay at hand. "Well, I guess I could go to my grandma's Pentecostal church. Or there's this woman I'm just starting to date—she goes to a church somewhere around here, so I might try that out."

Dave nodded. "Well, if neither of those work out for you, you could give us a try. I think you'd feel welcome here. With most people here, your experience with Jesus would be honored and not mocked."

The nuances of various Christian enclaves meant less to Philly than the various wines grown in Southern France, or the assorted species of freshwater snails in the world. At least, it *had* meant less to Philly in the past.

Dave watched him squirm a bit in his chair. "I'm thinking that you'll need some help figuring out how to keep the realness of your connection with Jesus going after he goes invisible. Even if you don't choose to attend this church, my door's open to you. I may be able to help a bit."

Philly appreciated that open door, along with the sympathy

for what losing his unique contact with Jesus would mean to him. "Thanks, Dave. I think I'll take you up on that."

Philly saw Jesus nodding agreement out of the corner of his eye.

He and Dave talked a while longer, each filling in some of his history. As they wound down and Philly made the first move to leave, Dave offered to pray for him. Philly agreed.

As the pastor spoke frankly and comfortably with his heavenly Father, Jesus stood up from behind the desk and knelt next to Philly, wrapping his arms around his friend. He seemed to favor that over sitting behind the desk listening to petitions sent to him from a distance.

To Philly's surprise, parting from Dave left him with the impression that the pastor had benefited from their meeting more than he had, though that seemed hardly possible. With thanks on both sides, the two shook hands, then hugged, and laughed goodbyes.

On the way home, Philly remembered that he should finally get his hair cut.

"Why? It doesn't look so long to me."

Philly laughed at his long-haired friend. And he pulled into the lot for one of the franchise haircut places in his neighborhood. He poked back at Jesus. "You can stay in the car if this place makes you feel uncomfortable."

Jesus laughed heartily all the way to the glass-and-metal front door.

Inside, Philly took the last chair in the waiting area after putting his name in with the receptionist.

Jesus stood in the corner, leaning against the wall and looking kindly on all the patrons waiting, as well as the employees at the cutting stations. He seemed especially interested in a short young woman working at the far chair.

When that young woman called his name, Philly wondered if he should have anticipated that, based on Jesus's attention toward her. Had Jesus manipulated the timing of the various employees and customers to get Philly into that girl's haircut station?

The young woman introduced herself as Rosa, smiling with closed lips at Philly as he approached the chair. Her own hair hung to her collar perfectly straight, though perhaps artificially so. Large, dark eyes and a round face gave her the look of a twelve-year-old street urchin from a barrio south of the border.

Philly liked her right away.

Jesus simply mooned over her.

After exchanging ideas regarding how to cut Philly's hair, they settled into the usual conversation about weather and work.

But Jesus had another topic that he wanted to pursue. "Ask her about her family."

When Philly did so, somewhat awkwardly, Rosa started cutting more slowly, her voice wavering as she told about her family in Mexico. They had returned there so that her mother could get medical care for cancer. Her father had feared being deported once he began winding his way through the medical care system in the U.S. But Rosa had stayed behind to keep earning money to send home. Separation from her family seemed to leave a less painful mark on her, however, than did her fear for her mother's life.

Philly knew why Jesus had chosen this chair, this young woman, and her family. But he wondered how they could help Rosa's mother in Mexico. All his healing experience had been with people he and Jesus could touch, or at least see.

Jesus answered Philly's question. "Don't worry, Philly. I can handle it."

Rosa sniffled, grabbed a tissue, and wiped her nose quickly. She finished the final snips on Philly's hair and blow-dried the loose hair off him. Her sniffles faded beneath the whir of the dryer.

When she finished and removed the smock that had kept all

that hair off Philly's clothes, he barely noticed his image in the mirror. He focused instead on how to propose helping Rosa's mother.

"Just ask if you can pray with her for her mother."

Philly fished his wallet out as he stood up. "Rosa, I'd really like to pray for your mother to be healed of cancer. I've seen Jesus do some really amazing healing lately, and I feel like he wants me to do this for her."

The petite girl looked up at him, as motionless as a store mannequin. Her lower lip quivered slightly. Her voice didn't rise above a whisper. "I would like that. Thank you."

Philly stepped close enough to Rosa to pray in a low voice—to protect her privacy there at work.

Jesus, on the other hand, moved up next to them and wrapped an arm around Rosa's shoulders. As soon as he did that, she began to sob.

To Philly, it felt as if Jesus had released the parking brake and this vehicle was rolling downhill fast, no brakes, no steering. But he only knew to keep doing what Jesus had instructed. He started asking God to heal Rosa's mother, but Jesus intervened.

"Philly, you have to tell the cancer to leave her mother, just like you told the spirits to leave Allen."

With half a dozen people obviously straining to see what was happening at that hair-cutting station, Philly kept his voice down. But he commanded sickness and cancer to leave Rosa's mother.

When he finished, she squeaked and exclaimed in Spanish. "Oh Dios mío!" She was panting. Then she dropped to the floor amid all the little blades of damp hair.

A collective gasp chorused through the salon. Philly looked around apologetically and knelt next to Rosa, much the way Jesus had knelt next to him the day before.

Rosa was repeating something over and over. "I see her, I see her being healed. I know it's true. I see my mother. I see her being healed." She wept cathartically.

The manager of the store ran interference for Philly and Rosa, telling the concerned customers and staff something that seemed to relax the worried onlookers.

After a minute, Philly helped Rosa to stand. She brushed the hair off herself and glanced around, clearly embarrassed, but also giddy. She looked up at Philly with the sincerest mortal face he had ever seen. "It is true! She is healed! I just know it."

This sent chills up Philly's back and into his newly cropped hair. He felt like hugging the small young woman but restrained himself, sympathetic about appearances at work. Instead, he smiled at her and glanced at Jesus. "Jesus says it's true, so I believe it too." Leaving her a sizable tip, Philly turned toward the door.

But Rosa stopped him. "Are you a pastor? I might want to come to your church."

Philly smiled, shaking his head. "No, I'm not a pastor. But I do know of a church that you might like." He gave her the name and location of Dave Michaels's church.

Rosa thanked him for that and thanked him again for healing her mother, impressing Philly with her great faith.

When he sat down in his car, Philly realized that his hands and knees quivered with an adrenaline overdose, much as they had the previous night with Allen. Though he felt the weight of these healings resting on Jesus and not on himself, Philly still vibrated with the rush of stepping out, speaking up, and following the instructions Jesus gave. Doing this had never failed, and he was getting used to that downhill-out-of-control feeling.

Early that evening, sitting in a little neighborhood Mexican restaurant that Theresa recommended, Philly recounted all of this, beginning with playing chess with Jesus. The momentum of the emotions bursting through all those events ran Philly through the telling, even though he sensed a bit of discomfort from Theresa as the narrative tumbled out.

When he finished with Rosa's story and the main course arrived, Theresa stabbed ineffectively at her enchiladas. "Philly, I have to tell you something. I want there to be no secrets between us."

Philly stopped cutting into his combination platter and squinted at her. He watched his appetite get up to leave.

"I'm overwhelmed at the beauty of what you've told me about seeing Jesus. And I'm so glad you're telling me so openly and honestly. But I also want you to know what I heard from one of my friends from church when I told her about your experience. It sounds like this pastor Dave sort of knew what to expect, but I was pretty stunned." Theresa drank some water and then urged Philly to go ahead and eat. She cut a mouthful of enchilada as if to encourage him.

As he ate, Philly listened cautiously to Theresa, glancing at Jesus sitting next to her—an arrangement that Jesus had requested. It worked for Philly, because he could monitor Jesus's reactions to what he or Theresa said. As Theresa told Philly about her conversation with a woman she trusted, Philly could see a sort of cloud arising on Jesus's countenance, a weather change that reminded him of the meeting with Father Tim.

Theresa's counselor and friend had reacted strongly to Philly's claim to see Jesus visibly. "I would stop seeing this man if I were you. He clearly has some serious issues, and you shouldn't have anything more to do with him." Theresa finished her story with a hollow tone, as if she had worn herself out by repeating what she'd heard.

The personal insult of that woman's advice bit into Philly. His feeling of being misunderstood—by his parents and most of the rest of the world—flared like live coals fanned in a rising wind. But just as those feelings threatened to overwhelm him, he saw Jesus begin to shake his head.

"Father, forgive them; they don't know what they're talking about."

Theresa, seeing Philly's glance to her side—where he had already told her Jesus was sitting—wanted to know what he said. When Philly repeated it, Theresa nodded. She took a long breath. "I'm glad you told me that. It helps me. I guess that's pretty much what I was feeling too."

Philly smiled meekly, relieved to have Jesus and Theresa on the same side. If he had to choose between them, it would have torn him in half. Theresa had already become that precious to him.

Jesus asked Philly to deliver a message to Theresa. "Tell her that when her friend Debbie made that little noise before saying those things, you could hear the sound of the fear that grips her heart. That fear is really about herself, and she projects it on you because you're alone, as she fears being alone."

Theresa hadn't provided Philly the name of her confidante, nor given so much detail about how Debbie responded. When he relayed what Jesus said, Theresa smiled with relief, blinking rapidly. Impulsively, Theresa reached across the table and grabbed Philly's left hand, tears welling in her eyes.

Philly missed some of the significance of Jesus's words to her about being alone, and worried that Theresa was feeling the loss of her ex-husband—until she combined those tear-filled eyes with a firm hold on his hand. He breathed easier, sensing that his connection with Theresa had only grown stronger.

Rather than solve the problem of antagonism for Philly's revelation, they agreed to avoid the issue by only mentioning seeing Jesus to select people, especially at Theresa's church. They also agreed that Philly would attend church with Theresa in the morning, at least so she could introduce him.

Theresa said she assumed that Philly would attend Dave Michaels's church long-term, based on the story he told. But Philly had assumed nothing about that, still stumbling his way into the world of Jesus and churches.

For Philly and Theresa, the night ended with a long

conversation over a glass of wine in her living room. Jesus just listened contently. Philly had spent most of his emotional and spiritual energy over the previous twenty-four hours and was glad Jesus didn't push him to accomplish more. Jesus, it seemed, was invested in the relationship between Theresa and Philly.

Knowing that he would see her in the morning released Philly from anxiety about leaving Theresa that night. They kissed goodnight with Jesus pretending to look the other way.

And Philly drove home with Jesus on a windy April night, just one more day of their miraculous encounter remaining.

Seeing Jesus

Chapter Sixteen

Jesus spared Philly from a late night of conversation but attended many of his dreams. The one Philly remembered best was about Jesus taking Philly's cell phone with him when he disappeared. Philly seemed to struggle all night to find that phone, or to get Jesus to come back and bring it with him.

When his alarm sounded on Sunday morning, Philly turned it off and then checked that his cell phone was still on the nightstand.

Jesus laughed at this move.

Philly squinted at Jesus. "Humph, you can laugh—you're the one that took it from me."

Jesus laughed louder.

After his usual wake-up trip to the bathroom, then to the kitchen to feed Irving, Philly paused to check for a rising dread he had noticed last night when he contemplated going to church for the first time in over a decade.

"This church is different than the one you attended last. For one thing, there won't be any corpse at this church."

Philly grinned and shook his head. He wondered why no one had ever told him that Jesus was such a comedian. But he had real questions. "Different in other ways too?"

"Not so solemn and dressed up."

That helped with his wardrobe choices but only dulled his multiplying dread. During his usual breakfast and dressing routine, Philly kept up a conversation with Jesus about what to expect and what would be expected of him.

"Very little is expected of you in this kind of church. Just be polite and follow the crowd."

"Follow the crowd?" Philly grunted as he tied his shoes.

"You know, stand when they stand, sit when they sit. But

there's less of that here than in the Catholic churches you've visited."

Philly remembered attending church with his other grandmother. His ma had cajoled him and Eileen into joining her and her mother at the local Catholic Mass when that grandma came to visit a couple times. Those occasions had taught Philly that complaining didn't help, and that compliance, which sheltered unspoken discontent, worked best.

Jesus obviously knew these ghosts arose for Philly with church attendance looming.

On the way down the back stairs, Philly spotted Mrs. Kelly in her kitchen, dressed and probably waiting for a friend to pick her up for church. Generally Philly lay in bed when that transaction occurred each week. The homey voices of the two nearly deaf women often penetrated Philly's peaceful Sunday laziness. Including himself now with those two old women—on his feet and out the door early on a Sunday—heartened Philly.

The sight of Theresa at her front door slowed Philly on his way up the walk. His object of infatuation looked even better in good daylight than in the low lights of restaurants and evening living rooms. She smiled at Philly, who couldn't stop grinning at his good luck.

"Good luck?" Jesus wasn't only looking over Philly's shoulder, he was peering right through his head.

A short drive on that warming Sunday morning brought Philly and Theresa to the tan brick building in a near suburb, where Theresa had been attending church for several years. When they climbed out of the car along with Jesus, it was Philly that felt like the odd man out. Theresa and Jesus both acted like they knew where they were going and expected to be welcomed. Philly scooped at his hair against the steady morning breeze, out of habit more than necessity, since Rosa had tamed it. His guilty neglect of church had been compounded by Theresa's friend doubting Philly's miraculous experiences. He struggled to avoid slipping from feeling like a stranger to feeling like an intruder.

Theresa seemed to sense his nervousness and took hold of his near arm with both hands.

Philly caught a smile from Jesus when she did this. Philly hoped that Theresa's friends would allow her display of affection for him to dampen their resistance. He could at least hope.

Not being a church-going person, Philly hadn't thought before what Jesus would do at church. He felt like a man attending a gathering in a building that bore the name of the man who accompanied him, like visiting a museum in the company of the one who donated all the funds for it, and who also filled all of its displays with treasures.

When they entered the sanctuary, Theresa steered Philly to a seat ten rows from the back. She assured an empty seat on each side of them. Philly wondered if this was to put space between herself and her church family or just a way to include Jesus.

At first Jesus sat next to Philly, as he might have expected. But Philly could sense that same wandering desire that he had seen from Jesus whenever they encountered other people. Jesus reminded him of a small boy filled with excitement that something amazing would certainly happen soon.

Several people took the stage, each to an instrument or microphone. Already, before the first chord was struck, Philly could tell that this would be different from church as he knew it. Song lyrics appeared on a screen above the musicians, and Theresa signaled time to stand up, as others began to do the same around the auditorium of blue-padded seats.

Jesus stepped into the aisle and clapped his hands above his head. He looked as if he were limbering up for some strenuous activity. As the first song began to build and the crowd began to sing the words on the screen, words about a great and loving King, Jesus danced in the aisle.

Philly scanned the stoic mortals around the auditorium and marveled at the contrast between them and the Jewish carpenter dancing near him. As late arrivals passed, Jesus would dance with them briefly, smiling, welcoming them. When the first song wound down, Philly leaned over to Theresa. "Jesus is dancing in the aisle."

Casting a glance at the open aisle, Theresa caught a laugh with four fingers over her lips.

Philly welcomed Theresa into his ironic experience, smiling at her and again watching Jesus's dance build toward the rousing chorus of the next song. He held his hands over his head and spun like a dervish for a moment, shouting above the voices and laughing through the song. From the corner of his eye, Philly noticed people behind him watching his misplaced attention, distracted by his distractedness. He rotated his head slightly toward the screen and stage, only sneaking peeks at Jesus.

By the end of the third and final song, Jesus seemed refreshed and ready for more. But he followed the direction of the man on the stage and returned to his seat.

Philly imagined the pastor singling out the rowdy dancer, insisting that he return to his seat to stop distracting the sedate worshipers around him. In this way, Jesus enhanced the overall entertainment value of church for Philly on that first Sunday.

"Is he done dancing?" Theresa said quietly, with a nod toward the aisle.

Philly nodded his head and grinned at Theresa.

Jesus sat next to him and smiled, as if immune to their playfulness. He appeared more focused. When the sermon began, however, Jesus put his left arm around the back of Philly's chair. Philly frequently caught Jesus looking at him. He seemed to be reconnecting an invisible link that required care and precision. The net effect of this behavior erased the sermon from Philly's consciousness. He later remembered some words and a few phrases from the preacher, but he couldn't explain the main point or the theme of the talk.

At the end of the service, he met some of Theresa's friends

and endured their diagnostic glances and interrogative stares. Finally, Philly followed her out to the parking lot.

He unlocked the car door for Theresa and looked at his long-haired companion who stood on the other side of the car. Jesus was turning his face to the moderate morning breeze and smiling like a spring flower making its annual debut to the accolades of the sun.

When Philly reached his seat and Jesus magically slipped into the back, Theresa sat smiling at Philly.

"How about some brunch?" The man in the back seat sounded hungry.

Philly looked over his right shoulder where he found Jesus smiling, as usual, with his eyebrows raised in a sustained facial question mark. "Jesus wants brunch." Philly allowed a dash of irony in his voice.

"She wants some too." Jesus spoke just before Theresa started her reply.

"That sounds great. But I didn't know he actually ate anything."

Philly started the car. "No, you're right. He doesn't actually eat. But he sure seems to like restaurants." Internally, Philly reminded himself to get something healthy and low calorie, beginning to add up all the times he had eaten restaurant food in the past few days.

Within less than an hour, the three of them sat around a small square table on the patio of a restaurant on the border between Evanston and Chicago. The day had begun to warm toward the first convincing promise of summer.

Philly tore at a regrettably healthy omelet, chosen out of guilt. Half of his attention available because of the uninteresting food, Philly wondered at why Jesus had suggested brunch and had tipped the vote toward this particular restaurant. He had grown to accept Jesus's constant agenda. That acceptance, however, hadn't erased Philly's own innate introversion. It was one thing to celebrate the satisfying rush of a *completed* healing, but it was another to ride the stomach-startling careen past the boundaries of his control.

The rest of Philly's attention rested, of course, on Theresa. She chatted pleasantly about a memory of this restaurant, which led to memories of this neighborhood from ten years ago—before her marriage and before her conversion to an active adult faith. Philly welcomed these quaint artifacts of a life similar to his own, laying another beam in the bridge between him and Theresa.

Philly reached for his iced tea and noticed Jesus looking at a couple seated on the opposite side of the patio.

Jesus smiled slightly, perhaps slyly.

Philly was beginning to relish some of the nuances of Jesus's many smiles, reading in them words that his companion preferred not to speak.

Theresa noticed Philly's attention to the other couple and then to the seat which Jesus occupied. She stopped in the middle of her explanation of the changes that had taken place on Howard Street over the past decade.

Philly noticed her sudden self-interruption and regretted neglecting what she had been saying.

Theresa, however, seemed to entertain no such regrets. Instead, her eyebrows arched, and she adopted a sly smile somewhat similar to the one Philly had seen on Jesus's face. "What's he going to do?"

Philly didn't know the answer to that yet, which explained his rising pulse rate. But he marveled again at Theresa's total acceptance of his claim that he saw and heard Jesus.

Jesus answered her question. "I want to show them my love."

Philly decided not to relay that answer, not wanting to assume responsibility for such a vague promise.

Jesus, on the other hand, knew that Philly thought primarily in terms of moving pieces on a visible and solid board, and he added more of what Philly would consider specific content. "That man, whose name is Matt, has diabetes. Once you tell him that you know these facts—his name and his disease—he might allow you each to lay a hand on him to heal him of that condition."

Philly smiled at Theresa's expectant pose as she waited for his translation from Jesus. "He wants us to heal that man's diabetes."

"Us?"

"That's what he said."

"Oh. Well, I guess ... if *he* says so."

Philly took another drink of iced tea, wiped his mouth with the burnt-orange cloth napkin, and nodded to Theresa.

She nodded back.

Jesus stood up and laughed, elevating Philly's mood and expectations with the sound of it. On his way across the patio, Philly wished he could always remember the sound of that laugh whenever he had to do something that Jesus pushed him to do.

The other couple looked up at the two people approaching them, the woman a bit twitchy at the surprise encounter.

Philly pulled up next to their table. "Sorry to bother you, but I want to ask you something." He paused a second, then addressed the man, who greeted him with stunned silence. "Is your name Matt? And do you have diabetes?"

The stunned effect deepened. Matt seemed to be trying to remember where he had met Philly. He didn't seem to be making any progress at that search.

In his mid-forties with a thin, tanned face and a country club look about him, Philly had a hard time imagining being in Matt's social circle.

"Do I know you?"

Philly shook his head. "No. I just had this idea come to me that your name is Matt, you have diabetes, and we're supposed to heal you."

The woman at the table spoke with the tone she might use

after discovering a large, poisonous spider on her husband's shoulder. "Matt?"

Matt regarded his wife and then turned back at the two strangers. "My name *is* Matt, and I *do* have diabetes. I guess we can test the rest of what you said by just giving it a try. What can it hurt?"

Theresa smiled, turning to the wife. "My name is Theresa. I've never done anything like this before. But Philly has healed a few people of some pretty serious conditions." She extended her hand in greeting.

"I'm Rosalynn." She maintained a monotone. "I don't really believe in that kind of thing." She shook Theresa's hand mechanically.

"I'm Phil." He shook hands as well. "I never believed in this sort of thing either—until it started to happen to me."

Jesus had positioned himself behind Matt and held his hand over the shoulder nearest to Philly. He nodded toward his hand.

Philly took that as his cue. "Okay if we put a hand on your shoulder?"

"Sure." Matt seemed slightly amused, as if indulging children playing a game.

Theresa scooted up close to Philly and reached with him for Matt's right shoulder, resting her free hand on Philly's shoulder.

Jesus joined them immediately.

Then Philly spoke. "Be healed in the name of Jesus." He waited a moment, checked Matt for a reaction, and then looked at Jesus.

"Break the genetic connection of diabetes in his family."

"I break the genetic connection of diabetes from Matt's family." Philly increased his intensity a little.

At that moment Matt sat up straighter, raised his eyebrows, and grabbed his stomach. "Whoa! What was that?"

Theresa tilted her head toward where Matt's hand had landed. "That's where your pancreas is." Her voice escalated a bit. "God must be healing your diabetes."

Matt looked at Philly and then at his wife. Rosalynn appeared to be fighting back tears. This seemed to puzzle Matt. He bent his head to check what must have been his insulin pump. He reached for his belt, pushed a button, and waited. As he noted the result, his eyebrows arched high and his mouth curved into an upside-down smile.

"What's happening?" Rosalynn, sniffling, reached a hand to touch Matt.

"It's going down. I knew it was a bit high from the muffin and I was just going to adjust. But I don't need to adjust anything. I've never seen it level off like that without a dose of insulin." He sounded fascinated and yet strangely removed from the impact of the miracle.

Jesus spoke to Philly. "For now, tell him that he can monitor his levels and see that he doesn't need to program doses for meals anymore. Then he should go see his doctor to get tested."

Philly relayed these instructions to Matt. He stared at Philly, hopefully absorbing Jesus's instructions.

But Matt had apparently locked onto more than the medical implications of Philly's intervention. "Did God just heal me?"

Philly nodded and smiled. "Keep an eye on it and see your doctor. He'll let you know if you're really healed."

"But it was God that told you to do this—that told you my name and said he was gonna heal me?"

"It was Jesus."

Theresa boosted Philly's response. "It was. It was Jesus that said he wanted to heal you."

Rosalynn shook her head and held both hands over her mouth.

Theresa asked them about church and faith in God. And she encouraged them to check it out. She turned to Philly and said, "Tell them about Dave Michaels's church."

After a low hurdle of surprise, Philly gave them the name

and location of the church so they could research online and perhaps visit. He smiled at Theresa, appreciating her flare for follow-up and wondering at her apparent surrender of loyalty to her own church in favor of one she had never attended. Philly's inexperience at church matters left him uncertain of the significance of her recommendation.

Matt looked at his insulin pump again. He shook his head and then looked up at Philly. "What am I gonna tell my doctor?"

For a moment Philly missed the point of the question, then understood and smiled. "Well, I guess you could tell him you went to brunch on Sunday morning and, one muffin later, you were cured of diabetes." Everyone laughed at this.

"Or you could tell him that Jesus healed you." And he left it there.

Warm handshakes, a hug between Theresa and Rosalynn, and friendly farewells ended the encounter.

Back at their table, Philly left cash for the waiter and the brunch, and he headed for the car with his two friends.

"We make a pretty good team," Jesus said.

Philly chuckled, forgetting for a moment that Theresa couldn't see or hear Jesus. When he remembered, he filled her in on Jesus's joke. Then he responded to Jesus out loud. "You knew what you were doing when you included Theresa in this one, I can see."

Hearing Philly address Jesus aloud appeared to discomfort Theresa a bit, but she smiled weakly at the compliment.

Jesus smiled at both of them and then slipped through the body of the car into the back seat.

"Oh. I'm still not used to that. He just went through the side of the car instead of climbing in the door."

Theresa laughed, her response somewhat delayed.

"Let's take Theresa home. I have a gift to give her there. And then you and I need some time together."

Philly nodded and relayed the message.

"A gift?" Her voice faded like a passing bird call.

Parking on the street in Lincolnwood, Philly jumped out and circled the car, arriving in time to close Theresa's door for her.

Jesus stood leaning on the side of the car already, beating Philly there by virtue of his mastery over time and space. In the look on Jesus's face, Philly felt a poke at his finite humanity, as the Savior watched him huffing and puffing to get around the car.

On the way up the sidewalk, Theresa slipped her hand into Philly's. His heart rate accelerated, and he smiled covertly.

Jesus, seeing all and hearing even Philly's thoughts, slapped Philly on the back good-naturedly.

On the porch, Theresa fumbled for the right key and then handed it to Philly to open the door.

Philly obliged and checked with Jesus, concerned for what was happening with Theresa.

Jesus took the lead, once they were all in the living room and had finished greeting the cat. "You two just have a seat on the couch."

Philly suggested sitting on the couch to Theresa, and she complied, appearing as relaxed as a person waiting for a dental extraction. Putting his arm around her to settle her apprehension, Philly looked to Jesus for the next step.

"I want you to heal her blindness."

"Blindness?" Philly said it aloud. He tried to guess at a metaphorical meaning to that word, given that Theresa seemed to see okay.

Theresa looked at Philly. "What about blindness?"

Philly twisted his mouth apologetically, suspecting Jesus was asserting that Theresa had some sort of spiritual blindness. "He says he wants to heal your 'blindness.'" Philly put *blindness* in quotes with his doubtful tone.

Theresa reached up to her left eye. "He means my eye. I can hardly see anything out of this eye." Her voice was hushed.

Philly raised his eyebrows. "Wow, I didn't know that." He

smiled. "But, of course, Jesus did."

Theresa stiffened, sitting up straighter and looking scared. "I feel a vibration in my eye. Is that normal?"

Philly glanced at Jesus, sitting on the other side of Theresa. He downloaded comfort from the pleased look on Jesus's face. "It's fine. I think Jesus is starting to heal you already."

"The doctors said there was nothing they could do about it. I won't ever be able to see out of it."

"I think all that changes now."

Theresa put her hand up to that eye, as if attempting to steady it.

Jesus nodded toward that hand, and Philly knew he should put his hand over Theresa's.

Sitting there, feeling the warmth of Theresa's shaking hand, his near arm wrapped around her, Philly grew more conscious of their physical contact. Then he rebuked himself, just as he had that first time he caught himself admiring Theresa in the hospital lobby. That self-chastisement further distracted Philly from the healing process, doubling his sense of guilt. *"Boy, I'm blowing this,"* he thought.

Jesus replied to that thought. "Really? And her healing was up to you?"

Philly answered that rebuke by shaking his head and deleting the stream of thought that had drawn him away from the healing process.

Theresa, clearly still focused on what was happening to her eye, withdrew her hand, prompting Philly to do the same. She looked around, closed her good eye, and looked around some more.

Philly waited for the celebration.

"Hmm, it seems the same."

Philly checked with Jesus internally. *"Am I supposed to do something different?"*

"Put your hand up there again and tell the eye to be healed."

Seeing Jesus

Philly followed these instructions. Theresa dutifully closed her eye to let him gently touch her, mostly on the eyebrow. Philly's healing command came with a little more force than his first words to Matt at the restaurant.

When he pulled his hand away, Theresa looked around again and then just shook her head.

Again, Philly checked with Jesus. *"What else?"*

Jesus shook his head slightly, looking perfectly satisfied. "Nothing else. That's enough. She will be healed."

"When?" Philly said it aloud, impatient and a bit embarrassed.

"Later," Jesus said. And that was it.

"He says it's going to be healed later, but nothing more specific than that."

As the disappointment of the experience began to fade through the following silence, Jesus spoke to Philly. "It's time to give her a hug and a kiss goodbye. We need some time alone, you and I—and Theresa and I."

Chapter Seventeen

Philly sat in the driver's seat of his car, warm in the greenhouse-like enclosure. Thinking about what had happened in contrast to what he wanted to happen, Philly shuffled through a confused pile of thoughts and feelings.

"Don't worry about it, Philly. Just trust me."

Philly replied only with a brave smile.

Jesus supplied directions for what he planned next. "Home first and then to Grandma's."

Philly nodded and pulled away from the curb, glancing toward Theresa's house once, wondering what she was doing now.

Jesus punched the radio on and quickly found a classic rock station. He turned it up three notches.

Glancing at his passenger rocking to old U2 music, Philly adjusted his expectations one more time. A Tom Petty and the Heartbreakers song followed, and Jesus stayed with it, only switching when it ended—this time to Aretha Franklin belting a tune on another station. Philly noticed that Jesus didn't surf stations, rather punching quickly to exactly the FM frequency that he wanted. Philly shook his head at the advantages of omniscience and let the wind ruffle his new haircut as he enjoyed the music.

On the way up the back stairs of Philly's apartment building, Jesus stopped at Mrs. Kelly's door. "Let's just check in."

Philly shrugged a bit and then knocked on the glass of the kitchen door. After several seconds, Mrs. Kelly appeared in the kitchen. She still wore her Sunday dress, but shuffled along on bedroom slippers. She smiled when she saw Philly at the door. To Philly's surprise, Jesus offered no miraculous insight, and the visit seemed to have no heroic purpose. After inquiries about her health, about church, and comments on the fine spring weather,

Philly said, "Well, just checking to see how you're doing, and to say hi, I guess."

Mrs. Kelly thanked him and smiled in a way that reminded Philly of his grandmother. It occurred to him then to introduce the two ladies somehow, and he heard Jesus seconding that notion. They said cheerful goodbyes, and Philly renewed his climb to the top floor and his own kitchen door.

Philly poured himself a glass of apple juice and sat down in the living room.

Jesus seated himself on the easy chair opposite Philly, with Irving in his arms. Looking warmly at Philly, Jesus said, "I've really enjoyed our time together, Philly—much more than you would believe." He stroked Irving behind the ears and then drilled into Philly with his sparkling eyes. "I don't want it to end, of course, and I want to help you to be conscious of me even when you can't physically see or hear me."

Philly nodded. "That's what I'm counting on. I can't just go back to living on my own now. You've ruined that for me."

Jesus smiled. "It's good to hear you say that." He put Irving down and pointed to Philly when Irving looked back at him dejectedly. "I want to play a game." Jesus glanced from Irving to Philly.

Philly just stared at Jesus, waiting for the next surprise to finish being unwrapped.

"The game is called 'Can you hear me now?'"

Philly's stared a second longer, but then he felt like he knew what was coming and grinned in anticipation. "Okay, go ahead."

Jesus smiled. "Okay. You can see me and hear me now, of course ... but can you hear me now?" He spoke audibly, even though he disappeared from sight.

"Yes. I can still hear you."

"And can you see what I'm doing?"

At that moment Irving wriggled pleasantly, as if someone had expertly stroked his back.

Philly tilted his head. "You're petting Irving."

Jesus reappeared just a few feet in front of Philly, crouching down and rubbing Irving's insistently offered head. "Okay. You can hear me now. But can you hear me now?" This time he didn't disappear but projected his thoughts into Philly's mind without moving his lips, as they had done many times.

"I hear your thoughts in my head."

"Good. That's how it will be for us after today."

"Really? It's that easy?"

"Of course. I never leave my friends."

Philly tried to find the trick in what Jesus was saying. "How come I've never heard anyone talk about this? I mean, if Christians are always hearing your voice in their heads, you'd think I'd have heard about it."

Jesus stood up and walked to the other end of the couch. "Well, there are a few things you need to learn about Christians. The reasons you've never heard about it are numerous and tangled. Some of the people in churches around this country don't expect to hear me, so whenever I do speak they mistake it for their own thoughts, or the voice of some tempting devil. Some of those folks have learned to filter me out to simplify their lives. For other people who follow my teachings and love my Father, my voice is something that breaks through only in emergencies or in peak experiences of religious fervor. They tend to assume that they can handle most of their lives on their own, and that I'm too busy or too small to stay daily involved with all of them at once. Of the folks who fall somewhere along these two broad categories, most of them don't believe I can help them in substantive ways, such as healing their ailments. They certainly also doubt that I would use them to heal anybody else—the way I've used you."

Philly nodded. "That explains the people at Theresa's church being so suspicious of me."

"Yes. They're like children who leave home and completely

forget what their parents are like, assuming no one wants to take care of them or provide for them, just because their parents are out of sight for a moment." He lowered his voice slightly and peered at Philly. "This is the point of my little game just now. You can hear me even when you can't see me, because you expect to hear me. They don't expect to hear, so they don't hear."

"But what about Dave Michaels and his church?" Philly strained against a sinking hopelessness.

Jesus smiled. "Well, there you have another kind of child. In fact, Theresa is also another kind of follower—one who is ready to believe, given half a chance to experience what I can do."

"I guess I'm still wondering why I haven't heard anything about this stuff."

Jesus sighed. "There are at least two more reasons for that. Among my followers, wherever they may fall on this spectrum of expectations, many are afraid of believing. They've had their hearts trampled—by parents and others they trusted—so hard or so often that they fear sticking them out there again. That risk is what it would take for them to learn to trust me enough for you to feel the impact of them in the world.

"Another reason is bad press." Here he named some prominent Christian leaders that Philly had heard of in the recent past. "You're familiar with their names, aren't you?"

"Sure, I've heard of those people—mostly 'cause they got in some kind of trouble."

"Exactly. The people who publish and produce the news seem to get a lot more mileage out of a sex scandal involving a Christian leader than they do out of a simple physical healing by that same leader or by someone less famous in their church. You need to understand, Philly, that the people who aren't on my side are working against me. The world is still under the control of my enemy, and that includes most of the institutions of your society—even some of my church."

"Ugh. That sounds really depressing."

"Only if you focus on it. If you focus, instead, on my voice and on what I show you in the world around you, you will be full of joy instead of fear and depression."

Philly nodded thoughtfully. "I believe that. I remember my dad once showed me, when I was a kid, that if you stare at someone's nose for a while it starts to seem really big." Smiling, he continued. "The point being that the thing you focus on tends to seem bigger than it really is."

"Wise words."

Philly took a deep breath. "This all sounds really complicated. Will I find people who can help me keep it all straight?"

"You already have. And I'll show you more. Just stay tuned to me, and you'll be fine."

Philly relaxed a bit, smiling self-consciously at Jesus. "Ready to go to Grandma's?"

Jesus nodded.

"Can we practice me hearing you inside my head on the way over?"

"Yes. That's a good idea."

Philly and Jesus carried on an invisible conversation as they walked out to the car and as they drove west toward Grandma's house.

The phone interrupted their conversation, however, when Eileen called to check in with Philly and to update him on her recovery from the breakup with her boyfriend. But, most of all, Eileen called to tell Philly that she had gone to church that morning with a woman from work who had invited her to numerous church events in the past.

"So, how was it?" Philly withheld his news that he had also attended church that morning.

"I liked it. It's mostly African American, but it reminded me of Grandma, the way the people talked and seemed to feel about God. I think you'd like it."

"Yeah?"

"Yeah. They talked some about healing."

"That sounds good." Philly told her the news of his own visit to church, which led to a lot of probing regarding Theresa. His fear of this probing explained Philly's hesitation to reveal his church attendance earlier in the conversation, But Eileen kept her questions light and her comments sympathetic.

Jesus reappeared in the passenger seat as the conversation wore on. That reminded Philly of their agenda. But Jesus merely mouthed, "Say hi for me," waving his hand in the direction of the phone.

Philly snickered.

"What's so funny?" Eileen said.

"Oh, Jesus just said to say hi from him."

A moment of silence on the other end concerned Philly until it ended in a low laugh. "Well, hi back at him." She paused a moment. "So, you still see and hear him, then?" The laugh was gone out of her voice.

"Today's the last day."

"Oh. You sound sad."

"Yeah, of course. It won't be the same. But I'm practicing hearing him when I can't see him."

"You can do that?"

"Yep."

"Well, I guess anything's possible." Eileen sounded more hopeful in the way she said that than Philly ever could have imagined before his visit with Jesus.

"I'm beginning to believe that," Philly said.

"Have there been more miracles since Grandma?"

Philly tried to update Eileen on the healings he had seen since she left for New York. He finished his account while sitting in the car next to Grandma's house.

"Wow, Philly. That's amazing."

"I could almost start getting used to this stuff."

"Hmm," Eileen said.

"Good," Jesus said.

Philly looked at Jesus, adding that little comment into his growing comprehension of what lay ahead of him. "Well, I'm at Grandma's house. I should go in. This is the night that she and I say goodbye to the 3-D version of Jesus."

"Oh, okay. It was good to talk."

"Yes. I'll call you later this week when we can talk longer."

Eileen's goodbye included a slight hesitation, perhaps because of the unusual promise of a call from her brother.

Philly hung up, and Jesus opened the passenger's door as Philly got out of the driver's side. As Jesus shut his car door, Philly noticed an older woman walking a scruffy little dog, the woman staring at him and at his car. He nodded at her but decided against an explanation, real or fabricated. He looked at Jesus for some direction regarding the curious neighbor, but Jesus just headed up the driveway to Grandma's kitchen door.

Grandma greeted them at the door. Philly hugged her and then noted Jesus behind her instead of behind him.

"How are you Philly? Did you have lunch?"

"Yeah, I had brunch with Theresa."

"Oh, okay. Well, come on in and have a seat. I'll get you some iced tea. I guess Jesus has something for us, one last time in full view."

Philly nodded and walked through the kitchen to the living room. He smiled at the same familiar dark green carpet, dark green plaid couch and chairs, and Grandma's favorite rocker by the window. She hadn't redecorated for as long as Philly could remember, perhaps to protect her family from the shock of any changes to her familiar old house. He wondered for a moment whether his family had held Grandma back from being and doing what she wanted, free from the expectations of insecure generations of offspring.

Grandma appeared with the iced tea in a tall, clear glass with pictures of lemon slices on it. She knew better than to include actual lemon slices in Philly's tea. But that glass was part of the set that added to the sweet familiarity of Grandma's house.

Philly noticed Jesus watching him, as if observing the mundane thoughts stepping through his head. He could sense Jesus's pleasure with him, even without words passing between them.

When he thanked Grandma for the glass of iced tea, Philly thought he detected a touch of sadness on her face. "How have you been, Grandma?"

She smiled loosely, her eyes glistening. "I've had such a marvelous time seeing and hearing Jesus. It's so much easier to listen to him and talk to him." Here she hesitated, and her face changed, like a girl who realizes that summer vacation is almost over. "I'm gonna miss seeing him, though I know he'll always stay with me. It just makes me want to go home to be with him so much more than I ever wanted before."

Though Philly had never heard Grandma speak of death as going home to be with Jesus before, he knew what she meant. He even recognized that feeling of wanting to make their communion with Jesus permanent. In Philly, of course, Grandma had a sympathetic listener about the wonder of being with Jesus. But he also remained emotionally dependent on her and didn't want to see her leave anytime soon.

Jesus spoke up. "My hope for you two is that you won't have to struggle between your desire to be with me and your assignment to live and work here on earth. I always intended for you to stay constantly connected with me here. If you see with your spirit instead of your physical eyes, you'll still see me. If you listen with your spirit instead of only your physical ears, you'll continue to hear me. As I told my first disciples, it really is better for me to give you my Spirit to live inside you. With that internal contact, you'll never have to ask me to speak up. You'll never have to strain to see me in a crowd. I will be inside you and you inside of me."

Mysticism of any sort had baffled Philly at best. Without

religion or faith, he had constructed his life, and even his self-image, out of material he could hold and touch and throw away when necessary.

Jesus seemed to take this into account with what he said and did next. "You had an unusual introduction to being with me, Philly. So I want to leave you a connection between this way of seeing me and having me inside you." He stepped up in front of Philly. Gently touching Philly's chest in the recess below his left collar bone, Jesus started a small fire in him.

"Receive my spirit to live inside you now."

Time and space disappeared. Philly no longer felt the floor or chair beneath him, nor saw the room around him. He heard nothing except a heavenly music that didn't pass through his ears. He didn't spin, shake, or fall, though he couldn't explain why not. And he didn't scream out from pain or intense pleasure, though he didn't understand that either. Without leaving a mark on his skin, Jesus somehow branded him in both mind and spirit, leaving a handle to grab whenever he felt the presence of his friend slipping away.

Jesus removed his hand and spoke to Grandma. Philly knew that much, but no more. He remained suspended in between heaven and earth during Jesus's final interaction with her.

When he began to emerge into ordinary earthly sensations, Philly saw Jesus standing there waiting. He said simply, "I will never leave you." And then he vanished.

The next morning, Philly found a voicemail message from Theresa:

"Philly. I just wanted to tell you what happened to me." He could hear her catching her breath. "When I got out of bed to go to the bathroom last night, I noticed a weird sort of vertigo. I started blinking my eyes. And then I looked at myself in the mirror. When I closed my right eye, I couldn't believe it. So I opened it and closed my left." She made a little gasping sound. "With both eyes open, I realized that I could see perfectly with both eyes.

"Jesus healed my eye, Philly!"

Chapter Eighteen

Philly plunked the TV remote onto the coffee table. He scratched at two weeks' growth of beard and contemplated whether his stomach was expanding or whether that was just his imagination. He had a very active imagination, as it turned out. But some things had to be real, he reasoned, such as Theresa's sight restored in her nearly blind eye, his dad's hearing restored, and, of course, Grandma waking from her coma. He hadn't merely imagined those things.

Theresa's place on that list distracted Philly down a dark tunnel leading to the lowest level of his depression. He remembered that day, a week after Jesus disappeared, when he saw the picture on Theresa's computer ...

He sat at her kitchen table drinking skim milk and eating homemade cookies while Theresa checked her email. Philly's attention swayed between the sunset tint of the yard outside the window and his cookies, the laptop screen taking a distant third.

Theresa opened a message nonchalantly, clicking away, when a photo of her at work popped up. Her muted gasp drew Philly's attention. In the photo, probably taken with someone's phone, she stood with her hand on the posterior of a male staff member.

Immediately, Philly could tell she was embarrassed that he saw the image, but some part of him noted that she wasn't as embarrassed as he would have been were the roles reversed. Philly's cheeks flushed hot in that humiliating way that made it impossible to hide his feelings at times like this.

Theresa released a forced laugh and closed the photo. "Oh, that's embarrassing. I didn't know she got a picture of that." Her voice quavered very slightly.

Philly stared at the screen, though the offending image had vanished.

Theresa squirmed in her chair, as if irritated by the sick look on Philly's face.

They parted earlier than usual that night, a smothering silence between them. Philly knew he couldn't find fitting words.

Theresa had tried to laugh off the incident, to attribute it to office culture and "good, clean fun." But, in the midst of her attempts, she seemed to give up on an explanation.

This discovery split open Philly's soul, and his confidence in everything spilled out of him like kernels of popping corn pouring from a damaged bag. He could almost hear the noisy little grains pelting the hard floor—faith, love, joy, and hope escaping from the opening in his heart. Then, in the days when he struggled to recover from this shock to his relationship with Theresa, the darkness grew even deeper.

When Philly had returned to his office on LaSalle Street back in April, after his long weekend with Jesus, he found that Craig had spent much of Friday debunking rumors that Philly had been fired, as well as rumors that he had done any number of fictitious miracles. Managers throughout the company resorted to threats to contain the cascade of hearsay and gossip. The clampdown simply drove the talk underground and fueled the more drastic speculations. That Philly appeared at the office the next Monday, and without boxes for clearing out his personal effects, reduced the pressure, as had a weekend away from work for everyone.

In the days that followed, coworkers made surreptitious requests for healing that allowed Philly to take his ministry outside the office, undercover, for a while. But the occasional healings started an even broader flow of new rumors—until one day when Dennis caught Philly in an unguarded moment.

"Phil, are you talking to yourself?" Dennis had checked in the network room two weeks after Jesus disappeared.

Tired of ducking and covering, Philly told the truth.

"Actually, I was talking to Jesus."

Dennis shook his head. "I know there are rumors that you believe you can see and hear Jesus talking to you, but I thought that was just crazy talk."

Philly looked at Dennis, trying to decide how much to say. "Well, I don't see or hear Jesus the way I see and hear you—not like a regular human being—but I do believe in talking to him and listening to him. That's really all that prayer is."

Dennis didn't seem to like being told what prayer was. He rolled his eyes and huffed. "Can't you do that in church and leave it out of the office?"

"I could. And I'm sorry I was talking out loud just now. That's not necessary. I just got carried away a little."

Dennis toned down his disdain, but he wasn't done. "I want you to go and see someone for an evaluation."

"Evaluation?" He associated the word with Dennis, who had always been his boss, evaluating his work performance.

"I mean a mental health evaluation."

"You want me to see a psychiatrist?" Philly was recalling that his mother had the same idea. This conjoining of Dennis and his ma represented a perverse symmetry that nearly made Philly laugh. Perhaps that was hysterical laughter.

"The health plan covers it. I'm sure you can find one that's on the network."

One mercy of this mandate, for Philly, was the time delay. It took several days to find a counselor and to schedule an appointment. Then there were two more weeks of visits. The process of finding a therapist would have been easier if Dennis hadn't insisted on a counselor who would report his or her findings to him.

Eileen heard about this on the phone and nearly cursed in front of Philly for the first time since her visit. She said she was certain that this wasn't legal for the kind of job Philly had, with no prior agreement to such an evaluation.

Though his sister certainly had grounds for these concerns,

Philly had never been the sort of person to press a fight to its bloody end. As it turned out, the counseling meetings benefited the psychiatrist, a gargoyle-like man in his late sixties. Philly healed the old atheist's lower back pain in their second meeting. The following week, the counselor apparently reported to Dennis that he found nothing wrong with Philly.

Thus, the firm had to resort to firing Philly for violating company policy against proselytizing in the office. Philly ignored recommendations from Craig and others that he hire a lawyer and contest that interpretation of what he was doing at work, since it excluded him from receiving unemployment benefits or severance. Though he never tried to convert anyone *per se*, Philly could see that healing someone in the office might be even more dangerous than an evangelistic pamphlet. Even though he didn't choose to fight, a handful of other people left the firm as a result of Philly's firing.

After he had packed up his personal belongings and left his office for the last time, Philly struggled with a drowning sensation. Fears flooded all around and into his soul. *"How will I take care of myself without a job?"* And that familiar voice that used to reassure and comfort him seemed a muffled shout from a faraway shore, his anxiety splashing away the clear reassurance carried by that voice.

During the first week of looking for a new job, Philly stopped repeatedly to try to hear Jesus still speaking to him. But at home, trolling on the internet for vocational hope, he lost track of his guide.

Then desperation pounced. Philly called his grandma to arrange a visit and found her sick in bed. Her longing to go home to be with Jesus rose in Philly's frazzled mind. But Grandma didn't die. She did, however, remain sick for nearly two weeks, even after Philly tried three times to heal her.

Ignoring a dozen phone messages blinking at him on his machine and cluttering his cell phone, Philly spiraled downward. He stopped shaving, bathed seldom, and didn't leave the apartment for ten days straight. The wall of emotional pain that loomed over him lacked the familiar proportions of past depressions. This depression dominated his emotional landscape like a tottering tower much bigger than in the past. This was the first time that he feared he had lost contact with Jesus and God.

After several tries at reconnecting with Jesus, pausing to pray and trying to listen for his voice in his head, Philly gave up. Instead of stirring him back to faith, his attempts only lead to crippling frustration. And then there was the anger, the angry accusations directed at the invisible God, who had withdrawn not only himself, but also the budding relationship with Theresa. Philly also stewed in his resentment that Grandma, his emotional anchor, would be leaving soon.

In that irreligious venting, Philly found an open door to God. Though he thought the heavenward howling would seal God's absence, he was surprised to find that God recognized his temper tantrum as an invitation to reengage. While focused on his losses, daunted by the task of finding new employment, and feeling alone in the world, Philly held God at arm's length. When he turned to complain about God's distance, his arms dropped to his side and God drew near once again. But this time the visible and audible projection of God in the form of his Son didn't appear. Instead, Philly had to return to that game of "Can you hear me now?"

Like whispers in a wind-rocked forest, Philly caught only faint voices, slim slips of sound of which he couldn't be sure. To gain that surety, Philly hunkered down and waited. He planted himself on the couch and waited for God to appear to him again, to speak to him again.

If not for Irving's insistent pleas for attention, Philly might not have left the collapsed cushions of his old couch. He ate and drank and relieved himself as an afterthought, on the heels of meeting Irving's basic needs. The cat didn't mind the vigil of course—it placed Philly right where his four-legged friend could find him, providing a warm place to sit and an idle hand to scratch his head.

On a warm and sunny Wednesday afternoon, Dave Michaels knocked on the glass of the back door. When Philly didn't answer, Dave tried the doorknob, though any veteran resident of Chicago would know that it would be locked. In his mind-fuzzing funk, however, Philly had left that door unlocked when he threw a reeking bag of garbage off the porch and into an open dumpster behind his building.

Dave stepped into the kitchen. "Philly? Philly, are you in here?"

Philly lay half asleep on the couch, his left hand cupped to that spot on his chest where Jesus had last touched him. At the sound of Dave's voice, he awoke fully and tried to sit up. The acute angle of his arm against his chest had put that limb asleep, such that Philly couldn't immediately move it. As he regained full consciousness, he looked down at his numb arm and remembered that he had been thinking of Jesus's promise that he would never leave him.

"Philly? I'm coming in." Dave was closer now, on his way into the central hallway of the apartment.

For a moment Philly couldn't place that voice, but he knew that it was familiar and felt that it was welcomed.

Dave hesitated at the entry to living room.

Philly twisted his stiff neck and looked at Dave. "Hey."

"Hey, yourself. Some of us were gettin' worried about you." He continued into the living room, surveying the unkempt apartment around its unkempt resident. "But I guess we shouldn't have worried."

Philly smiled at the ironic joke, then remembered his left arm as the blood began to flow and a hundred needles tried to shoot their way out of his fingertips. His hand flopped into his lap as partial control returned with the pain.

"Theresa called me." Dave was watching Philly trying to flex his hand at the end of an arm that was creased like a wet shirt left in the washing machine too long.

"Really? You know Theresa?"

"We talked."

"How did you find me?"

"Craig has started coming to our church."

"Really? Huh." Philly stared at Dave. "Theresa kinda cheated on me. But I guess I'd better forgive her for that."

Dave nodded and pursed his lips.

It wasn't clear to Philly whether Dave knew anything about it. What had Theresa said to him?

Dave stepped toward an old brown armchair and scooped up some garbage so he could have a seat. "Forgiving her would be a great place to start." He sat down, dropping the small pile of paper plates, napkins, and plasticware onto the floor next to him.

After coaxing Philly to tell his version of what happened between him and Theresa, Dave looked at Philly, nodding. "What would it mean for you to forgive her?"

Philly thought a moment. "I guess I would give it another try—a relationship with her, I mean."

"Forgiving her is really important, even if you don't get back together with her."

Philly's sleeping arm was almost back to normal. He tried to imagine that he could forgive Theresa and not get back together with her. He didn't argue with Dave, even if he couldn't form that imaginary scenario.

Dave ventured on. "You know, Jesus said that if we fail to forgive someone who does us wrong, then his Father won't forgive us. So, it's important—apart from whether you get back with Theresa, or even whether she stops doing things like that at work."

A sickness bubbled briefly inside Philly's emotional cauldron. Philly was thinking of his ma and the plethora of ways she annoyed and angered him. If he had to forgive Theresa no matter what, he would probably have to forgive his ma as well.

"I don't suppose this stops at Theresa. For some reason, my ma comes to mind just now."

Over the course of the next hour, Dave listened as Philly cataloged his recent collapse and then the back story for each of the people he realized he needed to forgive—Theresa, his ma, and even Grandma and Jesus.

"There's a principle around things like this, that you should start with the biggest pain first, which will loosen up a lot of the others. So, where do we start?"

"Gotta be Ma first." Philly took a deep breath.

"Yes. You need to forgive her, Philly. You need to let her go on being whatever unpleasant thing you think she is and still forgive her. Forgive her for what she couldn't be or couldn't give. She's not really the source of all of your troubles."

Philly felt a sort of grimace overtake his face. The sensation reminded him of the dragon he had fought that night with Allen Breen.

Dave seemed to respond to that change in Philly's countenance and began the process of setting Philly free from a tangle of cables he had twisted around himself in the process of attaching and maintaining resentments against the imperfect people he loved.

Not since that night on the kitchen floor with Jesus, after the chess match, had Philly exhausted his emotional stores to the extent that he did that afternoon with Dave. And, likewise, not since then had Philly felt so free. When they finished, and the late sun began to illuminate the apartment through the kitchen and bathroom windows, Philly sat across the room from Dave and almost felt as good as when the man sitting in that seat wore the robes of a first-century rabbi.

Just as he had promised, Jesus had shown up again when Philly needed him.

Chapter Nineteen

Philly scooped a spoonful of instant coffee into the cup of nearly boiling water that he had just removed from his microwave.

Irving crouched on the floor near his master's feet, contently capturing and consuming bites of odoriferous canned food.

Philly smiled when he thought of how Irving used to wander around the apartment looking for someone else besides his feeder and caregiver. The cat seemed to have given up lately, convinced that the visitor with the perfect touch couldn't be found in the other room, no matter how many times Irving prowled hopefully through the door.

A familiar ringtone startled Philly and his feline friend. Philly grabbed his phone off the kitchen table.

"Hello, my handsome man."

"Hello, my beautiful woman." Philly was smiling. His smile turned, however, to a rebuking scowl directed at Irving, who looked on critically at the playful love talk between the man and his noisy little electronic device.

"You ready for work?"

"Just about. A bit nervous, I gotta say."

A sigh of recognition crossed the cell signal into Philly's ear. "Yeah, a new job is a scary adventure. But you know they already love you there, and you're gonna have a blast."

Philly's nodding didn't make it back over the cell signal, but he finally spoke up. "I know. It'll be great. I think the part with the kids makes me most nervous."

"Oh, you'll be fine. Just be yourself. They'll know if you try to fake anything. Just do your stuff the way you do it."

Philly remembered asking Jesus whether he would send him help keeping things straight after he disappeared. This warm, encouraging voice on the phone sure helped fill that need, just as Jesus had promised.

"Thanks for the encouragement."

"I love you, Philly."

"Yeah. That's pretty great too." They laughed together, though miles apart. "I'll call you as soon as I get done, to let you know how it went."

"Okay. I'll make sure I have my phone with me. I'm working 'til seven, ya' know."

"Yeah. How about a late supper then?"

"That would be great. We can eat leftovers from Sunday."

"Nah. I start my new job. We should go out. It's been a while."

"Okay."

"I love you."

"I love you too."

Though he had waited over two months to start a new job, Philly was glad he didn't have to wait that long to reconcile with Theresa. Against expectations, friends from her church had encouraged Theresa to pursue forgiveness from Philly. For some of them, their antagonism toward the man who claimed to see and hear Jesus had turned around at the healing of Theresa's eye.

On the night of the purging forgiveness session with Dave, Philly had sat down by himself at home, prepared to call Theresa. In that moment of hesitation before he dialed, Philly felt the absence of his dearest companion and mentor. Out of habit, he placed his hand on the spot on his chest where Jesus had touched him that last night. He wished Jesus was back in his living room, holding Irving in his lap and smiling. As soon as he allowed that wish to dock in his heart, Philly felt a thrill, a warm confirmation, and he thought he heard a familiar laugh.

"Go ahead, she's waiting for you to call."

Spurred by that voice—or was it just a thought?—Philly tapped Theresa's name in his cell phone.

Theresa answered, her voice tame and hesitant. "Hello, Philly."

"Hello, Theresa. It's good to hear your voice. I'm sorry I didn't return your calls before."

Theresa took a relieved breath. "Oh, Philly, I feel awful. I'm the one that should be apologizing to you."

"I've forgiven you already. Jesus is pretty insistent about that sort of thing."

Theresa hesitated for a moment.

Philly intuited the reason for her hesitation and filled in a disclaimer. "I'm just going by what Dave was telling me from the Bible. Though I wish I could see him now, Jesus isn't back with me the way he was. He is with me though, especially when I started to forgive people."

"People besides me?"

"Yeah. You weren't even number one on the list." Philly chuckled. "And just now I realize I gotta forgive my old boss too."

"That sounds healthy. So, you called to tell me that you forgave me?"

"Hmm, well, not only that. I guess I called because I already have forgiven you. But I really called to hear your voice and see if you could still be my friend."

Theresa laughed a wild, sobbing laugh for two seconds. Eventually she regained her breath. "Oh Philly, I nearly ruined it. But you still wanna be with me?"

"Yes, I really do. I'd be crazy to let you get away."

That was weeks ago now. His relationship with Theresa had grown and matured since then through the process of reconciliation and recommitment.

When Philly hung up the call on his first day of his new job, Irving had finished eating and had turned his focus on a good tongue bath after his meal.

"You're disgusting."

Irving ignored the prejudicial remark.

With his car key on the same ring as his house key, the adjustment to driving to work altered little of Philly's old pre-work routine. The bus pass remained in his wallet and would stay right there today, but the rest was familiar and welcomed after two months of unemployment. *"Back in the saddle again,"* he thought.

"Are you gonna sing?" A subtle voice in his head teased him.

Philly laughed. "Don't count on it." He spoke aloud before sipping his coffee and locating the last supplies for his journey to work—sack lunch, sunglasses, cell phone.

He thought about how he had been trying to get used to his own singing voice over the last several weeks. That church on the north side of Chicago sure did a lot of singing. To Philly's relief, the music was more than old hymns or even the folk songs of his mother's contemporary Mass. The best thing about the loud drums, guitars, and the full spectrum of voices was the cover it offered a self-conscious singer like Philly. Theresa had a beautiful voice, and he loved worshiping next to her. But he felt that he was simply learning to bellow more freely instead of anything that could legitimately be called singing.

"It's all treasure to me." That voice in his head answered his thoughts.

For a moment, getting ready in the morning and thinking of worship, Philly forgot that he was going to work and felt that he was getting ready for church instead. While he put on his shoes, he marveled at how much he looked forward to church meetings, large and small. And he smiled at the realization that his anticipation of worship and healing leaked over into his new job.

This job that he now headed toward—out his kitchen door, over the shiny gray paint of his back porch, down the imperfect wooden stairs, past Mrs. Kelly's kitchen, and down to his car— this job stood head and shoulders over what he had dared imagine. Theresa had cried and laughed at the same time when she heard his new job description: computer support manager and chess coach. She barely seemed to notice when he told her about the big pay cut.

His new employer, a community center backed by his church and two others, needed a computer network manager and computer trainer. Among their expanding services to the community, they wanted to offer computer support for families in need. Here, of course, Philly could see a place for himself. Coincidentally, the director of community outreach had begun searching for a chess coach to oversee a cadre of young prodigies. As he sat listening to the program director apologizing that there might not be full-time computer work at first and throwing out a random comment about the chess program, Philly had to stop himself from staring with a slack jaw and watery eyes. The smart young woman interviewing him had stopped talking and fixed on him a querying look before he accepted both positions.

And, in contrast to his former employer who sent him to a psychiatrist as a condition of continued employment, his new employer would welcome him to offer healing at any time.

Philly laughed and swiped a tear off his cheek as he drove west toward the community center. Jesus had once told him that losing his job would be survivable and might even enrich his life. Though it seemed a lunatic proposition at the time, Philly remembered that promise and embraced a higher opinion of lunacy. Pastor Dave would have said something about foolish things beating out the wise, Philly thought.

One benefit of his unemployment, or perhaps one *more* benefit, was the time Philly had spent with Dave Michaels and others at church. After he and Theresa visited together a few times, they had agreed that this should become both Philly's and Theresa's church. Grandma would stay with her Pentecostal prayer group, of course. Her testimony and renewed faith in Jesus had sparked a small revival in that congregation.

As Philly met frequently with Dave and began to participate in church, including healing ministry, it turned out that he was in the right place to hear about the computer job at the community center.

Now, a half hour from home, Philly parked next to the director's car in the lot east of the rehabilitated warehouse. Various construction equipment and vehicles parked in that lot testified to ongoing work. Arriving so close to the launch of the project would allow Philly to help formulate the various elements of his job, including the chess club.

The chess players had mostly come from a Hispanic Pentecostal church where they had formed a club and participated in tournaments as individuals. Philly would join the club and add some of his chess skills to boost it into a team. The opportunity to engage so fully again in chess felt like a crisp new gift, though working with kids had been nowhere on his wish list.

Swinging through the brand-new glass door of the community center, Philly spotted Benny Hernandez, a guy from church that he had seen healed of an ankle injury.

The stocky young man greeted Philly warmly. "Hey, Philly! What's happening? Good to see you, bro."

"Hey, Benny. You working here?"

"Yep." Benny made an introductory sweep of his left arm. "I'm doing all the new flooring. I bet you didn't know that's what I do."

"I thought you played for the Bears. Isn't that how you banged up that ankle?"

"Oh, yeah. I got tackled by one of them three-hundred-pound linemen." He laughed. "This is my retirement."

"Hmm." Philly look at him skeptically. "I think you might want to renegotiate that."

They laughed together, and Philly clapped Benny on the back on his way to the director's office. "Gotta get serious and do something productive. My first day of work."

"Hey, great." Benny called after him. "I'll pray for your new job. That's really great."

Carmen Evans greeted Philly when he peeked in her office door. "Philly, come on in." She stood from her seat behind the desk. Carmen wore her hair collar-length, black with a streak of red highlight framing her face. She smiled readily, with a face that had won the trust of local politicians as well as little children.

For Philly, the solid-gold welcome settled some of his anxiety about a new job. He could tell that his new boss would be as open and accommodating at work as she had been during the interviews. He could shed some of his instinct to duck, to keep his head down and try not to be noticed. He could be himself—once he finished discovering exactly who that was.

At the same time, he welcomed Carmen's drive to get things accomplished, and they started right into discussing budget, computer equipment, and software—after Carmen got him a cup of coffee in his new Community Center mug.

Altogether, that first day resembled a job, but no job that Philly had ever held. The most outside-the-box activity on that day came just before quitting time at five o'clock.

Carmen came into the new server room that Philly was wiring. "Do you have a minute, Philly?"

He looked up from the switch he had just finished connecting. He smiled at his new boss. "Of course. What's up?"

"Well, there's a woman in my office right now with a severely swollen wrist. She fell at home and says she can't afford to get it looked at. I think she's more afraid of the hospital than anything. Would you be willing to come and give it a try?"

Her low-key request made Philly want to do whatever Carmen asked. "Sure, I can give it a try."

A short woman with graying hair that curled free of her ponytail in wiry wisps looked up at Philly when he entered the office. A small boy, perhaps her son, sat next to her, perched on the edge of his seat so that his toes would reach the floor. The boy's eyes fixed on Philly, and his eyebrows arched high.

Carmen introduced Philly to the woman in Spanish, then

told Philly that the mother's name was Philippa, and her son was Herman.

Philly shook their hands, taking Philippa's left hand instead of the one with the awkward Ace bandage on it.

She made a comment in Spanish that included her name, and Carmen translated. "She's says it's funny that she and you have the same name."

Philly smiled and nodded. "*Si, si, es verdad.*" That nearly exhausted his entire Spanish vocabulary, and the woman seemed to know that, because she continued to rely on Carmen to translate.

Carmen explained about Philly healing people, and the mother and her son both looked at him with new eyes as they listened to her description.

Little Herman stood up from his chair and looked as if he wanted to get close to Philly and perhaps touch him.

Philly just watched the boy with quiet amusement.

Philippa complied when Philly held out his hand and asked her to rest her sore hand in his.

Then Philly used another Spanish phrase he had learned recently, saying simply, "*Se sano,*" meaning "Be healed," as far as he knew. For a moment, nothing seemed to have happened. Philly paused to listen to Jesus for a different approach.

Then, without a word, Philippa removed her hand from Philly's. She smiled and nodded, standing up as if to leave.

Carmen looked at Philly, perhaps to see if he knew what had happened.

Philly just watched the petite mother as she reached out her left hand to gather in her son.

Carmen asked Philippa, in Spanish, how her wrist felt.

Philly waited patiently as the mother spoke plainly, always with the same little smile on her face.

Then Carmen laughed and looked at Philly. "She says, 'Thank you, it's all better now.' She says she's going to tell her family so they can come here and get healed tomorrow."

With that, Philippa casually started to unwrap the bandage.

Philly smiled, still holding his hand in nearly the same position in which he had healed Philippa's hand.

Before he could lower it, Herman reached his little hand up and rested it in Philly's. Then, as if someone had blown in his ear, Herman pulled his hand back and grabbed at the side of his head, a wide smile animating his face.

Carmen asked Philippa about Herman's ear and listened profoundly as the mother explained the situation.

Before the translation, however, Herman looked up at Philly. "Hey, I can hear on both sides now, Mister."

Philly laughed, cheered by the good news and amused by Herman's way of addressing him.

Carmen translated Philippa's explanation so that Philly had the complete picture. Herman had been born deaf in one ear. He had never heard a sound in that ear before.

Philly reached out to shake hands with Herman. "You have great faith, my little brother. Listen, and Jesus will talk to you in your new ear."

Herman nodded, as if taking Philly at his word.

When they had all said their happy goodbyes, and Philippa and Herman left the office, Carmen shrugged and grinned at Philly. "Well, I hope you have time to do some computer work around here in between all the healings." She let out a big laugh.

On his way home, Philly set his cell phone on the center console and connected it to his charger. When it rang, he saw Brenda's picture appear on the display. The mixed multitude of feelings that arose resembled a tangle of Chicago highways with traffic zipping in all directions. As agreed, Philly had told Brenda when Jesus stopped his sight-and-sound tour of Philly's life. Philly had hinted to Brenda then—not very bravely—that he might be interested in another woman, however, and the silence between them had resumed. Now, nearly three months later, here came a call from Brenda at the end of the workday. Philly tapped the phone screen, checked traffic around him, slowed down, and flipped the phone to speaker mode. "Hi, Brenda."

"Hi, Philly." She sounded at least as tentative as he did. "You driving home from work? You sound like you're in the car."

"Yeah. It sounds like you know about my new job."

"Oh, word gets around." After a moment, she adjusted that response. "Actually, I was at your church last night."

After another shocked pause, Philly said, "Really? You were at the evening service?"

"Yeah. I saw you there. But it was pretty crowded, and I slipped out early—when you were just starting to do that healing thing at the end."

"Well, I'm glad you checked it out."

"Actually, that wasn't my first time there. I've been visiting once in a while at your church and at that other church over on Devon."

"That's good. I'm glad to hear it."

"I guess it took me a while to recover from the feeling that Jesus was poking into my life and that he could just pull up anything from the past that he wanted to at any old time. But then I got to thinking that he must be real, and if he's real, then I better get more acquainted with him."

"I know what you mean. How's that going?"

"Good, I guess. I'm feeling like I should probably commit one way or the other."

Philly stayed silent for a few seconds, not comfortable to say what he was thinking, let alone able to sort through all that he was feeling.

Then Brenda filled in. "I'm not doing this to get you back, Philly. I saw you with your new girlfriend, and you look really good together. I mean you really look like you're in love, so I'm not doing all this for those reasons. I just need to get my life together for *me*."

Philly breathed easier. Then he realized he owed Brenda something. "I'm sorry I didn't do a better job of telling you what was going on with me and Theresa. I owed you more than the wimpy sorta way I told you."

"No, it was okay. It was pretty awkward, I know. All of this stuff just happened. You weren't in control of it any more than me."

"You sound like you're doing really well, Brenda. I'm glad to hear it." Though encouraged, he still held back, tempered by years of experience with Brenda in volatile emotional situations. She did seem to have found a good footing—at least a better one than when they last had a serious conversation.

"Thanks. Well, I'm gettin' on the train now. I should hang up."

"Yeah. Well, thanks for calling. I'll remember to pray for you."

"Thanks, Philly. That would be great."

"G'bye."

"Goodbye."

That Monday night, after his first day on the new job, Philly stopped at home to bring in his mail, have a snack, feed Irving, and check his email before he headed over to Theresa's. While at home, he stepped out onto the back porch, intending to check on Mrs. Kelly. But he heard her talking to someone in her kitchen. He reversed course and stepped back inside, glad to escape the July heat a bit longer. He decided to call his grandma, but got no answer at her house, so he just sat down in the living room for a few minutes to pet Irving and read ads from his mailbox. As he sat on his couch, he stopped reading when the voice downstairs with Mrs. Kelly hit a familiar note. Holding his breath for a moment, Philly listened more carefully to the two elderly women speaking loudly to each other.

The other voice downstairs was Grandma. Philly laughed. Given the hour and the direction of their voices, he guessed that they were having supper together. They had done this at least once before that Philly knew of since he had invited Grandma over to meet Mrs. Kelly. They seemed to get along like old sisters that simply hadn't seen each other for years.

A bit later than he intended, Philly gathered his keys and stepped absentmindedly through the kitchen and out the back door to pick up Theresa for supper, stopping just briefly to say hello to Grandma and Mrs. Kelly.

As he walked to his car, cicadas buzzed raucously in the old trees around the neighborhood, one even crying out from some attack by a bird or wasp as the summer creatures feasted on the noisy food source. For Philly, the sound of the cicadas was the sound of heat, as if the sultry summer air not only laid its hot hand on his skin but buzzed against his brain as well.

Gingerly sitting on the hot leather in his car, Philly spoke to an invisible companion. "I see why you came to ride in my car in April and not July." And he remembered the sound of that companion's contagious laughter.

Chapter Twenty

When Philly started attending the church, Dave Michaels shepherded him in, aware of the unconventional manner of Philly's conversion and the gifts he had received. Only members of the church leadership heard the details of Philly's story at first, allowing him some anonymity during his first weeks. Philly had blown his own cover one Sunday, however, prompted by an internal voice.

During an evening worship service, Philly's attention drifted from the music—generally his favorite part of the service—to a young man with an orange cast on his left leg. The cast allowed the man to stand for a while, apparently, but his frequent need to sit during the extended set of worship songs gained Philly's sympathy.

Then Philly became aware of a stream of thoughts that ran something like this: "You know I can heal that, and you know I can use you to do it. You also know that the people here are glad to see me heal. So why don't you go ahead and do it?"

Philly knew internal self-talk when he heard it, but this seemed more like Jesus speaking to him. Though he hadn't attempted to heal anyone for over a week, since he tried to heal an old woman in a wheelchair, he felt strongly that he was supposed to make another attempt. As the music rolled on and the young man sat down again, Philly slid out of his row of seats and crossed the aisle to where the injured man sat.

The young man, in his late twenties with short-cropped red hair, looked up at Philly and offered half a smile and a question in his eyes.

"I think Jesus is telling me to heal your leg." He spoke into the young man's ear, past the volume of the music.

The guy with the cast looked over at his friend to the right who was observing their interaction. The seated man motioned for his friend to bend down, and he repeated what Philly had said to him. The second stranger seemed more excited at the prospect than the injured man had, but Philly lost some of the nuances of his response in the air saturated with sound and motion. Finally, the red-haired man appeared to nod his head for Philly to do what he proposed. His friend sat down next to him and watched.

Philly knelt in the aisle and reached one hand toward the fluorescent cast. For ten seconds Philly knelt this way, until he felt his hand getting hot. With the music still rolling over them, he spoke to the leg, telling it to be well.

The man with the cast started shifting uncomfortably in his seat, and then he suddenly stood up and pounded his foot on the floor. He probably figured out at that point that the hard fiberglass covering could damage the wooden floor. He lifted his foot instead.

Philly leaned back as the young man waved his foot back and forth like he was trying to put out a fire. Philly stood up, understanding now what was happening. He leaned into the young man. "That hot feeling is the healing power." Just then the song ended, and the crowd grew quiet—except for the man with the orange cast.

"It's really hot!" His loud comment deepened the silence of the people around him. All eyes turned toward Philly and the man hopping around on one foot. About the time the young man became self-conscious about drawing so much attention, he also seemed to relax. He set his foot back on the ground and turned to his friend with an amused smile. Then he looked at Philly. "It feels great now—no pain at all. It feels great."

The injured man and his friend introduced themselves to Philly. The friend, Jim, told Philly that Don was attending the church for the first time.

Philly introduced himself, shaking their hands.

When the young woman leading the worship stood at the

microphone looking at the disturbance, she received a wave and a nod from Jim. The resulting trip to the microphone, Philly's stage-struck responses to questions, and the electric escalation of the tone of the worship service introduced his gifts to his new church.

Dave Michaels, who hadn't been attending the service, arrived toward the end, responding to a text from one of the leaders of the meeting. He smiled ecstatically when he found Philly and heard the story.

During the weeks that followed, that church crackled with excitement as more people received miraculous healings and more church members began healing others, including people outside of the church. Though Philly lost his anonymity, he remained the introverted computer guy—at first an unemployed computer guy. Theresa seemed to enjoy Philly's healing ministry more than he did. But, for Philly, the satisfaction of knowing that he was still hearing Jesus was worth the attention.

Dave tugged Philly into healing ministry opportunities, but Philly sensed that he was careful not to put him on the spot, especially at first.

The church saw new members drawn in during those days, including Craig and Allyson from Philly's old office. Their solidarity with Philly had only gotten them in the door before. But the friendly and vibrant church kept them there.

In contrast, neither Philly's ma nor his dad attended, maintaining their status as non-church people. Philly didn't attempt to persuade them, of course. But he noted that a brand-new Bible lay next to his dad's favorite chair now. Since Ma remained true to herself, her husband of over forty years didn't leave her behind, even to join Philly at church.

Eileen, for her part, continued to struggle with relationships, repelled by the austere expectations of church people regarding sex before marriage. As she told Philly, this issue kept her on the periphery of the dynamic church she attended with her friend in

New York City.

Philly also felt the challenging constrictions of his newfound religion. But Theresa's steadfast determination to conform to expectations at church overpowered her desire for physical intimacy with her boyfriend. On the back shelf of their relationship remained negotiations regarding engagement. Once Philly found his new job, that question moved to the front of his mind.

But Jesus had another agenda first. One night, Philly had a dream set in the new network room at the community center. Hunkered in the little closet that would serve as the nerve center of the computer network, he became aware of Jesus standing in there with him, separate but close. Then the scene of the network closet became something else. Instead of grown-up Philly and Jesus alone in the small space, there were four or five little kids, and all of them looked like Philly.

Then, as if he were sitting in that chair in the corner of Philly's bedroom again, Jesus spoke to him. "Philly, I'm right here, so close. But you keep as far away from me as you can, even in this small space inside you."

In the morning, Philly remembered that odd scene and the nearly audible voice of Jesus commenting on what he saw in that picture. It was Saturday, and Philly lay awake at eight in the morning, ignoring Irving's persistent mewing. Then, just as on that Saturday three months before, Philly heard Jesus telling him to go to Dave Michaels's office to see him. This time, Philly texted Dave to see if they could meet.

Dave texted back, **Already got the call, will meet you there.**

"*Who needs a cell phone?*" Philly thought, glad Jesus had reserved some of Dave's time for him.

Leaning back in one of the comfy chairs in his office, Dave nodded at Philly's account of his dream. After a moment of listening in the silence at the end of Philly's story, Dave responded. "I'm remembering a guy who used to attend the first church we started. He was there with us through all the early stages of building that church, was ready to help with anything we did. I think he had the most consistent attendance of anyone in that church. But one Sunday he shocked me by coming to the front at the end of the morning worship service, ready to commit himself to Jesus." Dave laughed ironically. "We all assumed he was a committed Christian because he was so faithful at worshiping and at working with the church." Looking at Philly as if to see if he knew where he was going with this story, Dave finished. "It's possible to just show up where Jesus is and not get right in close where he wants to touch us and heal us. Sorta like going to the emergency room but refusing to go in any farther than the waiting area. I think Jesus is calling you further in."

Something in what Dave said, even the way he said it, reminded Philly of someone else. Sitting in Dave's office, looking at the middle-aged, slightly overweight pastor—with what looked like egg on the collar of his sweatshirt—Philly felt like he was still seeing Jesus.

After giving him the contact information for one of the church counselors, Dave led Philly outside where the gray day hung cool and damp for July. On the landing at the top of the steps where Philly first met him, Dave offered an afterthought. "You know, a woman wants to be pursued. If you really want Theresa, it might be time to commit to getting closer to her as well."

Throughout his life, Philly had struggled with being wanted, accepted, and understood. That struggle usually left him too knotted up to really know his own desires. But just then the wisdom of Dave's words found an easy docking place in Philly's soul. "Thanks. I know you're right."

With that, Dave headed toward his car, and Philly started to plan what he would say to Theresa, when he would get the engagement ring, and when he would ask the question.

In the meantime, he decided to get a haircut. Though it had not been so long since his last trim, it just seemed the thing to do on a Saturday morning with no plans.

When he entered the franchise haircut place, he spotted Rosa collecting a tip from a customer near the register.

For a moment she didn't acknowledge Philly among the moms and kids coming and going. But when she did recognize him, she shrieked. This caught the attention of everyone in the store. It rocked Philly too, who generally aspired to never being shrieked at in public. After the momentary pause, during which everyone had to process whether the shriek was negative or positive, Rosa broke into tears and laughter. "It's you, it's you! Oh, I'm so glad to see you." She pushed past a stunned little girl and grabbed Philly in a breathlessly tight hug.

Philly reciprocated, at least a little, and collected his wits to start a question. "Your mother?"

Rosa recovered enough to cooperate with moving aside—to let customers get in and out of the busy shop—and she let go of Philly. "She's well. My mother is totally healed, just like you said. Her cancer is all gone. Oh, praise Jesus!"

Though he politely congratulated and rejoiced with Rosa, her public display of emotion and faith sent Philly looking for cover. Still he didn't run away when a woman waiting for her daughter's haircut sidled up to him and asked if he would pray for her.

The woman, in her early forties with short salt-and-pepper hair, held out her arm and said simply, "Bone cancer."

Philly moved farther from the little reception area, as if trying to hide himself in the little artificial tree that separated the waiting area from the service area of the store. He held out his hand, and the woman rested her arm in it. Philly had done very little healing outside of the church building since Jesus had gone invisible. But today he genuinely felt accompanied by his dear friend, and he imagined Jesus reaching up and holding that arm along with him. As he formed this mental picture, he simply said, "Cancer, be gone."

The woman started to quiver and then to cry. "I can feel it. The pain is getting less and less, and it feels like someone is working inside my arm." She took a shaky breath. "I can feel it."

Theresa's call a few minutes later pulled Philly away from the growing celebration of that healing. When he stepped outside he hadn't even had a chance to put his name in for a haircut. "What time can I see you tonight?" He looked at his reflection in the store window.

"Come to my house after three thirty."

"Okay. I'll spend some time at Grandma's house until then."

He didn't really need a haircut very badly anyway, so he didn't go back in to start the process all over again. Who knows? He may have been busy healing people there all day without ever feeling so much as a comb touch his hair.

Philly called and warned Grandma that he was on his way. She sounded a bit distant, but from that distance she also sounded happy to have Philly come to see her.

Grandma greeted him, as usual, at the kitchen door. She seemed more present than she had on the phone. It was just like old times—cookies and iced tea, catching up on the news—the bond between them still strong.

Looking into Grandma's eyes, Philly detected some change, however, and the first thing that came to mind was her health. "Are you feeling all right, Grandma?"

As if catching herself at some bad habit, Grandma winced slightly and shook her head. Then she smiled. "I'm feeling quite well, Philly. I'm as healthy as I've been in twenty years."

"What is it, then?"

Grandma took a big breath and scooted farther back in her seat at the breakfast nook. "I've been listening, and I'm still hearing him, Philly. I can still feel him in the room with me. And I go away with him more and more it seems these days." She tilted her head, assessing her grandson. "I'm an old lady. I've lived well past eighty years. We don't have to say how far past." She grinned. "And I've had a full life on this earth. But I know that he has a better life waiting for me where he is. And I'm feeling the pull into that world more every day."

Philly crunched his brow, and Grandma apparently recognized that look. "I'm not sick. What I'm talking about is not like that. It's not that I feel bad, or regret living here. It's just that I know, more clearly than ever, that there's a better place for me, and I'm ready to go there." Then Grandma looked at Philly, as if just realizing something. "But for you, young man, there's a lot of living yet to do, and you should go about doing it."

In that last phrase, Philly heard confirmation that he should ask that question of Theresa. And here again, Philly recognized the orienting experience of hearing Jesus speak out loud to him—this time from Grandma's mouth.

But he was struggling to understand what was happening to her. Wasn't she supposed to keep on living, like Jesus told them both to? "This doesn't sound like more of that same feeling from when Jesus was visible. You're hearing something specific, aren't you?"

Grandma nodded. "It won't be long. Oh, not days, or maybe not even weeks, but certainly months. I expect this will be my last year on this earth."

And Philly saw again that look that had launched his concern. He knew it now as a look of sorrow mixed with hope, the sort of expression no one could consciously mimic.

Again, Grandma took one of those purging deep breaths. "We mustn't talk about this anymore. And I want your promise not to tell anyone else. This is just for you and me and Jesus."

Philly slipped forward in his chair and leaned over to hug Grandma, and then he let himself feel the loss that lay ahead. Within a couple minutes he was sitting up, wiping tears, and blowing his nose on paper napkins and tissues.

Grandma had to take off her glasses to wipe at her eyes, though she seemed to remain remarkably calm.

Philly and Grandma generally talked about less weighty matters the rest of that afternoon, even watching a few innings of the Cubs game on TV. Philly told Grandma about what happened at the haircut place that day, and about his talk with Dave Michaels before that. As usual, she made comments, but offered little advice and no criticism. In the quilt of Grandma's contented life, Philly felt like one of her favorite squares. And she certainly was his favorite too. He expected that everyone needs to be somebody's favorite.

When Philly got the call from his dad that November, just three and a half months later, and learned that Grandma had died in her sleep, he instantly pictured her flying like an angel toward heaven, right past where the Russian cosmonaut couldn't find it, to where Jesus and his Father would greet her once and for all.

In the days between, Philly became as familiar in the counseling center of the church as he was in the healing lines, with appointments twice a week—once with, and once without Theresa. He had, of course, asked his question, and she had said yes, which explained the nature of their weekly counseling session together.

As the community center took shape, and Philly built a computer network and a computer training program for the neighbors, his chess team also developed. He enjoyed the kids even more than his network and found deep satisfaction from watching one particular boy discover his own genius at the game. Ricardo had no father at home, and his grandfather, who had taught him chess, had died recently. To Philly, the stocky eleven-year-old looked like a boy he once knew—with a little darker skin maybe, and the occasional spiky blue hair. In Ricardo, Philly saw a boy who needed someone to share his passion for the game, someone to understand him, and someone to accept him just as he was.

All that Philly could give freely, because he had received the same—after he met a remarkable stranger on the bus one day.

Acknowledgments: Thanks to the many readers of this book, for your generous reviews and support. Thanks too for the help of Penny Johnston, providing valuable proof-reading.

Made in the USA
Monee, IL
18 July 2025